Planet of the Jews

The Planet of the Jews

Philip Graubart

CREATIVE ARTS BOOK COMPANY
Berkeley • California 1999

Planet of the Jews is published by Donald S. Ellis
and distributed by Creative Arts Book Company.

For Information contact:
Creative Arts Book Company
833 Bancroft Way
Berkeley, California 94710

ISBN 0-88739-186-9
Library of Congress Catalog Number 98-72713

Printed in the United States of America

This novel includes some Yiddish phrases and sentences.
For reasons the author cannot go into right now,
the Yiddish is completely incorrect.
In other words, don't try to learn Yiddish from this book.

This book is for my brother, Jon Graubart, and my sisters, Beth
Graubart and Amy Katz.
In memory of my mother, Marilyn Graubart.

A special thanks to the members and directors of
Congregation B'nai Israel for giving me time and
support to write this book.
Thanks also to Susan Freeman,
Laura Michaels, Dennis Hudson
and Jay Neugoboren
for reading the manuscript and providing
thoughtful comments.

The Planet of the Jews

1: Moishe and Esther

For weeks after my father's death, I found myself running into strangers I could have sworn I'd seen at the funeral. I'd approach them, try to talk to them, but they'd either walk away, shrug and look puzzled, deny any knowledge of my father, or just ignore me. My father had been a major philanthropist, giving generously to Jewish institutions here and in Israel. Over a thousand people attended his funeral – grateful rabbis, executive directors, college presidents, and even a large contingent of black-hatted Yeshiva boys. I barely knew anyone there. But starting the very next day, I had the odd impression every stranger I'd bump into in the subway, or brush against on the sidewalks had been a fellow mourner.

Moishe and Esther were the strangest of them all. They appeared, as if by magic, one hot Friday morning in my office at *Astounding Tales*. I was standing, hunched over my desk, studying a story called "The Killer Robots of the Fourth Millennium," when suddenly I looked up and there they were.

"We have a story, for you," offered Moishe, a young man dressed in black, with a full brown beard, black bowler hat, and ritual fringes dangling from his dusty, black sports coat.

I stared at him. I was about to ask him how the hell he got past security and into my office, when the odd feeling of recognition washed over me. "I remember you," I heard myself say. "You were standing at the very front, right next to the grave." I looked at his companion, a gaunt, frail looking young women, whose wide peasant dress almost completely obscured her bony arms and legs. "You were there too," I said to her.

"Standing right next to him. You wore the same dress you're wearing now. I remember you couldn't stop crying."

"It's a good story," Esther told me, thrusting out a fairly thick manuscript. For some reason, I grabbed it, as if by reflex. I glanced at it, then tossed it on to the couch next to my desk.

"It's about my father?" I asked. "A story about him? About the funeral?"

They looked at each other, Esther's olive eyes narrowing in both confusion and annoyance.

"Excuse me, Mr. Loeb," Moishe said softly. "My name is Moishe. This is my. . . uh . . . my wife, Esther. We've written a story for your magazine. You should publish it, soon, we think, probably in your next issue."

"It's a good story," Esther added.

But I still hadn't recovered from the shock of recognition. "But my father," I insisted. "You must have known him. Why else would you. . .?" I stopped. I could see they had no idea what I was talking about.

Esther took a step forward. "You are Mr. Judah Loeb?" she asked. "Fiction editor for the magazine *Astounding Tales*?"

I nodded.

"We have some fiction for you, Mr. Loeb." She pointed to the thick wad of papers I'd thrown on the couch.

"Some very *good* fiction," added Moishe.

I looked over at the manuscript without making a move to pick it up. I could see the title: "The Planet of the Jews."

"I'm sorry," I said, trying to shake off the weird feeling I'd seen these two before. "This is not a religion magazine. We don't print religious fiction, or Jewish fiction. This is a science fiction. . ."

"This *is* a science fiction story, Mr. Loeb," Moishe said, in a meek, high pitched voice.

Esther interjected, in a much deeper, more confident tone, "It's a very *good* science fiction story." She pointed at the other manuscript on my desk. "It's certainly better than a story about warring robots." she added, with a nod.

How did she know what that story was about? I hadn't told anyone about it, not even Alan, my boss. I was about to ask, but I suddenly grew annoyed with these two oddly dressed Jews. They were wasting my time.

I shook my head. "This isn't the way we collect manuscripts," I said. "We deal with agents. Our writers don't submit directly to us. And anyhow, I wouldn't be your first reader. There's a process. . ."

"This is a story *you* will read first," Esther interrupted, her voice brimming with an odd mixture of self–assurance and irritation. "This is a story for *you*."

"I'm sorry," I said, beginning to show some irritation myself. "I can't accept. . ."

But they didn't let me finish the sentence. They turned around to leave, Moishe at such a fast pace it seemed almost like he was fleeing. Esther stopped at the door, and turned to look at me – her dour face brightening a bit. "We'll be back next week, Mr. Loeb," she said. I gaped at her round, sun–tanned face, and was astonished to see her wink one of her green eyes at me. "Have a good *Shabbes*," she added and scurried away in the direction of Moishe. I ran out and watched as the elevator doors snapped shut on the two of them.

I asked my secretary how the hell they got past her. She told me she had no idea. She hadn't left her desk all morning, and hadn't seen anyone go in.

I went back to my office and tried to work. I picked up the story about the killer robots and started to read. It was just the kind of story our readers loved, the kind of story that made us easily the most commercially successful science fiction magazine in the country, and one of the most popular fiction magazines of any kind. Robots from the year 4029 inexplicably show up in the twenty-fifth century. Without any attempts at communication, these futuristic robots begin destroying all modern electronic equipment. They only attack machines, never people, and no one can figure out why. After a while, it is discovered that the attackers are not really robots at all, but cyborgs – half machine, half human. It's very difficult to defeat these creatures since they combine the intuition and creative instincts of human beings, with the superior strength and durability of robots. The only possible way to combat the "robots of the fourth millennium" is to create a twenty–fifth century breed of cyborgs who could match their counterparts in strength and skill. The first installment of the story (it was to be a serialized novel – our specialty) ends with the first successful twenty–fifth century union of man and machine.

Under ordinary circumstances, I would have been thrilled with the story. There was precisely the right mixture of hard science, action/adventure suspense, human interest, and bloody violence. But since the death of my father, I'd somehow become less patient with these melodramatic gore–fests.

And I couldn't get Moishe and Esther out of my mind; absurdly, I even pictured them – with all of their ultra–orthodox garb – as two of the protagonists in the robot story. I imagined Moishe as the driven scientist who finally creates his own version of a Frankenstein monster. And I pictured Esther as the monster, the newfangled twenty fifth century cyborg.

I threw the story on my desk and massaged my eyes. Who were these two strange Jews, I asked myself, and why was I so convinced I'd seen them at my father's funeral? Once again, I wondered if I should have taken some time off after his death. Alan had insisted I take at least a week, but I knew I'd feel totally lost without my work. It's not as if I would have been inundated with well-wishers, and, since my divorce, I lived alone. I could have taken a few days, but what would I have done – watch television by myself? Besides, I was pretty sure I didn't need any extra time; I wasn't all that upset when my father died. We'd never been close, and he'd been sick for years.

But now it occurred to me that Alan might have been right. If every stranger I saw reminded me of the funeral, then I must have been more disturbed than I thought. I slowly rubbed my temples, keeping my eyes shut tightly, trying to forestall the headache I knew was coming. I decided to grab a cup of coffee from the company cafeteria, and then finish with the story I was reading. But instead, I dropped my head on the desk and fell asleep.

I woke up, startled, when my secretary buzzed to remind me of my appointment with Uncle Max. Stumbling away from my desk, I knocked the manuscript of the "Killer Robots" on the floor, scattering the pages in all directions. I was about to stoop down and collect them when I realized I didn't even have time for that. I dashed down the stairs (four flights) and caught a cab for the Flatbush section of Brooklyn.

Max was waiting for me on the front porch of his tiny brownstone. Despite the heat and the humidity – it was past ninety, and I was perspiring from head to toe – he wore his usual uniform: a brown cardigan sweater over a white shirt, a black bow tie, and wool pants. In the winter, he added a beat–up, dusty bowler hat and sometimes a scarf, but never an overcoat. Max wasn't one to let the weather dictate his wardrobe or, for that matter, restrict his movements in any way.

As soon as he saw me he jumped out of his seat and suggested a walk around the neighborhood. I begged off, not without some embarrassment. Max was in his mid–seventies, I was thirty–six, but I was the one who nearly swooned at the thought of strolling through the streets of Brooklyn on the hottest day of the summer. I convinced him to do the interview indoors. I also talked him out of making hot tea.

I was fond of Max, which was fortunate for two reasons. First of all, not counting my ex–wife, he was my last surviving relative. My mother had died ten years earlier, two days after my wedding. My father had just passed away. And, since I was an only child and both of my parents had lost their siblings and parents years before, that left only Max and me. And we liked each other.

The other reason was my latest project. I was writing a comic book novel about Max's experiences in the Holocaust. For the past six months, I'd been interviewing him about the war. In his dark, shabby Brooklyn brownstone, or on walks around the decaying neighborhood, I'd record his stories. I'd been writing science fiction and superhero comic books for years and I'd made a name for myself in the market; my editor and boss Alan Shapiro always assured me I was his "best comic book writer." But I'd never written a book-length comic, and I'd certainly never tackled a subject as serious as the Holocaust before. I started playing with the idea of a Holocaust book after my father, suffering from liver cancer, began attending healing services led by a Hasidic Rabbi named Chaim Boronsky. My father mentioned that this rabbi, a gnarled white-bearded old man with deep wrinkles and an inscrutable expression, had led a partisan band of Jewish fighters in Poland during the war. A warrior rabbi – the idea fascinated me. I spent three weeks meeting with the frail, stooped-over scholar every morning after his prayers. But, try as I might, I couldn't get the old guy to discuss the Holocaust at all. All he wanted to talk about was healing, or God. When I told my father how frustrated I was – how badly I wanted to hear details of the rabbi's story – he stunned me by revealing that Uncle Max had survived the Holocaust in much the same way as the old Rabbi, by fighting Nazis in the forests of Poland. In fact, he said, Max and Rabbi Boronsky had fought in the same unit. I wondered, briefly, why Rabbi Boronsky had never mentioned that to me – he knew Max was my Uncle. But then I assumed he just wanted to forget the past. In any case, I called Max right away and he agreed to tell me his story.

My idea was to depict all the various peoples involved in World War II as animals. It was easy to choose an appropriate beast to depict the Germans; they would be pit bulls. The

Americans would be horses – cocky, strong and good. The Christian Poles would be pigs; the French, poodles. But what about the Jews? I needed a creature that represented both fear (the Nazis had a strange inordinate fear of the Jews) and vulnerability. After experimenting with some sketches of sheep, cattle, and mice, I finally hit on cockroaches. I would call the comic book *Roach*.

Interviewing Max was both exhilarating and terribly frustrating. Exhilarating because he really did have quite a story to tell – he lived in the forests outside of Stascha for five years and, according to my father, led one of the most active Jewish partisan groups in all of Europe. Frustrating because getting him to tell his story in a linear, coherent fashion was like pulling teeth. He'd begin a story about capturing a German war prisoner in 1943, lurch back to a vague encounter with the gentile gym teacher who saved his life in 1939, veer forward to his final escape with his partisan wife Aliza to Switzerland in 1945, without ever coming back to the German prisoner. I quickly realized I could only rely on him to provide a mood, a main character, and a broad narrative structure. I'd have to make up most of the details myself.

That day I was anxious to get back to the beginning of the story. When Max was nineteen, right before the German invasion, most of his family fled Warsaw and crossed the Vistula River into the Soviet Union. For reasons still not clear to me, Max stayed behind.

"Tell me about saying goodbye to Rivka (his sister) and your parents," I asked him as he handed me a diet creme soda. "You were standing at the Vistula bridge, waiting for them to cross over. What did you say to them?"

Max took a loud slurp of iced tea and began with "Well, you must understand." He started every answer, every war story with the imploring phrase "you must understand" as if – really – it were impossible I would ever understand.

"I was with Voytek still," he continued, "the instructor of physical education. He gave me and Anshel a place to hide in Warsaw."

"He was with you at the bridge?" I asked. "He was with you when you said goodbye?"

"No, no, he was never at any bridge, Judah," Max said. "Why should he be? You see, he never met my parents. Except for when they met him at the school, but this was not. . . well, they never really met him."

"Is that why you didn't go with them?" I asked. "Because Voytek offered you a hiding place?"

"Well, at the bridge it was, of course, sad. Who knew if I would ever see him again?"

"Who?"

"My family. This is what you asked, Judah. My family at the bridge."

"But you said 'him.' You said 'who knew if I would ever see *him* again.'"

"Ahh," said Uncle Max.

This was not an a-typical Holocaust conversation with Max. I could rarely get him to answer one of my questions. Eventually, I learned if I hung in there and let him direct the conversation – which followed from my questions only in the loosest sense – then some story might emerge, sometimes even an interesting story. But the process was always frustrating.

You might have thought old Max was just getting senile, so it was unfair of me to expect any focused narrative from him at all. But, in fact, Max was as sharp-witted as I, and in every other area of his life, he spoke intelligently and lucidly. Only the Holocaust turned him into a scatterbrained old man.

"Why didn't you go with them?" I asked. "Why didn't you cross the bridge?"

"You must understand he was my best friend. He was my teacher, but he was also my friend. I know it seems scandalous; he was ten years older than I, and there was all sorts of talk, all sorts of gossip, but. . . fehhh," he said and waved his hand in disgust. I waited for him to continue. He took another long sip of iced tea.

"My father told me to look for him in Leningrad," he continued. "The Red army had set up some kind of refugee relief bureau. They would go there and I would join them in six months."

"So you were planning on joining them? You didn't plan to wait out the war in Poland?"

"The hiding place, Judah. Voytek wasn't ready to give up everything. It's not like you see in the movies. This wasn't some kind of Anne Frank closet. This was the forest, Judah, the fields. It was impossible. . ." His voice trailed off, and he frowned. His pasty white forehead filled up with wrinkles. "When he turned on us, I *knew* it, I knew I had to find a gun, to fight somehow, just to stay alive. But. . ." he shook his head, and looked up at me with sad gray eyes. "Everyone who crossed that bridge died you know. No one survived the war. They all ended up at Aushwitz."

I nodded.

"And you know, you understand, almost everyone who didn't cross the bridge also died."

"I understand," I said.

"Anshel, Malki, Jacob, Sasha. . ."

I nodded.

He shrugged. "This was the war," he said. "It got almost everyone."

I sighed. I can see, I thought to myself, I'm not going to get anywhere today. But that was Max; he had his good days when he could talk uninterrupted for hours, and give me a genuine feel for his experiences. And there were days – most days actually – when all he could do was shake his head and marvel at the number the people who'd been murdered, and I could barely understand a single word he said. That day I decided to leave him with his ghosts. I patted him on the shoulder and headed back to my office.

The first thing I noticed when I opened the locked door

was that someone had shifted Moishe and Esther's manuscript from my couch to the center of my desk. The second thing I noticed was that the Robot manuscript, which I distinctly remembered leaving scattered on the carpet, was nowhere to be seen. But no one ever came into my office without either myself or my secretary Sandy knowing it. And Sandy knew *never* to allow anyone to touch my papers, not even the janitors. She had left for the day, so I couldn't ask, but at this point, I was more annoyed than puzzled. Who cares how the thing ended up on my desk, I thought, I don't want it, and I don't want to read it! I had deadlines from four comic book publications; I had to copy edit eleven stories for *Astounding Tales* and I had at least two dozen manuscripts to go through from agents I respected. And I was way behind where I wanted to be with *Roach* – my own graphic novel.

The last thing I wanted to do was read a story about a planet of Jews.

But I did read it. Right then and there.

I'm not sure how it happened. I know I intended to look for the Killer Robot story, maybe even call Sandy at home and ask her to dig up another copy if I couldn't find it. But right after I sat down at my desk, I noticed inky fingerprint stains on the title page of Moishe and Esther's manuscript. Apparently I'd been perspiring, and had gripped the pages so tightly, I left an impression – like a fossil. I was fascinated because I'd never seen fingerprints on paper before. I thought about some of the crime stories I'd edited, and for a split second I fantasized about using the "Planet of the Jews" manuscript as a murder weapon, then burning the pages so no one could trace the crime to me. For a moment, I actually thought about who I would rub out, and when. But instead, I picked up the story and read it straight through.

I loved it, I was profoundly moved by it. It brought tears to my eyes, several times. Four or five pages into it, I realized it was quite possibly my all–time favorite science fiction story.

I had never read a manuscript that affected me so deeply.

Which is not to say it was any good. I couldn't tell. I was so personally affected by the story, there was no way I could judge its esthetic merits. I thought it was probably okay. It seemed to work well at the artistic level of our audience, which is to say bright thirteen–year–old boys would probably read it with a certain amount of pleasure. But I couldn't be sure. For some reason, judging this story seemed suddenly like judging my own work; I felt too close to make editorial decisions. But I knew I wanted to publish it. I decided to take it to Alan, our editor–in–chief.

"Is this some kind of joke, Judah?" he asked, studying the cover. He was in the middle of eating a submarine sandwich. "A planet of Jews," he said between mouthfuls. "Jesus, can you imagine? But the joke's not working, Judah. I know you don't like to write prose. Even the novel you're working on – what is it called – *Ladybug?*"

"*Roach*" I said.

"Yeah, yeah, right. *Roach*. That's a graphic novel, right, not old–fashioned prose? So this is some kind of humor piece, but I don't think. . ."

"It's not a joke, Alan." I said.

He looked at me, the lamp reflecting off his thick glasses, the way sunlight often bounced off of his bald head. "*You* wrote a short story called 'The Planet of the Jews?'"

"Me?" I asked. "What makes you think. . ?"

He pointed his chubby thumb to the credit lying at the bottom of the title page. It read: BY JUDAH LOEB.

"Jesus Christ," I whispered, staring at the page. "They used my name."

"Who?"

"Moishe and Esther," I answered. "Two Jews, I mean, two writers. A team. Orthodox Jews – with side curls, a *sheitel*, the whole bit. They showed it to me today." I shook my head, thinking about the credit. "Alan, I don't know how I could have missed it."

"Never mind, Judah," he said, shaking his head. "You say two Hasids *handed* you this story. They just gave it to you? Today?"

I nodded.

"What's the matter with you, Judah?" he asked, his wire glasses sliding down his nose. "You now we don't publish. . . wait a second." He sat up. "Judah," he said. "Is this about your father? I *told* you to take some time off. I told you! I should have insisted. It just wasn't right, you didn't even. . ."

"This has *nothing* to do with my father!" I snapped. Perhaps a little too sharp.

"Okay," he answered, his eyes widening. "Okay!"

I sighed. "Look," I said. "Just read it. That's all I ask. If you don't like it, we'll give it back to the Jews – I mean, back to Esther and Moishe. But I think you'll like it."

He took a large bite out of his sandwich and studied the title page. I could tell he was looking at my name.

"Please Alan," I said.

He turned to me, his face suddenly appearing rounder and fatter than I could ever remember. "I'll read it," he said finally, and took another bite. "For you, Judah, I'll read it. I'll read all about the planet of the Jews."

That night, at 1:30 a.m., the phone rang. It was Alan.

"It's wonderful," he said.

"Hmm," I answered, groggy.

"Superb," he added.

"Oh," I said, switching on my night lamp.

"Judah, I cried, I literally wept. I don't know what came over me! I cried when the old Jew – you know the Rebbe – when he got knifed in the back. It was just too much. And that scene on the planet by the sandy beach – it gave me the *chills*. Judah it was so inviting, so. . .so enthralling, I. . . I just don't know what to say!"

"That's how I felt."

"But the thing is, Judah," continued, "I loved the thing, but, well, I'm not sure if it's any good. I'm not sure it really *works*. You know what I mean? Is it really a decent story? I don't know."

"I don't know either Alan."

He paused for a second. I could hear him catching his breath. "Judah, did you know I'm Jewish?" he asked.

"I figured you were, Alan." His name was Alan Shapiro, so it wasn't terribly surprising.

"Never meant that much to me, to tell you the truth. I hated Hebrew School, hated the whole damn. . . well, never mind. I just never considered it important. But somehow this story, it made me. . . it made *think* about things I'd never thought about. I started having ideas I never dreamed would be in me. Spiritual shit. It was incredible, invigorating. Judah, you know I'd love to talk to you more about this stuff. We could have a wonderful discussion, you and I. About my life, your life. About Judaism. About God. Our parents. About this story."

"Of course, Alan. But it is – uh – it's almost two in the morning."

"Oh, is it?" He sounded startled. "I've just been re-reading the story, and thinking, and reading some more, and thinking, and – I guess I just lost track of the time. Of course, of course Judah. We can talk some other time. But there is something I need to ask you. What *is* the deal with the credit? You say it was written by some Hasidic couple."

"Orthodox, Alan." I said. "Orthodox."

"Whatever."

"Well, it's strange, Alan. They've got some kind of interest in me. I think they knew my father, and well, I guess they want me to have the credit."

"Look, Judah, we can credit it to Jesus Christ, for all I care. I just want to run it as soon as possible."

I was finally wide awake, and a little startled. I'd never

known Alan to make a publishing decision based on his own preference. There were always consultations with our marketing people, polling of focus groups, editors' conferences. How a story personally affected him was simply not relevant. I was not sure I'd heard correctly.

"You mean, we're going to publish it?" I asked. "Just like that?"

"We're publishing it!"

The next issue of *Astounding Tales* sold more copies than any other magazine in our company's history. Thousands of fans, not all of them our regular thirteen–year–old male readers, wrote to us, clamoring for a sequel. Within days we sold the anthology rights, and started taking bids from Hollywood agents. *Newsweek* ran a full page feature just on the reaction to the story in the science fiction world. I received requests for interviews from *The Jerusalem Report* and *Forward*. We were the new sensation.

2: The Planet of the Jews

Evan Isaacs was sinning. To be more precise, he was violating the seventh commandment; he was committing adultery, and not for the first time, nor even for the tenth time. He occasionally noted the irony of how his life of adulterous sin began right around the time he'd starting talking to God. Sometimes he allowed himself to feel guilty. But for the most part, Evan didn't like to waste time thinking about sin and punishment, and he didn't enjoy theological speculation. When God spoke to him, he followed orders. Well, more or less. In any case, he'd defintely dedicated his life to God's word. He was the Moses of his generation — the king of the Jews. But what he did with his spare time was not really God's business. At least, that's how Evan saw it.

He was about to consummate the act when he felt the Headache come on.

"Oh Christ," he said out loud, "Not now. Please."

The Headache meant a message from God was coming. Which, in theory, Evan didn't mind. God hadn't spoken to him in weeks, the project was nearly finished, and he could use some guidance. But this was not the time. Not with Lianna (was that her name? He couldn't be sure; he'd just met her that evening) lying beneath him, ready and waiting.

But of course, he had no choice. He rolled off of Lianna, covered himself with a sheet (since it couldn't be proper to address God in a state of nakedness), and waited. The young woman stared at him, and started to ask, but Evan rushed his finger to his lips and let out a hideous "Shhhh!" Then he heard the Voice.

"You have to go see the president again," it said, sharply. The Voice spoke directly into his head. He'd learned from hard experience that when *God* spoke to him, no one else heard.

"Oy," Evan thought, without saying the word. He'd also learned to communicate his ideas without speaking, a skill which came in handy when there were other people in the room, and he didn't want to come off as a total lunatic.

"And you must tell him your organization is responsible for the robberies."

"What the hell!" he shouted, out loud, again startling his young companion. Grabbing a towel, he ran to the bathroom, and turned on the faucet.

"I'll go to jail!" he whispered tightly, watching the water flow into the sink. "Is that what you want?"

"You must tell him your organization is responsible for the robberies."

"But we can't just. . ."

"You must tell him your organization is responsible for the robberies."

"Shit!" he whispered. "Goddamit!"

And he felt the Headache lift. The communication was over. It was one of the shortest encounters Evan had ever had with *God*. He wondered briefly if it was because of the circumstances in which *God* had caught him: cheating — again — on his wife. He shrugged and chose not to think about it. Staring again at the water, he decided to splash some on his face. Then he took a deep breath.

He would have to decide: obey or disobey. He'd never defied *God* before (at least not substantially), but this latest command — he just wasn't sure he could do it.

He turned off the sink and headed back into the bedroom. "Headache," he explained to the puzzled young woman.

Evan, a former financier and real estate mogul — and one of the richest men in the world — had been speaking with *God* for almost five years. The first time, he was relaxing in his den, drinking a martini after an difficult day of negotiations. Too tired to read a newspaper, he'd flicked on his holovid and was immediately drawn into one of the most fascinating holo–shows he'd ever seen. It was a documentary/re–enactment of an episode from the 20th century destruction of European Jews which had been known as the Holocaust. Evan watched, in the beginning only mildly interested, as a group of skinny but determined Jews in a doomed ghetto in an Eastern European city called Warsaw plotted a rebellion against the Nazis.

Evan recalled only vague details of the Holocaust — after all it had occured almost two centuries before, and he hadn't taken a history course in twenty years. Ordinarily, it would not have been a subject that interested him in the least; in fact at first he'd had the urge to switch channels. But after a few minutes, for some reason, he found himself transfixed. Could these starving corpses really be successful, he wondered. Could they defeat the German army? Would spirit overpower machine guns?

Evan had been watching for nearly an hour, despairing as the doomed revolt headed toward its inevitable denouement, when he suddenly felt something brush against his toes. He looked down and saw the electric chord from his holovid dangling loose next to his foot, the prongs just touching the outside of his sock. The cord was not where it belonged; in other words it was not connected to the wall. The machine was not plugged in. Yet he'd been using the thing, watching it, for over an hour. He slowly turned his gaze back to the holo—screen. The Holocaust drama had disappeared and in its place was an orangish light, the color of fire. Then Evan felt the first Headache.

It was not like the powerful, stabbing migraines Evan had suffered in college before his first nerve transplant. It was a dull, irritating pain that grew worse in the light, like a hangover, or the headache you get after riding a particularly obnoxious roller coaster. Evan blinked his eyes several times, turned away from the orange light, and then heard the Voice, coming from his holo—screen.

"You have to build ships," it said. "Thousands of ships. It's the only way to save the Jews."

"Ships?" Evan asked, massaging his temples.

"You will talk to your friend the president. You will raise all the money you need. Build these ships. Otherwise it will happen again. Only worse."

And then Evan felt the HEADACHE.

At first it was merely the worst, most searing, punishing pain Evan had ever felt in his life, or — for that matter — had ever imagined could be felt. Then it got worse. The only way Evan could describe it later was to say that he felt — not even in his whole head, really just in his forehead — the agony of each of the six million Jews who perished in the Holocaust. And it wasn't just their physical suffering — the choking gas, the burning gunshot wounds, the cold steel of the bayonets, the jackboots crushing skulls, the dirt in the lungs, the foulness in the bowels, the frost-bitten toes, the howls of hunger, the broken shards of glass cutting through veins in the throat. Evan also felt the terror of the roundups, the humiliation of naked girls standing defenseless in the mud, the horror of witnessing a child snatched away and beaten to death, the despair of seeing friends turn into enemies, the grief of loss, the crushing hate, and — above all — the terrible frustration and helplessness.

All these horrifying sensations, this complete physical assault — the entire Holocaust experience — descended upon Evan's brain in a ghastly symphony of death and deprivation. It lasted a fraction of a second. The memory of it would torture Evan for the rest of his life.

When it was over, Evan heard his holovid continue its bizarre narrative, as if nothing had happened.

"The new Ukrainian Alliance is about to embark on a war of expansion. During the course of the war, they'll implement Nazi-like policies against all Jews in the conquered territories. No one will help, and no one will care. Israel will try to intervene; she will be destroyed with the push of a button. You have seven years to get all the Jews you can off of Earth. You will go to a planet I will show you. A new planet. A planet for the Jews."

Evan had absolutely no doubt that everything his holovid told him was true. Even though as far as he understood, the new Ukrainian nationalists were not in the least bit hostile to Jews; in fact, they seemed to go out of their way to cultivate the Western democracies. Even though there had never been a successful manned space-flight out of the solar system; even though the state of Israel was easily the most powerful force in the Middle East, and it seemed more likely Israel could destroy the Ukrainian Alliance with the press of a button than the other way around; even though Evan understood that the most rational explanation for the whole experience was that he was dreaming. Still, Evan knew it was all true. No dream could be responsible for the Holocaust Headache, and nothing able to inject such unadulterated pain could ever be capable of lying.

So Evan understood: it was all true. He just didn't want anything to do with it. "No one will believe me," he told the holovid.

"Many will believe you. Enough for you to succeed."

"I really don't have much influence on the president."

"You will have a great deal of influence on him."

"I'm not a politician. I'm not a scientist. I'm not an astronaut. I wouldn't even know how to begin."

"I will find politicians. I will find scientists. I will find astronauts. I will tell you how to begin."

"I'm not well. I have asthma and achardic arrhythmia."

"You will live another sixty—seven years."

"I don't want to do this."

"You must."

The arguing continued for another twenty—two hours, until finally Evan fell asleep in the middle of objecting that his wife and daughters just wouldn't allow it. While he dozed, he dreamt he'd been given an entire strategy for transporting two hundred and fifty thousand Jews off of the planet — a plan that covered all the bases — political, scientific, and economic. In his dream, he executed the strategy to perfection only to have the entire project shut down at the last minute because he couldn't decide what to wear on the day of the Great Exodus.

He woke up after a two hour nap, feeling as tired as he ever had in his life, but remembering every detail of the dream. His head hurt. He showered, shaved, changed into a new suit and called the White House. Then he told his wife.

Before boarding his private jet to Washington, he stopped in to see Rabbi Judah Loeb, a wise old rabbi who'd been a friend of his late father. In the course of the past dozen years, Rabbi Loeb's sect had become the largest Hasidic group in the world. The Rabbi, through his own charisma, and through the efforts of a dedicated core of followers, had become the most widely admired leader in traditional Judaism, and a symbol of Jewish spirituality to the outside world. His blessings were now a valuable commodity among American politicians, who felt — probably correctly — that the sainted Rabbi had the power to sway hundreds of thousands of votes.

Evan had followed Rabbi Loeb's rise to prominence with a mixture of cynicism and amusement. A non-believer, he'd never put much stock in Hasidic piety; he regarded most Jewish ideas and rituals as superstitious relics. Besides, he remembered when the great Rabbi Loeb could barely attract ten Jews for a Sabbath service, when, as a struggling young rabbi, he'd depended entirely on Evan's father for his salary and for the maintenance of the small schull on Cleveland's west side. Still, Evan thought that the Rabbi's support would be helpful in winning over the president. He hoped he could convince him to fly to Washington, and at least sit in on the White House meeting.

"I don't believe a word of this," Rabbi Loeb spat out, sitting cross-legged on a synagogue bench like some Jewish Buddha, his graying beard hiding most of his face. "Why would you lie about such sacred matters?"

Evan looked at the old man and sighed. If he couldn't get this pious, spiritual giant to believe God really had spoken to him, how could he possibly convince his friend the president, who — for all he knew — didn't even believe in God?

"Rabbi," he said softly, "I. . ."

"You think because you are so wealthy and you own half the world. . . you think because of your riches and your privileges, God chooses to speak with you?"

Evan noticed the rabbi never looked directly at him when he spoke. Instead, his gaze just wandered. Evan wondered for a moment if the old man was blind.

"I know this sounds strange, Rabbi, but. . ."

"Such *chutzpah*. The Holy One should spare us from such arrogance!"

"Rabbi, if you'll just let me. . ."

"Your father — his memory is a great blessing — would be so ashamed. To have a son like you!"

Evan, who was not used to being spoken to in such a tone, worked hard to control his anger. He reminded himself that his story really was preposterous, and the rabbi's reaction was perfectly normal. Still, the virulence of Rabbi Loeb's attack surprised him. He began to grow annoyed.

"You're a disgrace to your mother's memory," the rabbi went on, looking everywhere in the room — at the bookshelves, the computer terminal, out the window — everywhere but at Evan. "At this moment, in the better world, she turns red with shame, she curses the day you were born, the very moment you were conceived!"

"Excuse me, Rabbi, I'm not sure. . ."

"She wails and beats her breast. 'Such a scoundrel for a son,' she cries out. 'A villian who perpetuates an unholy hoax simply to acquire even more glory and more money. How,' your mother screams, 'could God have cursed me so?!' She spends all her moments in Paradise crying and weeping."

To Evan, this began to seem a bit harsh.

"You consign your children to *Gehenna* — to the pits of hell — with these actions. Your demon children will not survive this joke, your pig of a son, your cow of a daughter, your whore of a wife. . ."

"Shut up!" Evan yelled out, suddenly furious. "This is not about me!" he screamed at the rabbi, his outraged voice filling the cramped office. "It's not about my family!" He stood up, balled his fists, and, with one sweeping motion, knocked all of the Rabbi's books and papers off of his desk. "It's about saving Jews!" he roared. His weak heart was now beating at an alarming rate. "I didn't choose to do this!" he continued. "I didn't ask for this! But if you don't accept me, the hell with you. You can go. . ." Evan stopped in mid-sentence. He noticed the rabbi was smiling, showing off a mouth full of yellowing teeth.

"At last," the rabbi chuckled loudly, his pale blue eyes glowing abruptly with warmth and acceptance.

"You believed me all along," Evan said.

"Of course."

"Then why. . ?"

"This is a terrible task the Holy One has placed on you. It is not a job for the meek, or the polite. You must learn to accept attacks. You must learn to talk so people will hear. You must get angry. We must hear God Himself in your voice, His spirit in your words. We must see the light of the Lord in your face. Otherwise," he said, his voice lowering, his eyes reflecting a despair so sharp it made Judah turn away, "we perish."

"You'll come with me to Washington?"

"I'll go with you wherever you ask," the Rabbi answered. He nodded his head slowly, as if responding to ancient wisdom. "You are my teacher now," he whispered. "My teacher," he repeated, and stood.

They flew together to Washington.

President Mortimer Michaels was Jewish but this was a secret known only to a select few. Evan was one of those few. He'd discovered it when both he and the president were fourteen years old. Mortimer had invited Evan to spend some time in the Michaels' palatial home in Shaker Heights. It was Friday night, and Evan, wandering around the house, noticed Sabbath candles burning in the master bedroom. "You're Jewish?" Evan asked, with only slight curiosity.

"Of course not," Mortimer answered, whisking them away from his parents' room.

"But those are Shabbes candles," Evan protested. "I've seen them at my grandparents' house."

Mortimer continued denying it, refusing even to acknowledge that there was anything special at all about "the goddamn candles." But Evan persisted. The candles were Jewish, so Mortimer's parents must be Jewish. Ergo, Mortimer, "You're a Jew!"

"What's the big deal?" Evan asked. "I know lots of Jews. I'm a Jew. It's nothing to be ashamed of."

"I'm not ashamed, goddamit, I'm just not Jewish! All right, my mother's Jewish. But it's just her! I don't even. . ."

"Wait a second, Mortimer. If your mom's a Jew, then you're one too. That's the rule: the mother's Jewish, then you're Jewish. You're a Jew! Just like me, just like Stanley Horowiz, just like Rabbi Loeb, just like Jesus."

Evan wasn't sure why he couldn't let go of the subject. He, himself, hardly cared about Judaism. But there was something about this rich boy's denial that irritated him. Evan's family was wealthy too — not as wealthy as Mortimer's, but still pretty well off. But they never tried to hide their Jewishness.

Nevertheless, he did finally back off, and — after repeated pleas from Mortimer — promised never to tell anyone about his friend's "secret." Years later, when considering Mortimer's odd behavior, he realized that even back then, his eighth grade buddy must have been planning a political career and had somehow calculated that being a Jew would put him at a continual disadvantage. Evan couldn't see why this would be so — after all, there were lots of successful Jewish politicians — but he was willing to respect Mortimer's wishes. He liked him and valued his friendship — a friendship which remained active through high school, Harvard College, and Yale Law school. He had no desire to cause him any trouble.

As a politician — and later as president — Mortimer Michaels dedicated his career to re-unifying the United States of America. By the middle of the twenty-first century, the racial polarization of America was an established political fact. For all intents and purposes, ethnic identification had become the only significant source of political identity. Black politicians represented black Americans, whites represented whites, Latinos — the largest group — represented Latinos, and so on. Mortimer led a multi-racial party called "The Melting Potters," whose primary purpose was to defeat the Ethnic Empowerment Act (EEA) — a proposed ammendment to the constitution which would divide the United States into self-governing racial enclaves.

A resourceful and eloquent man with a golden political gift, Mortimer managed to defeat the amendment and roll back years of separatist-style legislation. When he first ran for president in the year 2060, it was clear a vote for him was a vote for his vision of an America freed from race consciousness. He lost that year, and lost again in 2064, but in 2068 he finally squeaked by. Many commentators prophesied a bloody civil war, as different ethnic groups geared up to fight to preserve their political distinctiveness. Instead, Mortimer, through force of personality and sheer will, led a peaceful revolution. He and his supporters restored what they called "the Federal democracy." Mortimer told everyone he was proud to be following the traditions of his political hero, Abraham Lincoln.

Evan and Mortimer stayed in touch through the ups and downs of Mortimer's political career, the way all powerful American politicians stay in touch with all American citizens who happen to be multi-billionaires. Evan cared about Mortimer's political positions only to the extent which they affected his ability to continue making money. He contributed generously to his old friend's campaigns — neither out of the goodness of his heart nor for old time's sake — but so that one more politician in Washington would owe something to Evan Isaacs.

Evan noticed that Mortimer continued to hide his Jewishness through the years. As a young Senator, he'd married a Roman-Catholic, and the two of them worshipped regularly in a Unitarian church in Washington. As president, Mortimer mouthed religiously bland, but clearly Christian bromides every Christmas on the White House lawn. One of Mortimer's sons was now studying for the ministry.

Evan remained puzzled, and even slightly contemptuous at this continuing masquerade, but felt no inclination to unmask his former friend. Evan wasn't sure if Mortimer even remembered what he'd revealed to him as a teenager all those years ago in Shaker Heights. They never discussed it again, even at the bar mitzvah of Evan's oldest son, when Mortimer, already a powerful man, honored Evan with his attendance. In the back of his mind, Evan figured the information might someday be useful, but he rarely thought about it. Before God talked to him, Evan rarely thought about Judaism at all. For that matter, he rarely thought about his old friend, the president of the United States.

Rabbi Loeb, dressed in the Orthodox style with black coat and black homburg, stood next to Evan as they waited for the president to enter the reception room. The rabbi appeared nervous, shifting his feet, and running his hand through his thick beard. Mortimer surprised Evan by walking right up to Rabbi Loeb and embracing him.

"I was about to introduce you," Evan said, shaking the president's hand.

"There's no need," Rabbi Loeb said quickly. Mortimer nodded and motioned for his guests to find seats around an enormous mahogany table.

Evan looked around, clearly uncomfortable. He'd forgotten that a "private" chat with the president always included three note-takers, four secret service agents, Jerome Bazel — the president's chief of staff — and five other miscellaneous advisors Evan didn't recognize. The secret service agents, tall and muscular, stood in the background. But the advisors and scribblers sat on both sides of the president.

"Mortimer," he whispered, leaning toward his friend's ear. "Do you think we could be alone? *Really* alone?"

The president nodded and three advisors left the room. None of the others moved. "This is as alone as I get," Mortimer said.

Evan shrugged. Never one to waste time with small talk, he launched right into his request. He was going to build space ships, he said, so he could get as many Jews as possible off the planet. It may not be apparent now, he confided to his friend, but the Ukrainian nationalists would soon launch aggressive attacks against all the Jews on Earth. Yes, even the Jews in Israel. And there's no point in trying to fight, he explained. They'd lose. No one will come to the Jews' aid because no one really cares about what happens to Jews. So Evan would build the ships. He didn't need any money; he'd pay for it himself. He just needed permission from the government. He described the entire plan, leaving out only the small detail about the whole project being commanded by God who spoke to Evan through his Holovid. Evan felt it wise to leave out this particular detail, and Rabbi Loeb had agreed.

Mortimer gaped at Evan. He regarded him as one might regard a particularly dangerous mental patient.

"You're playing jokes on me, Evan?" he said. His face turned red with anger. "An important man like you? You and the Rabbi have nothing better to do than play a practical joke on the president of the United States?"

"It's no joke, Mortimer," Evan said softly.

Mortimer looked at Rabbi Loeb, who nodded. The president, normally a man of moderate temperament, flew into a rage. "How can I possibly take this seriously Evan?! Space ships, Ukrainians, Jews, what am I supposed to. . ."

"Mortimer," Evan said, interrupting. "I thought this might be a project of special interest to you. Given, your, uh . . . your history of interest in . . . uh . . . these matters."

"Mr. President," Rabbi Loeb said, looking deep into Mortimer's eyes. The president, at the sound of the resonant commanding voice, snapped his head around to face the Rabbi. "It would mean a great deal to me if you would. . ." he paused for a moment, searching for the right word, ". . . consider this. At least read the report Mr. Isaacs' people have prepared."

Mortimer gazed at the Rabbi, a look of concern and warmth spreading over his face.

Evan couldn't figure out what was going on. Wasn't *he* supposed to be convincing the president? Isn't that why *God* had chosen him? What was Rabbi Loeb doing? He was about to describe the technology he hoped to harness for his new spaceships when Mortimer spoke.

"I'll read the report," he said, looking straight at the Rabbi, ignoring everyone else in the room. Then he stood, nodded curtly at Evan, and went out the door, his entourage following quickly behind. Evan and Rabbi Loeb remained in their chairs. The meeting had lasted less than fifteen minutes.

"What was that all about?" Evan asked, as soon as everyone had left. "I thought it was my job to convince the president. Do you know him?"

Rabbi Loeb shrugged. "He's a politician. He looks for votes. He thinks I have them." He stroked his thick beard. "I may have some influence with him." He shrugged again.

Evan closed his eyes and rubbed his temples. "You know, I can't be sure of anything anymore. I don't really know what I'm supposed to do now. All this planning, all the money and we haven't — that is I haven't — heard from God since that first day. God's not guiding us at all!"

"Yes, well, Evan, this. . . this is not *entirely* true."

Evan glared at him. "He's spoken to you?" he whispered tightly, as if the president's meeting room might be bugged.

"Not . . . not exactly. Not in a voice. Not in a spoken voice."

"Then, what. . . ?"

"A dream. A feeling. A vision. A trance. A sense." He shrugged again. "I don't know what to call it. I thought I might be imagining things. I sensed you were coming. I felt I would have a role. I know the president," he paused, searching for the right word, "admires me. I figured he would listen to me. *How exactly did I know these things?*" He turned up his open palms.

"How was it?" Evan asked, softly.

"What, Evan?"

"Hearing from God."

The Rabbi thought for a moment, then shrugged. "How should it be?" He gestured toward the door, and they walked out together. On the way to the limousine, Rabbi Loeb asked, "How was it for you?"

Evan ignored the question at first as he settled stiffly into his seat and gave instructions to the driver. He watched as the glass partition between the back and the front seat snapped shut. Then, turning to his companion, Evan answered. "It was horrible." The Rabbi nodded.

Three days later, the president announced his approval, but called it a "private plan for colonizing space." He made no mention of Jews or Ukrainians in the announcement.

One month later, another Headache visited Evan. He was riding in his land car, heading toward his office at "Exodus" headquarters, listening to a Brahms concerto. The day before, at the advice of his accountant, he'd called an emergency meeting with his financial advisors.

"You must ask the president for money," his car radio told him. Strangely, the Brahms music still played in the background.

Evan blinked his eyes a few times, confused. He looked at his driver, who clearly hadn't heard anything.

"You must ask the president for money," the radio repeated.

"But I don't need the money," Evan said. "We have enough money!"

"You must ask the president for money."

"I promised him I wouldn't. This was supposed to be a *private* project. A private project," Evan repeated, his voice taking on a bit of an edge.

"You must ask the president for money."

Evan sighed, then clicked off the radio. It was clearly going to play only one song today, even if it was a nonsense song. He knew he couldn't possibly ask the president for money. The government deficit was large enough, and there was no popular will to finance a civilian space project. Luckily, he knew God was mistaken. They didn't need the money.

But as soon as he walked in the door, his chief accountant — who also happened to be his first cousin — had this to say: "We're looking at a twenty-billion-dollar shortfall in the first year, Evan." Evan glared at him, but the accountant kept his eyes glued to the computer screen. "Fuel costs, Evan. No one can control that." Evan noticed Rabbi Loeb sitting in the corner, looking out the window. "We could sink your entire fortune into Exodus," his cousin continued, "but it probably won't be enough."

Evan was still standing at the office entrance. He slammed the door shut, sat down, and swung his feet on top of his desk. Then he inhaled slowly, thinking about his weak heart, and took a sip of water. "Banks?" he asked.

"No bank in America will loan you money, Evan. A month ago you could have snapped your fingers. You were always a sound investment. Now they all think you're crazy. They don't know *what* you're up to." The accountant, who'd worked with Evan for over twenty years, looked as if he shared those sentiments. But there was nothing Evan could do. He couldn't shut down now if he wanted to, not when all legal barriers to the space flights had just been lifted. He thought about going back to his car and turning on the radio, but he was afraid of getting another Headache. Instead he kicked everyone out of the office except for Rabbi Loeb. The Rabbi, still staring out the window at the site where the ships would be built, told him softly not to worry. He would call the White House. He rose, smoothed out his black coat, and left.

Ten minutes later, Evan's private phone rang. It was Rabbi Loeb.

"Twenty–five billion dollars has just been transferred to the company's account," he said.

Evan didn't want to inquire, but felt he had no choice. "How?"

Evan could practically hear the Rabbi's shrug.

"I asked," is all he said.

"One hundred ships," Evan said. He was drinking a beer, sitting across from Rabbi Loeb. Since first hearing from God, he'd begun consuming eight to twelve beers every day. Somedays beer was all he ate or drank. "That's 100,000 Jews."

Rabbi Loeb puffed on his pipe. This was the habit he'd acquired after first "hearing from" God. It helped him concentrate on spiritual matters, he explained. "There's fifteen million Jews in the world," he pointed out.

Evan took a long swig, draining the bottle. He twisted open another one. "I guess the other 14,900,000 are out of luck," he said.

"Evan. . ."

Evan threw the open bottle against the wall, shattering it into thousands of pieces and sending out a warm spray of beer that settled on Rabbi Loeb's black coat. The crash was louder than even Evan had expected, though he was not surprised to see that the Rabbi didn't move a muscle. The old man didn't even seem to notice.

"Evan," he started again, calmly plucking a shard of glass from his coat, and still puffing serenely. "We need more."

Evan considered pouring an entire bottle of beer down the Rabbi's pipe, but understood that the old man would probably just keeping on puffing. He had explained it to him over and over: the money was gone; one hundred thousand was the absolute maximum number of people they could safely send to Alpha 2, the planet his scientists had recommended for the colonization project. His staff referred to it as The Planet of the Jews.

Until now, the project had proceeded with amazing efficiency and swiftness. The best scientific minds of the generation designed the ships, chartered the relevant regions of space and plotted the correct course. Tremendous technological difficulties were overcome in a relatively short time. Discreet advertising in Jewish newspapers easily garnered him not only several billion dollars in contributions but also 300,000 volunteers for the journey. Only five years after God first appeared to Evan in the middle of a holovid drama, one hundred gleaming blue-and-white ships sat in the Arizona desert, ready to cart

100,000 souls out of the solar system and into a whole new life.

But there wouldn't be any more. There was no money, and Evan didn't know how to get more. Besides, he wasn't even sure he was supposed to build additional ships. God hadn't spoken to him in over two years, and God had always been a bit fuzzy on exactly how many Jews he was supposed to transport off the planet.

"Rabbi," Evan said. "We may not even be able to get 100,000 Jews to sign up with us!"

"300,000 already have," the Rabbi pointed out.

"They've said they'd *like* to go!" Evan snapped. "It doesn't mean they'll actually do it! Give up everything they own, live in a spaceship for two years, land on a planet that might kill them the second they step on to it! You really think more than 5,000 lunatics will sign up for that? I'm not even sure I'm gonna go!"

"Build more ships, Evan. When the time comes, millions will want to go with us."

"How the fuck do you know that!" Evan spat out. It was the first time he'd sworn in the presence of the Rabbi, who raised his eyebrow slightly, but continued to puff on his pipe. He was examining a picture of Evan's wife and children. The two friends sat still for almost five minutes, Evan looking intently at the Rabbi, the Rabbi still studying the family photograph. Finally, he turned away from the picture and regarded Evan.

"How do I know?" he said. "Let me ask you this. How do *you* know what you know of this project?"

"God?" Evan softly asked, feeling an unpleasant pang he realized was jealousy. "God spoke to you?"

"Evan," he said patiently, like a teacher. "God doesn't speak to me. I don't own a holovid set or a radio or a private limousine. God speaks to you. But there are other ways to communicate."

Evan waited. The rabbi shrugged. "Why do you think I started smoking this pipe?" he asked. "Tobacco is a very unhealthy product. I was never a smoker, and never attracted to it. Even now, I don't particularly like it. It leaves a stale taste in my mouth, and my lips and tongue are often sore. But I smoke. Because, while passing a tobacco store some time ago, while walking home from *schull*, I had an. . . an urge. An urge to buy a pipe. And then an urge to buy tobacco. And then an urge to take these strange new things home with me, and to use them. Evan, as I smoked — and at first you must know I despised it — I coughed and I choked and my eyes felt like there were rocks in them. But the more I smoked the more I learned. I learned many things. I learned, for instance, that our scientists would have no trouble with the basic design of the space ships. And I learned they would find a suitable planet with no difficulty. I learned you are no longer talking with your son or daughters, and that you regularly cheat on your wife with a series of high priced prostitutes. . . ."

Evan started to protest, but the Rabbi held up his hand. "I'm simply telling you what I learned, Evan, and I wanted to show you that what I learned is truth. I'm not judging you. But you must understand: what I learn is *true*."

Evan nodded.

"I also learned this," continued the Rabbi. "We will need to transport at least 250,000 Jews off this planet, or the Jewish people will disappear completely."

"250,000!" Evan nearly exploded out his seat. Rabbi Loeb sat him down with a glance.

"It is the number, Evan. The minimum. But I also learned this. No matter how many ships we build, multitudes will be disappointed. When the time comes, we will never be able to carry all the Jews who wish to go. We will save many; but many, many more will be doomed to death. This I also learned."

Evan was surprised to see tears forming in the Rabbi's eyes.

"Every time I smoke this wretched pipe, Evan, every time I use this filthy tobacco, I learn these things. Over and over again. Some will be saved," he cried, tears streaming down his hairy cheeks, "and millions will die." He looked at Evan, his beard now wet from weeping. "Millions," he repeated.

Evan left the office without saying a word. He hopped into his hover car, waved off the driver, and sped to the house of his favorite call girl, a young woman who lived twenty minutes from the airfield. He stayed for one hour, and when he was done, returned to his office. He picked up the phone and began making calls. He made calls for fifty–six hours straight without stopping. By the end of the week, he'd raised another 30 billion dollars, enough for fifty more ships.

"Evan, we can steal. We can take the money from others. We can rob banks. This is what we must do." Rabbi Loeb was speaking in his calmest, most professorial voice. Evan was convinced the strain had finally gotten to him. Rabbi Loeb had gone insane.

"Is that what your pipe tells you?" he demanded, making no effort to hide the scorn in his voice. "To steal? Isn't there some commandment about stealing?"

"It's not the pipe," he admitted. "This is my own idea. But I see no alternative. All of our other resources have dried up."

Evan mixed himself a scotch and water. He'd given up on beer long ago. He mixed another drink for the Rabbi, who accepted it gratefully. Both men now drank heavily, though neither the drinking nor the smoking nor Evan's lengthy and varied sexual indulgences slowed either of them down. Since the beginning of the project, they both managed to live on three or four hours of sleep a night. Evan had all but abandoned his previous life — his friends, his career, his family. The Rabbi gave up his old pulpit, resigned from his teaching positions, and deserted his desperate Hasidic followers — all in order to dedicate himself to the project. They would go days without meals. But somehow they stayed healthy — though they both looked awful. Evan suspected God was keeping their lungs and hearts and livers and brains intact until the completion of the project. Then they'd both die from lung cancer, or cirrhosis of the liver, or gonorrhea, or HIV — or maybe from some colorful combination of these.

In one fashion or another, both men had sold not only their souls, but their hearts, minds, bodies, and morals to the Exodus project. Neither of them had any life outside of the project, neither of them could imagine a world without the project. Nothing was more important. But Evan, if only to keep them all out of jail, felt he had to draw the line at armed robbery.

He was about to articulate his objections when he felt another

Headache. Like his first encounter with God, this revelation left Evan wounded. However, unlike the first time, this wound was completely physical. For the rest of his days on Earth, Evan would carry a dull, occasionally throbbing pain one inch above his left eye. It would inter-fere — sometimes more, sometimes less — with his thought processes, and it would occasionally make him stutter. At the time, of course, he didn't know how long the effects would last. All he knew was it hurt like hell. And it went on and on. The great Holocaust—inspired pain only lasted an instance. This agony continued for more than twenty—five minutes. By the end, Evan would have done or said anything to make it stop. He noticed Rabbi Loeb rush up to him, massage his temples, pour water down his throat. He felt himself furiously shake off the Rabbi and send the larger man sprawling to the floor. In the next minute or so he became vaguely aware that — in one furious motion — he had swept every piece of paper and computer disk off of his desk, and had, in the next moment, pivoted, grabbed a book shelf, and sent fifty volumes on space aerodynamics crashing to the ground. He ran to the opposite end of the room and tore down every picture hanging on the wall. Still, the pain went on. This was a lonely, solitary, voiceless, senseless agony. There was no communication in the pain, only a furious, assaulting negation, a desperate stab at wiping out whatever Evan was thinking. After twenty-five minutes, he knew he couldn't take it anymore. He was about to crash his head into the wall and knock himself cold when, abruptly, the headache ceased.

Straightening up, he felt Rabbi Loeb embracing him from behind. He slowly disentangled himself and sat down on the soaked floor. The room reaked of tobacco and scotch. He accepted a glass of water and gulped it down.

"I g—g—gguess we'll go ahead with the robberies," he stuttered softly, but loud enough for the Rabbi to hear. He was breathing deeply, sucking in air as fast as he could.

The Rabbi nodded. "I'll arrange it," he said gently.

Stumbling to his feet, Evan called in his secretary and asked her to summon a maintenance team to clean up the office. She took a quick look at the chaos, shot a dirty look at Rabbi Loeb, and went about her tasks. The Rabbi shrugged.

The robberies were successful. Somehow, Rabbi Loeb knew exactly which targets to hit. He spread the jobs out over the entire world; only a few intrepid FBI agents suspected a pattern, and no one connected any of the break-ins to the Exodus project. For two years, Rabbi Loeb and his crew robbed banks.

During those robbery years, Evan barely saw or spoke to Rabbi Loeb. He left this entire "fundraising" project in the rabbi's capable hands. Rabbi Loeb didn't tell Evan how exactly he transformed himself from a Talmudic scholar and theologian into an accomplished criminal, and Evan didn't ask. Evan focused on Exodus, and kept it moving as more money poured in. In the course of the next two years, fifty additional ships were built, and several hundred thousand more Jews signed up to leave Earth.

The seventh year arrived. Evan was ready to stop, and this time Rabbi Loeb agreed. They'd managed to fit, staff, and equip 200 ships — enough to transport close to 200,000 souls. Neither the Rabbi nor Evan had heard from God in over two years. It was time to take-off.

In fact, Evan was in the middle of celebrating with Lianna, the young, long-haired prostitute, when God stopped him in the middle and ordered him to admit to the president of the United States that his organization had stolen money from banks all over America.

Like most of the other times, Evan was at first inclined to ignore this voice. This time, in fact, he was even more convinced he should just refuse. After all, he did obey God most of the time, at least 90% of the time. What other human being could boast of a similar percentage? He'd pretend this particular order — which would put him behind bars, and shut the project down altogether — had never come. They'd take off, as planned, the next month, and Evan would worry about the consequences when they reached the Planet of the Jews. When two weeks passed without any further headaches or revelations, Evan became even more convinced he'd done the right thing.

Ten days before their planned departure, Rabbi Loeb burst into Evan's office puffing furiously on his pipe. Evan noticed that the old

Rabbi was now almost completely gray, with only a few brown strands remaining in his long, full beard. Evan regretted that the two had grown apart the past couple of years. Since Rabbi Loeb had taken over "development," he'd kept his distance from Evan. A surge of affection and respect tugged at Evan's heart as he looked into his friend's powerful gray eyes. The good feeling evaporated immediately as the Rabbi vented his rage.

"What is going on?!" he demanded, sucking on his pipe and talking at the same time. "Something is not *right*, this is not the proper feeling we should be. . . something is simply not correct, something is altogether improper. . ."

Evan sighed and put up his hand. "Calm down," he said. "Stop. Sit. I should have known I couldn't keep it from you, it's just. . . I. . .well, never mind. This is what happened." He told the Rabbi of God's latest demand. "You can see why I absolutely couldn't go along with this. It would mean a jail cell and a complete shutdown of. . ."

Rabbi Loeb erupted in fury. Evan had never seen a man so angry. Underneath his beard, the old man's face turned beet red. Perspiration poured out of the many creases in his forehead, and his eyes suddenly emitted a deep orange glow, like bolts of fire. "And you are too much of a saint to be imprisoned?!" the Rabbi spat out. "You, with your whores! And your drinking! You — who abandoned your family, your children — you, Evan, you should never see the inside of a cell?! Remember Evan, where all this money comes from for our project!"

"But you also. . ."

"Yes, you *putz*, of course me! Of course me, also! And when you explain this operation to the president, has it not occurred to you I will also end up in prison? But God has not asked me to be the agent of our imprisonment, he has asked you! But you are too pure, and too arrogant, and too addicted to your liquor and your prostitutes. . . ."

"Shut up!" Evan cried out, balling his fists. Evan was now also furious—at the rabbi; he was ready to kill the old bastard. It only occurred to him later that Rabbi Loeb was, once again, baiting him, using his scorn and judgement to test Evan or to provoke him. Several months later, he realized this gentle person could not have been sincere in unloading this Old Testament–like wrath, not after everything they'd been through together. But at the moment, Evan was ready to grab the old scholar's beard, hurl him against the glass balcony door, and send him crashing to the concrete twenty–five stories below. Fortunately, the old Rabbi turned abruptly and stalked from the office. Evan was about to run after him, but he banged his shin on the way out, and sank to the carpet in pain.

Suddenly – for no reason he could think of – Evan started crying. Mostly, it was the pain in his leg. But he also felt a horrid sense of betrayal from Rabbi Loeb. The old man was the only person in Evan's life who could fully understand the awesome terror of the past years – the horror and the exaltation of being part of God's plan. Evan worried suddenly that he would never see the Rabbi again, and the thought filled him with an overpowering sense of loneliness. Rabbi Loeb had been more than an intimate friend, more than a confidante, more than a spiritual advisor. He was also a co–traveler in the most profound sense of the phrase, and the potential loss of his companionship left Evan in an oddly passive state of panic. He sat on his rug for twenty minutes weeping, his face buried in his hands. He longed for a headache, for a revelation from God, if only to relieve the awful feeling of loneliness. But he realized, finally, nothing would come, no revelations, no resolutions, until he followed God's plan. He stood up, blew his nose, drank down two tumblers of scotch, and called the White House.

President Michaels hung up on him ten minutes into the conversation. Twenty minutes later, Federal agents stormed the Exodus offices. On order of the government, the project was shut down. In quick succession, Evan was stripped, searched, blindfolded, handcuffed, forced into a helicopter and flown to a federal penitentiary forty miles south of Washington in Gaithesburg, Virginia. Until one of the bulky troopers tossed him into a dry, cold cell, removed his blindfold, and unlocked his handcuffs, Evan was certain he was going to be shot. Sitting in the corner of the jail cell on a lumpy mattress, staring at the cold gray bars, he still considered it a likely possibility.

Instead, he sat quietly for six days, mostly dozing, getting up only for meals and calls of nature. Only the clanging of the metal food tray disrupted the silence which had taken over Evan's life. Each day, with an increasing sense of resignation, he waited for some kind of judgement.

On the seventh day, two muscular guards appeared in his cell. Silently, they handcuffed him and put him in chains, though this time they left off the blindfold. They led him to the rear of an empty prison van and drove him through the countryside of Virginia. Evan was surprised to find that they were headed north, toward Washington. As the dirty white van passed through Virginia's green, rolling hills, the glare of the sunlight caught Evan's eyes. For a dreaded moment he though he was going to have another Headache. Instead, he found himself marveling at the simple beauty of the scenery. It was spring. Trees were in bloom; cows and sheep grazed on the broad farmlands; families rode bicycles along the road.

Tears formed in Evan's eyes as he reflected on all the years he'd lost to this insane project. What if it really had been insane? What if all his efforts had been merely to appease an illusion? What if God had never spoken to him at all? What if there really were no God? Maybe, Evan considered, psychotropic drugs would have been a more appropriate response to the voice from his holovid — better than spending seven years and seventy—five billion dollars building space-ships. In the midst of these thoughts, the glare from the sun suddenly shone too intensely. Evan was forced to shut his eyes, and close out the world. He kept them shut for several minutes.

At first there was only the orange colored, sun—tinged darkness, with a few yellow spots floating to the top of his field of vision. Nothing unusual. But, just as Evan was about to open his eyes, he saw a little yellow man, dressed in a black coat and a yarmulke, stroll into his line of sight.

"Keep your eyes closed," the man whispered. "And I'll try not to hurt you."

"You'll try. . ." Evan began.

"Shhhh," said the little man. "People can hear you. Don't speak; it's not for you to speak. Not to me, not now. I can't stay long. Listen to me, Evan. This is the longest conversation I've ever had with you. It's extremely unusual. I haven't showed myself this way even to Rabbi Loeb.

But I need you to see that this is real. That's my message to you, Evan. All this is real. Everything I've said, hinted and intimated to you is the absolute truth. Everything will happen as I predicted. So be strong. There's not much suffering left, at least not for you. Not until the real suffering, anyway."

At that, the small yellow man disappeared, replaced by total blackness. Evan slowly opened his eyes, not sure what he would see. But all his eyes revealed to him were more green hills, and a few tobacco farms. Evan sat back in his seat, reassured. It hasn't been for nothing, he thought. It's all been real. How do I know, he thought to himself. How can I be sure? A little yellow man with a yarmulke appeared to me in a vision and reassured me.

Evan started laughing. The prison guards stared at him, but he didn't care. He chortled all the way to his new home — a small red-brick prison which appeared to be only twenty miles south of Washington D.C. There he was given a large private cell — more a dorm room, in fact than a prison cell. It had a desk, a full size bed, a holovision projector with tape player, and a computerized stereo center complete with several music discs.

As far as Evan could tell, he was the only prisoner in the entire complex. The only people he ever saw were the ten guards, who all sported blue and orange warm up suits with yellow caps, a uniform he had never seen before and which seemed oddly cheerful for a jail. Evan was allowed to roam freely through the one-acre prison grounds. He could use the gym equipment, including the weights, without regulation. He was only locked into his room at night, for eight hours. He was not treated like a dangerous criminal, except for the inconvenient fact that he was not allowed to leave.

Six months passed. Evan, with no booze or cigarettes available — and with a steady regiment of both exercise and surprisingly nutritious meals — shaped up physically for the first time in seven years. His wrinkles began to clear up, his yellowish complexion whitened — a bit. He was not unhappy. He was, of course curious about his fate — would he be locked up for five years? Ten? Forever? But he learned to stop pestering the guards, who obviously knew nothing.

Then one day, he woke up and everyone was gone. No one let him out of his room; no one brought him breakfast. Or lunch. Evan quickly discovered that despite his relative comfort, this room was indeed a prison cell. He couldn't get out, not by jimmying the door with a leg from his bed, by smashing the window with his Deluxe Webster's dictionary, by fiddling for hours trying to decode the electronic lock, or by nearly breaking his leg in continuous but futile efforts to kick down the door.

Two days passed. Evan contented himself with swallows of water from the sink. Hunger crept up on him, but for some reason he wasn't worried. He understood that if no one showed up, his situation looked pretty grim. But he couldn't imagine no one would show up. He spent the days reading, meditating, and playing with the lock.

By the fourth day, he was worried, even more worried than he was hungry. By the fifth day he was just hungry. On the sixth day, the faucet and the toilet stopped working. Evan slurped down some dregs from the faucet, positive it would be the last drink of his life. He thought, briefly, about the little yellow man, and wondered what the creature (God himself? An angel?) was doing to help him. He scratched his chin, felt his head for signs of pain, went over to the bed, laid down, and waited to die. He wondered how long it would take.

Early in the morning on the seventh day he received a visitor: the president of the United States of America.

Mortimer unlocked the cell and handed Evan a ham sandwich and three bottles of water. Evan ignored the food and poured the water down his throat.

"You have two weeks to take your Jews and leave."

Evan nodded, tearing open the sandwich and stuffing it into his mouth. He felt new strength course through his bones.

"There's a helicopter waiting for you outside. It will get you to Arizona in two hours. Get back to work, Evan. Two weeks is all you'll get. You may get less."

Evan nodded again, and finished off the sandwich. He looked around for another.

"Evan," the president said slowly. "These are not my deadlines. It's the Ukrainians. It's about to happen. The war. A roundup of Jews.

Everything you predicted."

A guard handed Evan another sandwich. He chewed on it while Mortimer explained. Ten days ago, he said, the Ukrainian Alliance invaded three countries in Eastern Europe: The Romanian/Bulgarian confederation, Lithuania, and the Slavic Republic. Caught by surprise, all three countries surrendered without a fight. The day after proclaiming a "Greater European Empire," Ukrainian forces began arresting all Jews under their control. Thousands had already been captured, thousands more became refugees overnight. But none of this was the worst news, Mortimer said.

Evan waited.

"Eight days ago, the Ukrainians launched a nuclear tipped missile against Tel Aviv. They call it their Zyclon Fighter. Evan," the president continued. "It looks like the missile got through."

Evan looked up, surprised for the first time in the conversation. "Israel has nuclear protection," he said softly. "The same as the United States."

Mortimer nodded. "Just like us," he said. "But the missile got through. Just one missile. But it's more destructive than anything we've ever seen."

"How many. . ."

"We don't know, Evan. We can't get any information. There's no communication network open now to Israel. Phone lines, radio, cable, satellite surveillance — everything's cut off. And I don't need to tell you, the whole episode has created panic in the United States. Because if Israel's unprotected, then we. . . well, you understand. Big cities are emptying out. Washington, the whole damn state of Virginia, everyone's streaming to Canada or Mexico. People expect an attack at any minute. And since the deep disarmament. . ."

Evan understood. The United States stopped developing intercontinental missiles decades ago. They'd been rendered obsolete by the practically universal use of Nuclear Protection, a space based missile defense which not only intercepted 99% of all missiles, but caused all nuclear warheads to explode in the atmosphere, and automatically sent out a powerful gas which absorbed all harmful radiation. The United States was incapable of launching a preemptive attack on the

Ukraine. So they'd have to send troops, Evan thought, but that took time. Too much time.

"But Evan," Mortimer said. "None of this is why you have to take your people and launch. It's because of the message I received this morning from Serge Galitsky, the Ukrainian dictator. It's a pretty startling message, Evan. I don't believe either of us would have thought we'd live long enough to see a message like this. He gives me three weeks, Evan. Three weeks to round up what he calls 'my' Jews. Otherwise they send missiles to Los Angeles, New York, Chicago and Boston. And they'll keep sending them until we either comply, or everyone's dead."

"You're not going to. . ."

"Of course not!" Mortimer spat out. "But you have to get moving! Give me time! I'm going to tell him we're sending our Jews into space, that it's been our plan all along. I'll convince him we hate the Jews as much as he does. I'll try to stall, tell him I agree with him, absolutely, we have to get rid of the bastards, but I want to do it my way. Evan, since I arrested you, another one hundred thousand Jews signed up for your project. And donations poured in. You became a kind of martyr. This Rabbi Loeb of yours was able to put together fifty more ships in six months! But time's up now, Evan."

Mortimer went on to explain that the president's own private, souped-up heliporter was waiting for him, to transport him back to Arizona. He would be accompanied, said the president, by twenty five FBI and thirty secret service agents.

Evan looked puzzled.

"New intelligence," Mortimer explained. "We can't quite figure out why, but we think the Ukrainians are trying to shut down the Exodus project. We don't understand their motives, but we don't want to take any chances. Anyway, this explains those times Rabbi Loeb was almost killed. I'm sure you wondered. . ."

"What!" Evan burst out.

"The attempts on Rabbi Loeb's life. There have been three in past two years. I'm sure you thought it was just. . ." He studied Evan's face. "You didn't know about them, did you?"

Evan shook his head. "He never told me," he whispered, half to himself. "No one told me." He looked up at the president. "I wonder. . ." he started to say.

"Get back to Arizona," the president said, interrupting "Get your Jews into space."

Utter pandemonium greeted Evan at the Exodus space field. Years before, expecting a six month–long orientation for the pioneers, Exodus had built a huge dormitory complex with enough rooms to hold two hundred thousand souls. Those rooms now overflowed, and Evan saw what he thought must be another one hundred thousand Jews sprawled all over the complex, camped out in tents and sleeping bags, many lying dangerously close to the spaceships. Evan couldn't see any of his own private police anywhere near the ships' perimeter. Security's been violated, he thought; they'd have to thoroughly inspect each spaceship before taking off.

Evan quickly considered weight restrictions, thermodynamics, daily caloric intake, waste disposal, escape velocity, social psychology – all the disciplines he'd studied hurriedly the past seven years in order to lead the project. Another fifty ships, he thought, it meant they'd be taking at least two hundred and fifty thousand people. He had to talk to Rabbi Loeb. He directed the heliporter's pilot to land at the northeast corner, next to the "fundraising" compound.

Evan felt a surprising sense of anxiety at the thought of seeing Rabbi Loeb again. Would they be able to work together again, to regain their old friendship? Would the Rabbi be surprised to see him? Or was it, as Evan increasingly suspected, Rabbi Loeb who had sent the president to his cell in the first place?

He was never able to discover the answer to those and hundreds of other questions he'd been storing for years about Rabbi Loeb. Evan found the Rabbi's sizable body slumped over his desk. Black, day–old, blood was smeared on the papers and file–folders, and computer discs which lay strewn all over the office. A silver–handled knife protruded from the Rabbi's back. Evan gasped and took a step back in horror. Then he sank to his knees and started to cry out, first from sorrow and then pain, as another Headache assaulted him. His hands rushed up to his temples, massaging furiously as The Voice attacked his ears from all directions. "Leave!" the Voice commanded. "Leave, leave, leave, leave, leave."

They nearly couldn't. Ukrainian agents (or someone) had planted time bombs, set to ignite at lift off, in eight of the spaceships. After one pilot, who happened to have served ten years in the Israeli army as an expert in explosives, noticed a suspicious blip in the fuel line readings, Evan had to bite the bullet, ignore the president's ultimatum, and spend three excruciating weeks supervising a complete security inspection. By then, rumors of Ukrainian attacks had spread through the entire Jewish community. Evan, with great reluctance, was forced to use his own reconstituted security force to turn away Jews begging to be included on the trip.

Hours before lift–off, Evan spoke to his old friend the president on a secure holo–link up.

"Come with us," Evan said.

Mortimer laughed. Evan's face stayed dead serious; he wasn't joking. Mortimer stopped chuckling and apologized.

"They'll find out," Evan said. "Someone will find out. And you may not be protected. They may not want to protect you."

Mortimer shrugged. "I've already decided," he told Evan. "I'm going to announce it myself. But afterwards," he said. "After you leave."

Evan thought of reminding him that if the president suddenly revealed himself to be Jewish after the government had just spent forty–five billion dollars on a project to rescue some American Jews by sending them off into space, the public outrage could reach uncontrollable proportions. He may even be forced to resign the presidency. On the other hand, the entire United States might be blown up by the Ukrainians' strange new 'zyclon' nuclear weapon. Evan assumed the government was furiously working on a defense, and that the Americans had their own network of spies in the Ukraine. But he was also happy that he, for one, was getting off the planet. And he saw that his friend, who'd actively rejected his Jewishness all those years ago, was not about to throw his lot in now with a bunch of space–faring Jews in search of a new Zion, even to save his life. Evan mumbled a quick goodbye and cut off the connection.

In the end they only lost one ship. Somehow Evan's security team had missed the bomb, hidden in the food stores. It ignited exactly thirty minutes after take-off, killing one thousand Jews from Cleveland. But everyone else escaped and nearly two hundred and fifty thousand Jews became refugees from the planet Earth. A few days into the trip, scientists detected abnormal amounts of radiation coming from their old home-planet. The most likely explanation, the scientists told Evan, was a massive nuclear weapon exploding somewhere on Earth. Did it hit the United States? The Ukraine? Israel? There was no way to know; their instruments were not precise enough. To his own horror, Evan realized he didn't really care. And from a practical view point, it didn't matter which country now ceased to exist, or indeed if the whole planet had blown up. Their course was set; they couldn't go back. They could only go forward, toward the Planet of the Jews.

Evan was captain and commander-in-chief of the voyage, but really had very little to do. He wasn't a space pilot or a physicist or an engineer. The technical experts he'd hired on Earth ran the show. Each individual ship elected a government of sorts, and a kind of intra-ship council met occasionally through the use of shuttles and holo-projection. Evan chaired those meetings, but contributed almost nothing to the discussions.

He socialized with absolutely no one; he ignored his ex-wife and his children. He talked with fewer and fewer people, until by the end of the voyage he was speaking only when it was absolutely necessary. He spent most of his time in his private cabin (he was honored to receive the only private living space on all the ships) doing two things: studying the teachings of Rabbi Judah Loeb, and trying to figure who killed the old rabbi, and why.

The former endeavor was relatively simple. All he had to do was learn Yiddish, Aramaic and Hebrew, and familiarize himself with the most esoteric Jewish scholarship. But at least there was material available to him; he could try.

But solving the murder of his friend? The way Evan saw it, he had only one problem: no evidence. The killer had left behind absolutely no physical trace, not even a microscopic DNA fragment. Evan knew most of the voyagers assumed the murderer was a Ukrainian agent, and Evan tended to agree. But this killer somehow got through not only his private security team, but through hundreds of federal agents who were protecting both the project in general and Rabbi Loeb in particular. To Evan this meant only one thing, that someone on the inside, a traitor, murdered his friend. But why would the Ukrainians kill Rabbi Loeb? Granted he was important to Exodus, but the project could go on and, in fact, did go on without him. Both Evan and the Rabbi realized early on that the only essential personnel in Exodus were the scientists — the men and women who figured out how to get from here to there. The rabbi could rob banks, but he couldn't pilot a space ship. Evan felt it was no coincidence the Rabbi was killed the day he got out of prison; but, try as he might, he couldn't find the connection. In fact, Evan had only one clue — a metaphysical one. Every time he thought hard about Rabbi Loeb — either by studying his books, or puzzling out his murder, or just engaging in deep reminiscences — his chronic headache eased. And for Evan, the relief from the pain was so welcome, that by the end of the voyage all he was doing was thinking about Rabbi Loeb. He forced himself to think of nothing else.

Until the day before Arrival, when he closed his eyes tightly, and released his thoughts. He thought freely about his teenage daughters, his son. He thought about Lianna Smith, the last prostitute he'd visited. He thought of how he'd destroyed his marriage by saving the Jewish people, thought about the future, pictured in his mind a white sandy beach next to a blue, salty sea. Then the headache lifted. Now he knew who killed Rabbi Loeb. But not why.

Evan resigned from his command position an hour before leaving the ship. This was neither a surprise nor a disappointment to the voyagers, who'd long ago become alarmed by Evan's strangeness and had already selected other leaders. No one looked to Evan for guidance anymore, but out of deference to his work on the project, they gave him the honor of being the first to disembark. He asked for an hour to be entirely alone on the planet.

He wound his way through a forest, following signposts he somehow recognized, then climbed a steep, red, muddy hill, which levelled out onto an alpine meadow of yellow flowers. He strolled along, following a narrow (man–made?) path which cut through a field of multi–colored grasses, a swampy marsh filled with more red mud, and then descended to the sea. Along the way the red mud turned to sand.

When he arrived at the edge of a gaping blue ocean, spread out like a cataract along the horizon, he scooped up a heap of pure white sand and looked deeply into the tiny, speckled crystals. Bringing the handful to his nose, and inhaling their salty fragrance, his head felt lighter and clearer than it ever had in his life. No headache whatsoever. On the contrary a sudden sensation of complete clarity overcame him, a feeling of absolute confidence that his head would never again be a source of pain. Tears of gratitude filled his eyes. He kicked off his hiking boots, and stepped carefully into the water. Soft, cold waves brushed against his ankles. He knelt down and tasted the sea. Salty.

"It was you," he said out loud.

"Yes," the familiar voice responded immediately, and Evan knew right away it was coming from the sand. "I called you."

"And we came," Evan whispered.

"You came," the Voice agreed.

Evan stepped further into the ocean, the water now reaching his knees. He noticed the Voice was coming as much from the water as from the sand.

It's the planet, he realized, suddenly. The entire world. The Planet of the Jews summoned us. It's been the planet all along. He was neither shocked nor disappointed at this realization. He stopped crying and let the sand slip through his fingers. He wondered how he should feel. Anger? Gratitude? Relief? Sorrow? He tossed the remaining sand into the ocean, and waded toward the shore.

"What now?" he asked out loud, slogging back toward his ships, the warmth of the sand soothing his chilled bare feet. "What now?" he thought to himself, and started running across the beach, suddenly anxious to help his co–voyagers settle in.

"Life," the voice answered. But Evan had already stopped listening.

3: Partisans

"Judah, we need more material! Fast!"

It was two days before deadline, and Alan was screaming at me. Perspiration made his glasses slide all the way down his nose, giving me an unobstructed view of his eyes, which appeared to be bugging out even more than usual.

"A sequel, Judah!" he yelled. "This story *cries* for a sequel, it *weeps* for a sequel. I'm begging you," he said, "for a sequel."

"Alan, I . . ."

He came out from behind his desk and did something extraordinary. He embraced me – awkwardly. I'm nearly six inches taller than he is, and weigh a good seventy pounds less – and then he kissed me on my cheek, his bald head brushing lightly against my chin. "Judah," he said solemnly. "I've always thought you were the finest science fiction comic book writer I've ever worked with. But this short story, this Jewish planet story well . . . the reaction speaks for itself, doesn't it Judah? Judah, we made *money!* A great deal of money! So write me another one, Judah. Write some more about these Jews, this planet. We can have a series, a. . ."

"Alan," I said, finally interrupting, freeing myself. "I didn't write it. How many times do I have to. . ."

"Stop with this bullshit!" he yelled, staring up at me. At any minute I thought he would hop up on his desk, just so he could look me in the eye. "You expect me to believe two Hasids took a break from their *davening*, their *shuckling*, and their. . . whatever the hell else they do . . . and composed a best–selling story? In their spare time? In between the chicken soup and the gefilte fish?"

I remained silent, but he understood my meaning. That was exactly what I expected him to believe. Because it was true.

He plopped down in his chair, breathing heavily. Not for the first time, I wondered if he suffered from some kind of heart condition. He could certainly stand to lose some weight. I was about to ask, but he spoke first.

"Then find them," he said. "Find those Hasids."

I sighed. The fact is, as much as I would have liked to, I had no way of locating Moishe and Esther. They never gave me an address. Only a section of town, which, for some reason, I'd forgotten. "Alan," I said. "I don't know how. . ."

"Use your head, goddam it!" he exploded, the blue veins of his shiny scalp popping out ominously. "Go to Brooklyn! Put an ad in the goddamn *Jerusalem Post*. Look in every schull on Ocean Parkway, every *shtiebel* in Crown Heights, every yeshiva. Find me those Jews!"

"But Alan. . ."

"Judah, listen. You know this isn't just business for me. If it were just the money, just the sales, do you think I would have been so quick to publish it?" He looked at me. I could swear I saw tears forming just behind his glasses. "I *like* this story, Judah," he said slowly, shaking his head. "It. . ." he shook his head, and pushed up his glasses. They slid right back down. "It does something to me, though for the life of me I can't figure out what. Do you know what I mean?"

I nodded, and replied softly, practically whispering. "It does something to me, too."

He stared at me, then took off his glasses and wiped them on his shirt. "Just find them," he said.

But how was I supposed to find them? The day before deadline, out of pure desperation, I took the subway to Crown Heights and wandered around. It was a hot, sticky August morning. Ultra–Orthodox mothers in long plaid dresses, their heads covered with brightly colored scarves, strolled along the broad boulevard with their children. Many pushed multi–seat strollers which held three, sometimes four babies. Most of the women I saw were pregnant. In fact, I actually got tangled up in a large group of pregnant mothers in front of Fein's Fish store on Ocean Parkway. Alone with my thoughts, paying no attention to where I was going, I bumped into a large full–bellied mother coming out of the store holding two children and three packages. As I backed away, I ran into another pregnant mother who seemed to shove me into a yet a third protruding stomach. I felt like the ball in a pinball machine, knocked from bumper to bumper.

I searched for Moishe and Esther, but I really hadn't the foggiest notion where to look. I ducked into a couple of synagogues, saw plenty of men in beards, but none with Moishe's piercing green eyes. Once I thought I recognized him from behind – there was a man whose jacket looked rumpled in almost the same fashion as Moishe's – but after I called out, it turned out to be a much older, and more sinister, looking man. I gave up and headed back to the office.

Moishe and Esther were waiting for me inside. Esther sat at my desk, leafing through manuscripts; Moishe stood off to the side, his hands folded meekly in front of him.

"Thank God!" I said, suddenly out of breath.

They looked at me. "Baruch Hashem," Esther said.

"Where have you been?" I asked, a bit cross. "I've been searching all over for you."

They looked at each other. "Where should we be?" said Esther, shrugging.

"We've been at home," Moishe added.

As if out of thin air, Esther produced a thick manilla envelope and held it out to me.

"A new manuscript," I said, grabbing it eagerly.

They got up to leave. "Wait!" I cried, practically imploring. "I have, well, just some, a few, uh, questions."

They waited. Moishe fiddled nervously with his beard, and Esther stared at me, putting as much impatience in a look as any human face could muster. I noticed her turquoise dress looked tidier, less wrinkled than before. She'd obviously taken it to the cleaners.

"I, uh, I know so l-l-little about you." I stammered, devolving into my usual inarticulate, stuttering self in their presence. "I don't even know your last name."

"Cassanofsky," they both answered at once.

"Or where you're from," I said.

"Williamsburg," they both replied. "Park Street," Moishe added.

"Anything else?" Esther asked, checking her watch like a busy executive. Did they have an appointment at a comic book company? A power lunch at some kosher restaurant?

"Yes," I answered and cleared my throat. "In the story," I said gesturing toward their first manuscript, still lying on my desk. I'd suddenly forgotten its name. "That one," I said desperately, nodding at it with my head. They watched me, not moving a muscle. "Why?" I asked, then blushed. I'd even gotten that word wrong. "I mean *what*. What happens to the Jews left behind on Earth? The ones who don't manage to escape in the space ship?"

Almost imperceptibly, Moishe glanced at Esther, a worried expression on his face. "They get killed," Esther answered evenly. "By the Zyclon Bomb."

I became so distraught at this answer that I felt an actual weakening in my knees. I backed up toward a chair and fell down, breathing heavily. Moishe appeared concerned, but Esther again checked her watch.

"But doesn't that bother you?" I managed to say. "All those people? And this evil force – the Nazis, the Zyclon Bomb? I mean it's just so upsetting!"

"Of course it bothers me," Esther snapped. She glanced quickly at Moishe. "I mean it bothers us. But it's just a story. Just a science fiction tale for your two-bit. . ."

"Besides," Moishe said, interrupting. Apparently, he'd

discovered his own voice. "It's really a story about resistance. How the Jews don't just escape, they fight back. Because they're forced to fight. And they win. It's a story of how they finally win."

"Resistance," I said softly, almost to myself. "I see," I said, though of course, I didn't. It seemed to me the Jews in the story just up and left. There was hardly any fighting at all. I sat still and thought for a moment. I was about to ask another question, but they'd already left.

I settled into my chair, feet propped up on the desk, and was about to read their new story when the alarm went off, reminding me of my meeting with Uncle Max. I scrambled out of the office and rushed downstairs to grab a taxi.

This particular meeting offered a great deal of promise – certainly much more than my previous interviews with Max – because this time he'd invited a few comrades from his days with the partisans. Although I enjoyed Max's colorful stream of conscience Holocaust narratives, I was desperate for some kind of coherent story, and I realized I would need to get it from someone else. I'd been after him for several weeks to introduce me to some of his old friends. I'd learned from my father that most of Max's social life consisted of get–togethers with other survivors. I also knew that the surviving members of his partisan band met several times a year. So I knew Max was in touch with these people. Maybe, I thought, he could even get Rabbi Boronsky to talk to me about the partisans. But Max never seemed to understand what I was asking.

"Others?" he would say. "You wish to speak with others? The others are all *dead*! Mother, Alexander, the children. This is *my* story, Judah, which I am telling *you*."

"No, no," I would explain. "I mean others who survived. Others who were with you in the forests. The other fighters."

"Ah, well. You understand. The forests. It. . . it was not like home."

I understood, but he didn't. In his roundabout way, he

would always steer me off the subject. In fact, if I became too insistent, he would suddenly weave a fascinating and even coherent story, drawing me away, at least temporarily, from any interest in outsiders, while at the same time compensating me for his unwillingness to produce any.

But a week before, for no apparent reason, Max gave in. He invited three of his comrades to participate in the interview. When I began to thank him profusely for his efforts, he waved me off.

"You're doing them this favor, Judah," he said. "This is a service you are doing for them. They wish to talk. The are quite eager to talk. They've wanted to talk for years."

I found Max and four other old men sitting around Max's kitchen table. Oddly, the room smelled of aftershave, as if Max's friends had prettied themselves up for the meeting. At first glance, they seemed like a perfectly pleasant crew, but I quickly noticed there was something just slightly "off" about each of them; it was as if I'd wandered into a particularly subtle but still effective carnival side show. One of them, for instance, his name was Ira, wore gloves, inside, even though it was quite hot. Another, Mendel Greenberg, had only nine fingers. The third, David Idelson, the frailest looking one of the bunch, had exactly half a head of hair; thin white hair filled the left side of his head, but on his right side he was completely bald. The last comrade – I never learned his name – couldn't speak English, even though he'd lived in America for over forty years. Even that wouldn't have particularly bothered me, but he kept trying to talk to me as if it were perfectly natural for me to understand him.

After introducing myself, and accepting the weakest cup of coffee I'd ever tasted, I froze up completely. Max had already told me he'd explained nothing to his friends about my comic book project. He'd leave it to me, he said. But, sitting in his old–fashioned kitchen with the white metal cabinets and the dented, humming refrigerator, I suddenly couldn't explain why

I'd asked to meet with them. I mumbled something about my father, and Rabbi Chaim Boronsky who'd been a partisan himself, about my fondness for my Uncle Max, my curiosity about Jewish resistance during the Holocaust. But it became clear I wasn't connecting. They stared at me glassy eyed, as if I were speaking a foreign language, which, I guess, I was. Finally, I came out with it.

"It's this comic book," I said.

They gaped at me, each shrugging more dramatically than the other. Foreign whisperings filled the air. Max got up to make tea.

"I'm writing a comic. . . I mean a graphic novel. A novel about the Holocaust. I'm a comic book writer. My plan is to draw different animals to represent different nationalities. The poles will be pigs, Americans will be horses, the Germans will be pitbulls, Jews will be. . ." I froze, staring at the strange, gray faces. "I haven't decided yet on Jews," I lied. Then I stopped. I couldn't say anything more.

"Stories," Max sang out, as he joined us with a tray of hot tea and stale, crumbling honey cakes. "He wants our stories, my nephew. He is an author," Max added as if to forestall any complaint that a comic book may not be the most appropriate venue for discussing the Holocaust.

"Yes, stories," I said, gratefully. "About the partisans, the forests, the Poles." I put out my hands, palms up, in reverence. My hands were empty of stories; this was the treasure I was seeking.

After consulting with each other in what I guessed was Yiddish, they related the following tale. My uncle, they told me (of course, I assumed they meant Uncle Max) had led a group of Jewish partisans that operated from the forests outside of Cracow. They would harass German troops with sniper fire, steal German rifles, and try to rescue Jewish families. Mostly, Max explained, they tried hard to stay alive, stealing just enough food and oil from the Poles to survive the harsh winters. He seemed to take pains to reassure me that they weren't a particularly violent bunch. They hardly ever killed anyone, and he wasn't sure if the Polish underground, much less the Germans, even knew of their existence. They wouldn't have existed at all, Max said, if it weren't for Rabbi Chaim Boronsky, the young Stashover Rebbe who was a constant spiritual inspiration, and a pretty fair fighter to boot. He was the one hero in the bunch. No one, Max assured me, was tougher than he. The other men around the table all nodded.

Like tag team story–tellers, Max suddenly stopped speaking, while David picked up the tale. One day, he related, a Polish peasant – a non–Jew – happened on their hide out. He claimed to be fleeing from the Nazis, and begged the suspicious group for just a couple of nights shelter. David wanted to kill the "miserable goy" right away, just to be safe, but my uncle recognized him as a boyhood companion. So the grateful Pole stayed on, even helping out on a raid or two. But one night Rabbi Boronsky caught him stealing extra food and stuffing it into his thick wool pants. This was a serious offense in a place where you literally never knew where your next meal was coming from. But, as David insisted on reminding me, they weren't cruel people. They understood hunger. Yet if someone steals from you, even once, how can you ever trust them again? And remember – this poor peasant wasn't even a Jew. No one can live in a partisan group – cold, hunted, and desperate – without the feeling of absolute trust for each comrade. Once the trust died, the comradeship died with it. So the group didn't know what to do. They couldn't just kick the peasant out; as much as he offered assurances, there was still a chance he would go straight to the Nazis. But they couldn't let him stay, because they couldn't trust him. They were stymied. But while they argued about it, for almost half an hour, my Uncle took a pistol and shot the peasant in the face, killing him instantly. That ended the discussion.

"He never explained," David told me, scratching the bald

side of his scalp. "Not to anyone, not to any of us, why he did it. Maybe he felt responsible. After all, he'd convinced us to trust the Pole in the first place. Maybe he never liked him. Maybe he just got tired of talking about it. But I'll tell you one thing. He was the only one who could have done it, who could have killed someone in cold blood, right in front of everyone. We thought we were tough men, fighting the Nazis. But we weren't. We were just scared and hungry and frozen. We were just trying to stay alive. But Judah – he was different." He smiled at me, a sly, teasing grin. "Your Uncle Judah was something else," he repeated, and the other old men all nodded.

"Excuse me," I said politely. "You mean Max. My Uncle Max."

They stared at me, mystified. They shook their heads and babbled at each other in Yiddish. What was this crazy comic book writer talking about?

"You said *Judah*," I explained, with a bit of agitation. Normally I wouldn't have been so insistent on extracting a correction. This was obviously just a slip of the tongue, and these were old men. But hearing my name in the middle of this weird story gave me the creeps. First Moishe and Esther freely used my name, and now these gentleman did the same. I was beginning to get the uncomfortable feeling that odd forces were imposing my own persona onto some utterly bizarre narratives. I wanted it to stop. "You said *Judah* killed the traitor," I continued, raising my voice. Was I screaming? I felt my face redden. "But I'm Judah," I insisted. "I wasn't there!"

Silence. Puzzled faces, old, wrinkled, and puzzled, and also pitying. Max's poor nephew, they were thinking. Losing his mind over a Freudian slip.

"You must have meant *Max*," I said, quieter now.

"Judah," Max explained. "We were speaking of your uncle. My brother. Your grandfather's brother. You were named for him, Judah. This was your Uncle Judah."

"But," I protested. "I wasn't. . . I never. . ." I swallowed hard. Then I got it. An uncle. A man I'd never heard of. No one had ever told me.

The information startled me in ways I couldn't begin to understand. My hands started shaking. I became nauseous. I tried to take a sip of tea, but I couldn't grip the cup. I'm positive I turned completely pale. None of the old men sitting around the table looked at all concerned. "I never knew about any other Judah," I whispered.

Max shrugged. My discovery, to him, was entirely uninteresting. "So now you know," he said. "This was your uncle, the man for whom you were named. He led our little, uh, our little band in the forests."

"Well," David said. "He killed the Pole."

"Yes, yes," Max agreed, quickly. "He was the one to do it."

"He was something else," David said.

"Something else," they all chimed in.

Meaning? That he was a killer? Or a hero? Or what? I was about to ask, when one of them – the Yiddish speaker, whose name I never learned – started coughing uncontrollably. The others hovered around him like nursing hens, shoving water at him, patting him on the back, screeching at him to "stop already," but nothing helped. He slid off his chair, rolling on the linoleum floor, coughing, and hacking, like a sputtering old motor car. Finally, I grabbed a phone and called 911. By the time the ambulance arrived, he was barely breathing, though the medics did manage to stabilize him before roaring off to St. Mary's. Max and the others were considerably shaken by the incident, and I didn't have the heart to press them for any further tales. Or even to ask Max why they'd chosen that particular horror story to tell me. I was about to say goodbye when Max suddenly remembered there was a package he wanted to give me. It had belonged to Judah, he said. He ran into one of the bedrooms and returned with a small, blue velvet bag. For just an instant, I recoiled, thinking it was the gun my uncle had used to murder the Pole.

"It's his *tefilin*," Max told me – two long thin black straps attached to two small black boxes. Orthodox men wind them around their arms and heads every morning as part of their prayers. "Judah's," he explained.

"Ah," I said, making no effort to reach for it. Why on earth would I want his *tefilin*?

"You should take it," he insisted, and shoved the bag at my chest, like a quarterback handing off a football. I had no choice; I couldn't just let it drop, so I took it.

Right before I left, the tefilin bag stuffed into my pants pocket, Max embraced me and kissed both my cheeks, a show of sentiment utterly foreign to our relationship up to that point. Confused, I hugged him in return, but left without saying anything.

When I got back to my office, Moishe and Esther's new story was waiting for me, perched in the center of my suddenly clean, dust–free, orderly desk – like a dove proudly displaying her shiny new nest. Had I cleaned my desk before I left? Had I really placed the manuscript at the exact center, taken a ruler and spent minutes finding the right spot? I put these questions on hold, though they were decidedly of great interest. I would pursue them later. But now, I was eager to read the story.

I read it straight through and understood immediately and intuitively that it would be an even greater sensation than the last one. Again, this was not an issue of good writing, snappy dialogue, clever use of futuristic science, suspense, pace or any qualitative characteristic. I was simply enamored with it, and I knew others would be too. It provoked an emotional response, which I was almost ready to label as spiritual. Without even bothering to show it to Alan (I knew he'd like it), I sent it up to be typeset for the next issue, including my own suggestions for the cover art. I considered recommending we devote the entire issue to the story (even though it was fairly short) but decided it would have been too much, at least at this point.

After dropping off the manuscript, I went downstairs and grabbed a cab headed for Brooklyn. I wanted to find Moishe and Esther. I wanted to talk to them about a permanent contract, about putting them on staff. I wanted to discuss the stories, and maybe offer suggestions for future plots. I wanted to enter into a professional relationship with them, one of mutual understanding and respect. But mostly I needed to show them my Uncle Judah's *tefilin*.

4: Time-Travelling Jews

Of course it was the Planet, not God, who had been talking to Evan all along. At least that's how Evan explained it to Alan Shapiro, Evan's successor as leader of the Jews. But even though the Planet wasn't God (and – for that matter – wasn't Jewish, or even human), it did enjoy participating in Evan's weekly Talmud class, as did Alan.

The night the time machine was invented, Evan was leading a discussion on the obligations of saving lives. Alan sat in on the class, though he was having difficulty concentrating.

"This is the situation," Evan explained, distributing the texts in both Hebrew and English. "You're wandering through the desert with a friend. You have enough water in your canteen to make it to civilization. Your friend has no water. If you share the water, you'll both die. If you take it all for yourself, your friend will certainly die, but you at least will survive. What do you do?"

"You give all the water to your friend!" The Planet immediately replied.

As usual, the Planet's voice sounded to everyone like Evan's voice. It took a long time for Evan to convince his fellow pioneers on the Planet of the Jews, that the Planet had simply chosen Evan's voice as a means to communicate, that it wasn't Evan talking, but the Planet. Eventually Evan proved it by having the Planet carry on a simultaneous conversation with everyone in the community, while Evan went scuba diving with Alan and a few other friends. It did the trick; they finally understood that Evan's disembodied voice sounding in their heads wasn't Evan at all but a manifestation of the telepathic powers of the Planet.

Still, it was confusing when Evan taught his Talmud classes. The teacher and the most eager pupil sounded exactly alike.

"Hmm," Evan responded. "An interesting suggestion. But one, as you can see, the Talmud doesn't even consider. Rabbi Akiva suggests the exact opposite — you should take all the water for yourself. Ben Peturah says you should split the water with your friend and die together."

"Ben Peturah, then!" the Planet exclaimed. "Certainly not Rabbi Akiva! Certainly not!"

Alan stifled a chuckle. Out of simple human decency, he tried to resist laughing at the Planet, even though Evan had explained to him the Planet could never experience humiliation, nor hurt feelings of any kind. But he was often amused to the point of laughing out loud at the Planet's enthusiasm for Talmudic dialectics. It was especially striking, since the Planet hardly ever spoke outside of Talmud class.

Evan explained why the Jewish tradition, in fact, preferred Rabbi Akiva's opinion. "We're never obligated to actively give up our own lives for others, even our closest friends. Now, this doesn't mean that we're allowed to commit murder in order to save ourselves from being killed. We're not. If someone comes up to me and says, 'you kill Alan, or I'll kill you,' then I have to allow myself to be murdered. The Talmud says, 'how do you know your blood is redder? Maybe his blood is redder.' Everyone agrees about this. But, still, we have a responsibility to our own bodies. How can we serve God if we're dead?"

Those comments triggered a lengthy debate on the ethics of risking lives in order to rescue others, which led, inevitably, to the perennial question of whether the Jews on the planet had done enough to save the Jews of Earth. Alan stayed out of the discussion; for him it was pointless to dwell on the past. Besides, he couldn't really stop himself from stealing glances at his watch. He planned to stop by the Pesek Z'man complex after class to check on the progress of the Time Travelling project. It seemed like they were finally getting somewhere, and were perhaps finally ready for some initial testing.

Alan recalled how the scientific theory for time travel had originated in Evan's Talmud class. Ziony Zevitt, a bearded, eccentric physicist and Orthodox Jew, who had developed most of the science which allowed for star flight , sat in on one of the sessions — merely to kill time, he later explained — when the idea suddenly hit him. Evan had been telling the story of how *God* once transported Moses forward through time and deposited him in the back of Rabbi Akiva's second century Torah class. It was the first time Dr. Zevitt seriously considered the relationship between time and space since graduate school. According to Zevitt, he immediately ran back to his office at the Technion — the new scientific institute built just the previous year — and started making calculations. Three days later he, along with several of his young students, came to Alan with a proposal. He wanted to build a time machine.

Alan had urged Evan to take charge of the project as chief executive officer. Since the Landing, actually since the take-off from Earth, Evan had almost completely withdrawn from public affairs. For the first six months of settlement, he barely spoke to anyone except Alan, whom he advised on a regular basis, and the Planet. He began to come out of his shell when a group of rabbis announced they were forming the world's first Yeshiva — a religious seminary which focused on Talmudic study. Evan insisted on being among the first students. He studied intently, practically in isolation, for six years, communicating only with his teachers, some of his fellow students, and, of course, the Planet, who reportedly offered great help in unravelling particularly difficult Talmudic puzzles. Finally, after receiving Rabbinic ordination, he joined the faculty of the Yeshiva and gradually re-joined the community. But he consistently refused any public or political role, as his fellow pioneers struggled through their first decade on this strange, sentient world.

Until, that is, Alan asked him to work with Ziony on the time-travel project. At first Evan said no. Then he changed his mind. The Planet, he explained, had talked him into it.

That night, after class, Alan and Evan walked together to Pesek Z'man headquarters. Alan noticed that, except for a full head of gray hair, Evan appeared younger than he'd looked even on Earth, twelve years before. Back then, they had worked together on the Exodus project. Alan had been Rabbi Judah Loeb's right-hand man, his chief fundraiser. Back then, he'd been appalled to witness both leaders completely ignoring the needs of their bodies, practically working themselves to death. Before Rabbi Loeb's murder, they'd both acquired the wrinkles of men twice their age, and the yellowed complexion of advanced liver patients. At liftoff, Alan genuinely feared for Evan's health; he looked as if he were about to have a heart attack or a stroke. But here he was, over a decade gone by, ruddy-faced, vigorous, muscular, walking with the broad, confident steps of an athlete, looking at 55 like he was in the prime of his life. Alan wondered about this sudden return to health, since he'd never seen his friend exercise, but he didn't ask. He had his suspicions, but he held his peace. After all, as the leader of over 250,000 souls, Alan now had enough to worry about.

The Pesek Z'man complex took up more space than anything else on the planet; it filled two of their standard 4000-square foot prefab, plastic houses. No other institution could claim more than one. Building materials were scarce on the Planet of the Jews; the Ruling Council limited the use of trees and plastics to those tasks deemed absolutely essential to maintain life. Luckily, the climate was perfect all the time. The temperature was always seventy two degrees, and rain only fell during the two winter months, and even then only from nightfall till dawn.

Evan strode into the laboratory, Alan following closely behind. Fifteen tired looking men and women — the senior staff of Pesek Z'man — sat around a table drinking coffee, most of them dressed in the casual uniform of the colony: blue shorts and white t-shirts. Only Dr. Zevitt sported the traditional white coat of a laboratory scientist. Alan hadn't visited the complex in over a year, and wouldn't have recognized the time machine at all if Evan hadn't walked up to what looked like an ordinary computer terminal, tapped it three times on the side and asked, "Ready to go?"

Everyone in the room turned to Zevitt, who made a slight, twitching gesture, which Alan could only assume was a nod.

"How do we test it?" Alan asked, staring at the terminal. It was no bigger than a small computer screen. He wondered how on earth this little thing could transport something through time.

"No need for tests!" Zevitt snapped angrily, not even bothering to look at Alan. "The mechanics, the mathematics, the physics, everything is *perfect*."

Alan was not at all offended by the scientist's tone. Here he was, an outsider to the scientific community, someone who rarely bothered to check up on the project, suddenly demanding tests. Still, he wasn't about to authorize an untested machine. He pushed his glasses up his nose and turned to Zevitt.

"That's not your decision to make, is it Doctor? Look, Evan we need to. . ."

"Alan," Evan interrupted, politely, squeezing his friend's shoulder. "We've discussed this. We can't test it. How can we test it? The machine only works to send things into the past. We can try to send something back there, but how are we supposed to know if it made it? We can go back ourselves and look, but then we'd be using an untested machine. We can wait until the time distortion effect wears off and the object re-appears, but we still can't be sure what happened to it — whether it truly traveled backward, or whether it just disappeared for a few days. Believe me, we've been through this. Either we trust the science, or we don't. And that is up to us to decide."

Alan nodded. The night before, the Ruling Council had authorized Alan and Evan, in conjunction with the Pesek Z'man staff, to make the final decision on whether and when to use the time machine. In case of a disagreement, Alan was to arbitrate. He took a deep breath, wiped the sweat off his bald head, then walked over to the table and poured himself a cup of coffee. "Well, you must know what I'm going to ask. Don't we run the risk. . ," he scratched his fat chin. "Isn't it possible," he continued, "that if we send someone back, we'll wipe out all of history? Someone will trigger some event which isn't supposed to happen and suddenly, we'll never have existed. No one will ever have existed. I mean, I read all the science fiction novels. Isn't this the big issue — the contamination of the time line?"

Evan looked nervously at Ziony, whose bugged-out eyes betrayed a soul nearly bursting with frustration. "These are not questions we can answer, Mr. President!" he said, singing out the phrase 'Mr.

President,' so everyone would hear the contempt in his voice. Alan, as usual, ignored the insult and listened. "We're not Talmudists!" Zevitt continued. "We're not theologians! We're not philosophers, God forbid. We're scientists! We've expanded the field of human knowledge. We should use the machine, and not be afraid!" He slammed his empty coffee mug down on the table, grabbed some papers and began making calculations. "Time line contamination," he muttered angrily, loud enough for everyone in the room to hear. "We're not science fiction writers!"

Alan turned to Evan.

"Alan," Evan said. "We just don't know. We've involved the mathematicians, the logisticians, we've looked at it from every angle, we just can't. . ."

"There will be no contamination."

It took Alan a few moments to realize it wasn't Evan talking anymore. It was the Planet. It had interrupted Evan — who now shut his mouth and waited.

"No contamination," the Planet repeated. "Illumination. Redemption."

"His opinion," Ziony barked out. Alan smiled. He could only image Zevitt arguing with the Planet — a mysterious, serenely confident Talmudic entity having it out with a radically rational, skeptical, short-tempered human who still doubted whether the Planet had any real existence outside of Evan's imagination.

"Illumination," the Planet repeated.

Alan asked how the machine worked. Evan showed him, carefully explaining the function of every part. Alan understood nothing except the operating instructions which seemed fairly simple. You typed in a date, how long you wanted to be stuck there, put your hand on the screen, and voila: Time travel.

"How would we use it?" Alan asked, and looked around the room. That's when the real discussion began.

It turned out four factions had developed. The first was Evan. He wanted to send one traveler to ancient Israel. The mission: discover if God had really spoken to Moses at Mt. Sinai. What greater service can we provide, he asked, than to confirm deep religious truth? Alan was not surprised that none of the scientists shared Evan's spiritual curiosity.

The second faction was Dr. Ziony Zevitt. With great passion, he urged that the machine be used to send observers to study how the greatest scientific geniuses in history made their revolutionary discoveries. "We could be with Isaac Newton when the apple fell. Or with Einstein. Or with Hawking when he discovered the Unified Field Theory of the Universe. We could understand how genius works! Maybe get a glimpse at the process of true inspiration! Evan, this is religious truth, is it not? Is this not how God enters our souls, with the creative process of thought? Let us watch the geniuses! *Then* we'll discover God."

But no one else was much interested in the process of inspiration. No one even bothered to respond to his rantings.

The remainder of the Pesek Z'man staff — a carefully selected group of historians and scientists — made up the third faction. For them, the time machine could only be used for one purpose: to undo the historical circumstances which led them all to the Planet of the Jews. In other words, they wanted to go back only twenty five years, to Chmielnitsky, Ukraine, and prevent the rise of the viciously anti–Semitic Ukrainian Nazis. "For all we know," Elena Gold, the leader of this faction, explained to Alan, "every single Jew left on Earth was murdered." She pointed to the machine. "We have the power now that we didn't have before. Power, Alan. We don't have to run away," she said, her voice suddenly cracking with emotion. "We can stop it from happening."

The fourth faction had one member: the Planet. It wanted to go after Nazi Germany. "What Elena proposes," The voice said, ringing in Alan's ears with what he thought was an extra sense of clarity, "is historically just, morally correct, and filled with the proper sense of the love of neighbor. But she lacks both ambition and imagination. You all do. You can use this machine to right the worst wrong in your history. The Holocaust. Go back to Earth and prevent the Holocaust. And remember. By preventing the first Holocaust, you prevent the second one. No German Nazis, no Ukrainian Nazis. You will have repaired your world, for yourselves and everyone else on your home planet. Repair," it said calmly. "This should be your goal. Wipe out the Nazis."

Alan leaned his stout body back in his chair, and adjusted his glasses. At first, he was inclined to ignore anything the Planet might contribute to the debate. This was, after all, a human decision to make. And the Planet's precise role in drawing them all off of Earth was still unclear enough to Alan that he couldn't help associating a sense of the sinister with the Planet. He had no real reason to distrust it, but nonetheless, he had suspicions.

As moderator, he put all four proposals on the floor and opened up a full scale debate. If the Planet participated in the discussion, Alan was prepared to ask it to butt out. There was, however no need. It stayed quiet the entire four-day argument.

Even so, they took its suggestion. They would go after the Germans.

After almost another year of preparation, three teams were set up. Elena Gold would lead a commando team back to 1928 Germany and assassinate Adolph Hitler. The second team, led by Alan, would infiltrate the American political scene of the 1930's and work to create a powerful and motivated American force strong enough to deter (or defeat) Hitler before Germany could become a threat to anyone. The third group, with Evan in charge, would spread out all over Europe, urging Jewish communities to get out while they could.

The idea was if one group failed, perhaps the other groups would succeed. Zevitt programmed the machine so each team had enough time to complete its task. After a designated amount of time, all the travelers would be whisked back to the Planet of the Jews, reappearing just one day after they'd left. The return would happen automatically. Or, anyone taking part in the missions could press a button and come back home whenever they wanted.

Since they'd agree long ago to leave aside problems of timeline contamination, no one bothered to point out that if any of the groups really did succeed, none of them would ever return to the Planet of the Jews, because none of the events which had led to their journey would ever have taken place.

Elena Gold waited two years, until 1930. Then she shot Adolph Hitler, at point blank range, directly through the heart. She pumped twelve led pellets into his chest, watched him scream, his twisted face filled with anger and fear, clutch at his bleeding chest, and fall over dead into a pool of blood. Ignoring the panic which erupted with the suddenness of a gun shot all around her, she knelt down and felt for a neck pulse. Finding none, she holstered her gun (she'd kept it cupped in her left hand because she'd been prepared to blow the fuehrer's head off if any signs of life remained) and quickly walked off the stage. No one saw her, of course. She was cloaked, along with her gun.

The next day she read in the *Berlin Gazette* that the leader of the Nazi Party had recovered fully from the light wounds he'd received when his stage–microphone short circuited, giving him a slight electric shock.

"You must have missed," Aaron Walken, one of her companions from the late 21st century, told her. They were sitting at an outdoor cafe at the Blindenshplatz across from the Reichstag.

"Idiot!" she hissed, and then blushed. It was unlike her to insult the comrades under her command. But she was frustrated. They'd trained for two years, tested the equipment, followed Hitler's movements, studied the leadership of the Nazi party, took turns at target practice, and perfected the cloaking technology to such an extent that even the half centimeter led pellets would be invisible for over one hundred years. Every outdoor speaking venue in Berlin had been studied; their pros and cons as spots for assassination carefully considered.

The group aimed for perfect political timing. They wanted to kill the evil dictator far enough along in his career, to strike fear into any other potential Nazi who might pick up his repugnant ideas and attempt to foist them on Europe. They wanted to make clear that being a Nazi leader was dangerous to one's health. On the other hand, they wanted to take him out before he became Germany's chancellor, so his murder wouldn't cause rioting, civil unrest, and, inevitably, pogroms. They'd fed all of the detail's of Hitler's career into their newly designed political assasination computer and came up with what they believed was the perfect date, time, and place for murder. But, despite all their tortuous, painstaking planning, something had gone wrong.

"He's obviously dead," Moshe Rothblum whispered, while sipping a beer. "Twelve bullets in the heart kills you," he pointed out.

"So they're hiding it?" Aaron asked.

"Obviously."

"But they must know they can't keep the news secret for long," Elena said. "There were witnesses. We saw reporters at the stadium from all over the world. They saw his chest collapse. All the blood! How could anyone deny it happened? What would be the point?"

"Maybe they're planning on installing a replacement," Aaron answered. "A twin, or a look–alike, or maybe they'll use plastic surgery. . ."

"Oh, don't be ridiculous," Elena said. "We've been tracking them for two years. We know all those characters, inside–out. They don't have the ability. . ."

"Look," Moshe interrupted "Why don't we just go over to his house. They say he's resting, recuperating. They say he's in bed. Let's go see."

They did. Moshe, the technical expert, figured they had enough charges in the cloaker to hide them for approximately five more missions. One visit to Hitler's apartment on Striemelstrasse would still leave them adequate cloaking power for several more attempts if they needed it. Elena, who still felt the burn on her trigger finger – it stung, but felt good – was sure all they'd find was an empty apartment. She'd seen Hitler's blood leak all over Blethkom Stadium.

They set up a sound muffler outside the building, put a miniature charge into the door lock, blasted their way into Hitler's bedroom and found him in his bed, covered with blankets, muttering in his sleep. It was him; there was no mistaking the moustache, nor the pock–marked face which, to Elena, looked like the face of Satan himself.

Even though they all knew the computer had recommended that any assasination be public, Elena grabbed her gun, put the barrel right up against Hitler's nose and shot ten times. All three of them watched as facial tissue, brain matter, blood and bones splattered all over the room. By the time she finished shooting, literally nothing was left of Hitler's face; only a bloody red stump hung loosely from his neck. Elena glared triumphantly at her companions, and motioned them to follow her out.

The next day, they watched as Hitler gave a speech at the Windersturm Restaurant to a group of wealthy widows of the Great War. He was brutal, charming, and fierce. After the talk, he ate hungrily, slurping the cabbage soup with great noisy gulps. He was very much alive.

They made two more attempts. Moshe slit his throat from ear to ear with a twelve-inch carving knife. Three hours later, they heard him on the radio denouncing American President Herbert Hoover as a tool of Jewish Capitalists. The following Friday, Aaron placed a small explosive device in Hitler's limousine. A cloaked Moshe, Elena, and Aaron watched as the car burst into flames trapping Hitler, his driver, and his bodyguard in the black Mercedes. The car burned for forty–five minutes before an ambulance and fire truck arrived. Aaron, his cloaking device equipped with thermal protection, walked into the flaming wreckage and saw three skeletons, their flesh completely burned away. The next Sunday Hitler attended services at the Great Lutheran Church in Shloderstasse. Elena and her two traveling companions watched him nod enthusiastically as the chubby pastor inveighed against the fierce, vengeful God of the Jews, who'd been thankfully replaced with the Love of Jesus. In the middle of the hate–filled homily, Elena touched a button on her coat, instantly transporting the group through time and space, back to the Planet of the Jews.

Senator Alan Shapiro, his bald head glistening with sweat, his normally steady pulse racing, sat with his feet propped up on his desk. He stared straight ahead, at the open door, and waited. His comrade and chief aide, Marshall Bookbinder, who also happened to be adjutant to the Head of Intelligence at the War Department, a senior advisor to Secretary of State Cordell Hull, and the head of the German Embassy's legal department, slipped in quietly, closing the door behind him.

"He's not going to do anything," he whispered tightly. "He won't respond at all."

All the color drained from Alan's face. His feet dropped to the floor with an assertive clunk. "Impossible!" he cried. "We had an absolute commitment! As soon as Hitler made his first move, the fleet was supposed to sail. Roosevelt sat here in this office and promised us!"

Marshall shrugged. "Call Hopkins," he suggested, with little enthusiasm. "And grab your checkbook," he added.

Alan gave the younger, slimmer man a quick, irritated look. During the past five years both of them had been surprised at how amenable senior government officials in the United States and Europe had been to bribery. Using enormous sums of money, Alan had all but purchased his Senate seat, and then later his chairmanship of the Armed Services committee. He'd also managed to set up an impressive private intelligence operation in the middle of Washington D.C., with the aid of some stealth, some ingenuity, some 21st century technology, but mostly with lots and lots of cash. No one Alan or Marshall approached ever explicitly refused a bribe. Some, like President Roosevelt's chief advisor Henry Hopkins, were particularly gifted at linguistic obfuscations and rationalizations. Some, like Secretary of State Cordell Hull strung them along for years. The president himself insisted the cash go to subordinates or family members. But everyone took the money. Of course, Alan doubted whether anyone in the history of the United States had ever before offered bribes of such startling amounts. He liked to think that the country's leaders – normally, he assumed, men of great integrity – were only being bought because the price was so high.

His group, six time-traveling spies from the Planet of the Jews, had decided back at their home base that their primary political tool would be money. None of them, not even Alan, himself a former member of the American Congress, and currently president of his community, had enough confidence in their political skills to design an honest plan which could work within the system. So they brought along a money–making machine. So far they'd manufactured, and spent, five billion dollars. They'd enriched most of the leaders of the Republic. But they'd also failed. Despite all the promises, all the bribes, all the propaganda, despite the clear direction of public opinion, the U.S. government was not going to respond in any meaningful way to Hitler's clear violation of the Versailles Treaty – his march into the demilitarized Rhineland.

Alan lifted up his blue and white tie, and ran his fingers across the clip. "Maybe I should just press this button," he said. "We should get out of here before we get into any real trouble." Marshall smiled at the word trouble. Altogether, different members of the group had been arrested twenty four times in six years. Bribe money had released each of them almost instantly, but they'd certainly already gotten themselves into trouble. Of course, none of them were dead — at least not yet.

"We should wait," Marshall said, after a long pause. "Try again. At least one more time. At the next provocation." Alan nodded slowly, and tucked his tie back into his shirt.

The president, Harry Hopkins, assured Senator Shapiro, was appalled, outraged.

Somehow, he said, the military bureaucracy fumbled. Roosevelt, Hopkins continued, had fully intended that the third fleet sail the minute one Nazi soldier entered the demilitarized zone. But somehow the order never got conveyed, the chain of command, uh, well, it broke down, the ships never got sent. And now, well, certainly the senator understood, now any aggressive act would mean war, especially since none of the European powers had lifted a finger. An American military response would now function as not merely a deterrent, but as a *casus belli*.

"Of course, Senator," Hopkins declared. "The president is ready for war. He's ready to fight the Nazi menace at any moment. But can we really make this claim about Congress? There are many members who might need more. . . more of your unique form of . . . persuasion."

Alan sighed and handed Hopkins a dark satchel filled with hundreds, fifties, and twenties, which added up to three hundred thousand dollars. It never ceased to amaze Alan how easy this whole process was. Hopkins had all but spelled it out to him: he needed bribe money. He never used any but the thinnest euphemism for this outright graft. And Alan had given him the suitcase in broad daylight in front of three witnesses. A simpler time, Alan thought to himself, with just a slight bit of longing.

Over the next two years, Alan handed over quite a few suitcases, not just to Harry Hopkins, but to several members of congress, and one to Roosevelt's son. Carefully, methodically, Alan and his group formulated a response to what they knew would be Hitler's next provocation — the occupation of Austria. First they got the president to send eleven private messages to the German Chancellor warning him that any move across the international border meant war with the United States. They were also able to place the American economy at complete war readiness. Congress had reinstituted the draft, and factories made the production of war material their number one priority. All American newspapers supported this pro–war, anti–fascist activity. Editorials heaped opprobrium on Hitler, and urged Roosevelt to stand up to Nazi aggression.

And then Hitler invaded Austria.

And then nothing.

Alan waited two weeks. Each day he left Hopkins' office with a solemn promise ("on my mother's life", "on my daughter's head," "as God is my witness," "in Jesus' holy name") that the next day Roosevelt would bring a declaration of war to congress. The last day, Roosevelt joined Hopkins, wheeling himself into Alan's own office, and offering the senator one of his best cigars. "Listen to my fireside chat, tonight, Alan," he said. The man sounded sincere even to Alan, whose immunity to the charms of politicians had garnered him a lucrative career back when he'd lived on Earth 185 years in the future. "Have your friends listen. You'll be pleased."

Alan listened closely that night, leaning back in his plush leather chair while he fiddled with the dials on the radio. He tried not to notice the perspiration dripping off his scalp onto his suit jacket. Marshall stood next to him, a blank look on his face.

The president spoke movingly, using his most commanding tones, of the need to extend the new deal initiatives to urban areas. "The economy of our cities," the president intoned, "is our next and possibly our greatest challenge."

Marshall giggled once, then shut up quickly; Alan rubbed his eyes. The president wished the country a good night.

After the speech, Alan took one look at his comrade, who shrugged. Then he slipped his tie out from under his belt, and pressed the gold button in the middle of the clip. Alan and his group of six were sent home — back to the Planet of the Jews.

Evan Isaacs felt like Moses, demonstrating God's wonders before Pharaoh and his magicians. Except Moses only had to convince Pharoah of his magical prowess; Evan had to convince all of European Jewry. For his first trick, he took a cloaking rod — a black, narrow, fourteen-inch cylinder, with a silver keypad at its base — typed in three numbers, and disappeared. The stadium crowd of several thousand Jews oohed and aaahed, and then applauded vigorously as Evan reappeared. Not even bothering to acknowledge the ovation, Evan grabbed one of his three matter transformers — this one a silver box about the size of a small coffee table — showed the crowd the empty container, filled it with water, pressed six buttons, popped open the lid, and took out a Nazi flag, the jet black swastika dominating the red cloth background like a conquering army. The audience first gasped, then applauded even louder than before. Before the noise died down, Evan took out his holo-mask projector — a hand-held device which looked almost like a pistol — punched in some numbers, pointed the trigger at his face, and presto — suddenly Evan became the spitting image of Adolph Hitler. The crowd cheered wildly. After two minutes, his face returned to normal, provoking another wave of appreciative applause.

Over the course of the next hour, Evan performed nearly a dozen "tricks." He used his Holographic Imaging Processor to create the illusion of a thousand white mice scurrying through the stadium. The audience squealed with terror and delight. He used a hand-held laser equipped with an arto-computer to carve a menorah out of a World War I rifle. In full sight of the crowd, he stayed submerged under water for twenty minutes — by taking an oxygen pill. He produced twenty-five steak dinners, with mashed potatoes and broccoli, out of four white, aspirin sized, pellets. He flew over the crowd. He changed water into wine. The audience loved him.

Walking to the very end of the stage, he grabbed the microphone and began to speak. He explained to the assembled Jews that he was not a magician, and his acts were not magical. His purpose that night was not to deceive them, like some itinerate trickster. He was there simply to demonstrate the truth. He — Evan Isaacs — ostensibly an agent from Palestine sent to encourage immigration to the

Jewish homeland — was, in reality, a visitor from the far future, come to warn Europe's Jews about the impending Holocaust. The magical tricks, he explained, were merely superior technology; for people of Evan's era, they were routine acts. The crowd, of course, laughed with great pleasure; they were convinced this was part of the act. But, he told them — he boomed out to them using a 22nd century microphone which projected his voice into the eardrum of each listener — this was no act. A terrible Holocaust was coming, he warned. He knew this for a fact. It was part of his history. Every Jew needs to leave Europe now, he urged. Before it's too late.

For the next hour and a half, he told stories from the Holocaust. He described the gas chambers, the ghettos, the starvation marches, the chimneys. For Evan it was easy to describe it all. Fifteen years before, he'd received a telepathic imprint of the Holocaust, which included the personal experiences of every Jew who went through the war. This was a storehouse of memories, which for obvious reasons he kept blocked most of the time — but he could call on it at will. The audience chuckled at the stories for the first five minutes, coughed and shifted uncomfortably in their seats for the next ten minutes, and then sat utterly silent for the remainder of the speech. Evan was grateful to have finally gotten their attention, though in the back of his mind he suspected that what kept the crowd transfixed was not hearing a horror story of the near future, but witnessing the creative powers of an obvious lunatic. The end of his talk was greeted with utter silence. The young Rabbi Judah Loeb, Evan's ally of the past six months, came on the stage and explained that visas to Switzerland, Palestine, or Argentina were available, free of charge, to any Jew seeking emigration from Europe. If they were interested, they should see him after the demonstration, or contact him at his office.

Out of a crowd of six thousand, three elderly Jews approached Evan and Judah after the show and asked for visas. The two exhausted friends sat at a table in front of the stadium for two hours following Evan's performance, hawking emigration documents. No one else showed up. During the next three weeks, two more Jews — a homeless beggar and a newly widowed woman of eighty — came by Evan's make-shift office in downtown Cracow to pick up travel papers. The public demonstration, Evan's entire strategy of Truth and Revelation, failed completely.

It had been a strategy born of desperation. In the five years Evan and his group had been prowling around Eastern and Central Europe, warning of the coming onslaught, offering free visas for any Jew to almost anywhere, offering also loans and cash assistance for relocation, distributing phonographic recordings with text translations in Yiddish of Hitler's most notorious anti-Semitic speeches, five years of almost non-stop activity designed to get the Jews of Europe to leave voluntarily, perhaps a dozen Jews took them up on their offers and moved either to Palestine or the United States. Until Evan's stadium revelation, they'd all posed as sh'lichim — emissaries from Palestine whose mission was to encourage Jewish immigration to the Jewish National Home. But the apathy which greeted all of their effort was, to Evan, not only profoundly depressing, but instructional. Naturally they couldn't convince anyone to leave, he argued to his comrades. They don't believe us. We have to convince them the danger is real. Absolutely real. And to do that, we have to tell the truth. The horrible truth. Tell the Jews — or at least a select group — that we've come from the future to rescue them from the Holocaust.

Of course, Evan's suggestion was controversial. Before they'd embarked on their journey through time and space, there had been a rough consensus at Pesek Z'man that the time travelers not reveal their true origins and identities. No one could offer an absolutely clear rationale for this policy other than the obvious: if certain individuals from the past discovered what the future held, they could use this knowledge to amass great power. And this could cause a significant 'shift' (fearful of Dr. Zevitt's scorn, no one used the word 'contamination') in the time line. Left unsaid was the obvious flaw in this reasoning — the whole point of the missions was to alter the timeline, to stop the Nazis and save the Jews. Their mission was to contaminate the time line. Still, most of the time travelers left the Planet of the Jews committed to the idea that, while they would indeed try to prevent the Holocaust, they would make efforts not to mess up too much else.

After five years, Evan grew less cautious. And none of his group disagreed; after all their failure had been enormous. Evan asked the one contemporary ally they'd managed to acquire — Rabbi Judah Loeb — to organize a mass meeting of Cracow's leading Jews. Demonstrating his technological superiority, Evan would convince the crowd he'd come from the future. Then he would tell them truth: they all must leave, and they must urge others to leave with them. That, at any rate, was the plan. But it, like all the other efforts, failed.

Evan first met Rabbi Loeb at the tiny Sherover synagogue on Market Street. The Rabbi had invited him — by telephone — to offer his Zionist/anti–Nazi shpiel to his Saturday morning crowd of twenty elderly men. Naturally, Evan was surprised the Rabbi had the same name as his murdered friend. But Evan assumed Judah Loeb was a common Polish–Jewish name and didn't make too much of the coincidence. Until he saw the Rabbi in person. Then he was astonished (and terrified) to discover this Rabbi Judah Loeb was practically the spitting image of his old friend Judah. He was a young version (maybe twenty five years old) of his late friend — the same fierce gray eyes, the same athletic build, the same upright, confident posture.

While shaking hands with the old/new Judah, Evan considered the possibility that God (or some force) really was directing events; after all, this confluence of both name and appearance was truly a great miracle. He also considered the possibility that he'd finally gone insane. But then he remembered his friend Judah had been part of a revered Rabbinic line with roots in Poland, and the answer came to him: the two men looked alike because they were related. That Evan would be standing in Cracow shaking the hand of Judah's great–great–great–great (or more) grandfather was certainly a marvel, a great coincidence. But it was not a supernatural occurrence. It hadn't come from God. At least that's how Evan saw it. He'd gone through his God thing; he was, thankfully, done with that.

Evan's speech at the synagogue went over like the hundreds of others he'd given across Poland. He spoke forcefully, with great conviction and erudition — and no one believed him. Except, this time, he finally gained one adherent. None of the snoring old men were at all impressed, but their young rabbi, for some reason, became a convert. He followed Evan home that afternoon, to the large house Evan had bought on Shalover Road. They stayed up all night talking. Three days later, Judah left his wife and four children (temporarily, he assured them) and moved in with Evan.

That first night, they smoked cigarettes, drank Turkish coffee, and discussed the Talmud. Evan told Rabbi Loeb he'd been given an excellent Talmudic education, but he hadn't studied in years. The last passage he'd learned, he told the young Rabbi, concerned the responsibilities of rescue.

"If you're stuck in the desert. . ." he recited to Judah.

"Yes, yes," Judah interrupted. "Of course I know the passage. Every school boy knows it. You're with a friend in the desert, but you only have enough water for one. Should you share your water and die with your companion, or take all the water yourself and live? Rabbi Akiva says take all the water for yourself. A surprising answer, if you don't mind my saying so. But what conclusion did you come to?"

"You find more water."

"Ah. You cheat. But this is not really answering the question. What if you can't find more water?"

"It doesn't matter," Evan said. "I already found the water. I have more than enough. Enough for everyone. Enough for six million."

Judah stared at Evan, the scholar's deep gray eyes probing every corner of Evan's face. Evan felt like a cancer patient under the scrutiny of a laser scan.

"But they won't take the water," Judah said. "Is this what you're telling me? You offer to save their lives, but they refuse."

Evan nodded.

"They think," he continued, "perhaps the water is not kosher. Or more likely, it is not real water at all, but a kind of fake, maybe even a kind of poison. Maybe, they think, we're better off drinking our own water, even if it comes from Polish Jew haters. Well then, this is our challenge. We must sell them the water. Your water. Or else. . .?" He looked at Evan, waiting.

"They'll die," Evan said. "And," he added, "it won't be long."

Evan and the rabbi travelled together all through eastern Poland, occasionally sneaking across the border into Russia. They posed as Zionist agents — in fact Evan told his friend he was a Zionist agent — but, in fact, their only mission was to get Jews to leave Europe. If they wanted Palestine, fine, they'd send them to Palestine. But Argentina was fine, and so was Ecuador or South Africa or Cuba; and so was the United States if you insisted, though that would take some doing. Anywhere you wanted to go, they would send you. But no one wanted to go. They failed utterly, miserably.

Yet the two became friends. Evan, of course, was hopelessly drawn to the young Rabbi who looked and acted so much like his old comrade. And Judah clearly admired Evan's dedication and his skills as a pseudo-spy. Mostly, though, their relationship revolved around Talmud study. Neither man seemed to want to spend much time discussing their own personal lives, Evan for obvious reasons. So they spent the long, cold winter nights studying Jewish texts. Evan's only previous study partner had been the Planet. He was amazed at the personal intimacy that could result from the cooperative study of sacred literature. He grew fond of this Judah, probably as fond as he'd ever been of the later Judah Loeb, this one's great, great, great, great grandson.

One night in an expensive kosher hotel in Warsaw (Evan always had a great deal of money and always stayed at the most luxurious spot in town. Judah never asked where the money came from.), Evan told his friend the truth. He'd come from the future, he told Judah, whose only reaction was to put down his coffee cup and light a cigarette. He wasn't just predicting the demise of European Jewry, Evan continued, he knew it for a fact. He'd come on a mission — to rescue Jews who would otherwise be murdered. He showed Judah some of the gadgets he'd brought with him from his home planet. He put on a miniature magic show, a preview of the one he'd later use at Cassanofsky Stadium in Cracow.

Judah believed him without asking any questions. He didn't even need the demonstration, he said. He, himself, wasn't even particularly surprised, though the facts, on the surface, were certainly astounding.

"But true," Evan said. "It's all true. The water I'm offering is real. Because the danger is — it's more than real. It's. . ." he closed his eyes. "It's more than you could possibly imagine," he said.

Except for one suggestion, Judah had very little to say about Evan's revelation. Evan, he advised, should tell the rest of the Jews. Let everyone know you're from the future, he said. Let them know it's real, not some nightmare, or ugly fantasy. Tell them the truth, he said. And then, finally, they'll leave. So Evan did it, he told the Jews the truth. But they still wouldn't leave.

Two weeks after Evan's flop at the stadium, he realized his team had failed. He gathered his comrades from all over Poland, Russia, Lithuania, Latvia and the Ukraine at his headquarters in Cracow, a spacious law office in an old, tall building which towered above the heart of what in just a few years would become the notorious Cracow Ghetto. They sat around a large wooden conference table — all but Judah Loeb, who stood by the door, watching. Evan smoked — he'd picked up the habit again in Poland — but the rest sat completely still, like mannequins. No one had any new ideas. There were no successes to report. None of them had accomplished anything. There was nothing to say.

They'd just have to let history take its course, Evan finally told them. It was time to return to the Planet of the Jews.

Naturally, he wanted to take Judah along. But the time machine functioned through radiations which entered the body. There was no way to transfer additional rads into the young Rabbi. Anyway, Judah didn't want to go. After all, he told Evan, he had responsibilities, a wife and four children. And, he added, an American visa, for himself and his family. He, at least, would escape the Holocaust. He would flee right after Evan's group disappeared.

Evan nodded, snuffed out his cigarette, and removed his gold pocket-watch. Without bothering to look at the others, or even to say goodbye to his friend, he pressed the button. In less than an instant, they were home.

All three teams materialized in the woods in back of Pesek Z'man headquarters. They reappeared at exactly the same time — twenty-four hours after they'd left. Though each of the travelers had lived through many difficult years, they looked exactly as they'd looked the day before. No signs of stress, no more gray hairs, no new wrinkles. None of the petty injuries they received in the twentieth century followed them home. Physically at least, if not emotionally, it was as if they'd never left.

Three days later, after resting and re-uniting with their families, they met at Alan's cabin and swapped stories. Max spoke first, then Elena, and then finally Evan.

"Well," Alan said, stretching out on his sofa and taking a sip of coleander wine, a pleasant slightly intoxicating drink he'd invented using a strange local fruit. "At least now we know the answer. You can't change the past. Something miraculous — something *supernatural* — will always intervene. Reality, the laws of physics, all of science will turn upside down, but the timeline stays the same. It happened to all of us."

"Yes, yes," Ziony said excitedly. "And isn't it fascinating that. . ."

"Not to me," Evan said.

They looked at him.

"Nothing supernatural happened to me, Alan. No miracles. *I* provided the miracles. I just failed. I couldn't get anyone to leave. You all succeeded," he said nodding his head at the other teams. "Elena, you killed Hitler; Alan you talked Roosevelt into taking the Nazis seriously. You succeeded, but some laws of temporal dynamics intervened. My group on the other hand, we just plain failed. We couldn't get anyone to take us seriously."

They stared at their former leader. With those mournful, vacant eyes, he looked as gloomy and pained as he had the moment they left Earth, as bereft as the day he found his friend Rabbi Loeb stabbed to death in his office. Alan was about to say something, offer consoling words, but he realized he had nothing to say. He just nodded and took another drink.

That night, in his own cabin, Evan sat up in bed, speaking to the

Planet.

"You knew what was going to happen, didn't you?" Evan said. "You knew it wouldn't work."

The Planet stayed quiet for several minutes, though Evan had the feeling it was thinking.

"Rabbi Elazar is of the opinion that the oven remains impure," the Planet said, quoting what Evan recognized was a completely irrelevant passage from the Talmud. "Now this would imply. . ."

"Could you please just answer my question," Evan said softly. "Did you know we would all fail? Is that why you encouraged us to go, so we could discover it for ourselves?"

"I'm not here to answer your questions, Evan," the Planet replied, in its usual matter-of-fact tone.

"And will you ever explain to me why you murdered Rabbi Loeb?" Evan asked.

"It would imply that soaking the dish beforehand is useless as a ritual act," the Planet recited. "On the other hand, if you boil it in a pot of water, Rabbi Meir deems it impure. Still. . ." And the Planet continued quoting, then discussing portions from the Talmud late into the night. Eventually, Evan joined in. They studied together – Planet and Jew – until dawn.

5: *Friday Night Dinner*

"Judah, what the hell am I doing in the story?"

Alan and I were enjoying an unusually extravagant dinner of lobster bisque and shrimp scampi at a tony East Side seafood restaurant. Alan was "taking me out to dinner," which of course meant the company was paying. We both ate greedily, almost desperately, as if we hadn't eaten in days. Alan was polishing off his second entre.

"I'm sorry?" I said. I assumed he meant the latest "Planet of the Jews" story, the one that had literally changed the face of the science fiction publishing world, and revolutionized the magazine industry. The issue featuring the second "Planet" story sold three million copies at the newsstand. People literally snatched up the magazines faster than we could print them. I'd heard there was a plan to reproduce and distribute over a million more. The company, to say the least, was pleased, and Alan was demonstrating his personal pleasure with this little dinner. But I didn't understand his question.

"Come on, Judah," he said, chewing and talking at the same time. "You know. This Alan character the, uh, president, or prime minister, or king, or whatever, of the Jews. That's *me*. It's my name, he acts like me, he even looks like me. Don't get me wrong, Judah. I love the story. *Love* it. But why'd you put me in there? It's starting to get a little embarrassing, you know, with hundreds of millions of people reading the thing, and I'm the publisher. They must think I'm some kind of crazy ego–maniac. To tell you the truth, I'm sort of flattered. In fact, overall," he said, pausing to reach for a piece of bread. "I'd have to say it feels pretty good to be in the story." He shrugged and started in again on his lobster. "But don't you think you should have asked me?"

I put down my fork and shook my head. I was flabbergasted. How many times did I have to go through this with him? "Alan," I said, trying to keep the tremor out of my voice. "I didn't write these stories. It's not me. They were written by Moishe and Esther Cassanofsky from Brooklyn. They're the goddamn authors, Alan. And how should I know why they put you in their story? To tell you the truth, I hadn't even noticed."

Alan cocked his head at me, an odd sight. It made him look something like a curious St. Bernard with glasses. "Didn't notice?" he said.

I shrugged and downed a glass of wine, probably my twelfth of the evening. "They used my name too," I said. "They even use my name as the writer. I've learned to ignore it. Who knows what they're doing? But I didn't write it. I wish I had, Alan, but I didn't."

Alan looked at me, winked, and then polished off his second helping. He didn't believe me, but I didn't particularly care. One day, I thought, I would force Moishe and Esther to reveal themselves, to tell him the truth. But until then, let the company think I'm a gold mine. I've lived through worse accusations.

As if he were reading my mind, Alan grinned widely, put on his most officious–looking expression, took an envelope out of his breast pocket, and handed it to me. "Before we order dessert – and Judah I hear they have the best creme brule here in the city – I'll get the business part of the evening over with. Some of the higher ups in the front office wanted me to show our appreciation to you for, uh, let's just say *producing* these stories. We want to show you how valuable you are to this company, how we'll always be grateful and loyal to you, blah, blah, blah. . . So," he said nodding his head toward the envelope.

I was pleased. I'd been saving the magazine royalties in an account for Moishe and Esther, but this money I would keep. After all, they had come to me. I'd think of it as a finder's fee. "Thank you, Alan," I said. I stuffed the envelope in my breast pocket and picked up a dessert menu.

But Alan couldn't take his eyes off of me, and wouldn't wipe the strange grin off of his chubby face. "Aren't you going to open it?" he insisted. "Look at the amount?"

I shrugged. I'd gotten bonuses before – a couple hundred dollars here and there, sometimes as much as a thousand. Useful money, but nothing to get too excited about, especially living in Manhattan in a $2100–a–month one-bedroom apartment. But to satisfy Alan I took out the envelope, eased it open, and looked at the check.

I started choking right away. I grabbed a glass of water, poured it down my throat, then snatched Alan's water, and drank that too. The check was for $100,000.

Alarmed at the sounds coming from my throat, and my beet red face, Alan jumped up and ran over to my side of the table. He actually started to wrap his thick arms around me from the back – I guess he was thinking of the Heimlich maneuver – when I finally stopped gasping. "I'm all right," I said weakly. "Just a little shocked."

Alan smiled and danced back to his chair. "Enjoy the money, Judah," he said, his eyes twinkling behind his thick glasses. He was happy. He'd actually managed to surprise me. "Now," he said, rubbing his hands together. "How about dessert?"

Before saying goodnight, Alan reminded me that "one of these days, Judah," he wanted to have a "real heart to heart" about Judaism. "I'd like to get your opinion, Judah," he said. "You know, what does it all mean? Judaism and Jewishness and everything. The whole. . . thing. You know," he said. "You know. All this. . . all this . . . you know. All that. . . shit?"

"Of course Alan," I responded. "One of these days," I said.
"You know?" he said.
"I know exactly what you mean." I answered.

I made one stop on my way home – at a mailbox. I mailed my last alimony check, for me a decidedly strange moment. As

I watched the blue iron lid clang shut, I realized I'd just cut off my last human connection of any consequence. True, I hadn't spoken with Elena for almost two years, but at least sending her these checks had been a kind of contact. I even wrote her notes every once in a while, though, of course, she never wrote back. But now, even that slender tie had snapped. I wondered, briefly, if she'd been following my new 'success' in the newspapers. And then I realized I didn't really care.

It was nearly eleven when I finally made it back to my apartment, but I still wanted to work on some of my own writing. Since Moishe and Esther's fiction invaded my life, I'd fallen behind considerably in my own work. I was late with three novelizations, four FutureWorld stories, and two articles for fanzines. And I hadn't worked on my own graphic novel in weeks. Somehow, with all the hysteria surrounding the Planet of the Jews, I hadn't found more than one hour to sit and write on my own. But tonight, no matter what it took, even if I had to brew a gallon of coffee, I was going to catch up.

But first I listened to my messages, which was a mistake. First message: David Letterman's office; second message: David Letterman himself. Later, Jay Leno's office, then Jay Leno. Next, the *Today Show*, and then all the morning news shows. In between, the *New York Times*, the *Los Angeles Times*, the *Chicago Tribune*, the *Daily News*, the *Post*, etc., etc. . . Agents were calling. Desperate fans, aspiring science fiction writers, university professors, politicians. Politicians! What were they looking for? An interview with the author of "The Planet of the Jews." A statement from the author of the "The Planet of the Jews." A picture of the author. Help from the author. Advice from the author. Tonight, of course, the message load was considerably lighter than the night before, since I'd just switched to an unlisted number. But the intrepid could always get through, and where there's big money involved, or sudden fame, or both, the intrepid multiply.

Even if I'd actually written the thing, all the attention

would have been too much. I'm essentially a shy, reclusive type. I don't much like to talk to anyone. My wife divorced me, she claimed, because she couldn't stand the silence. I avoided interviews even in my relatively modest capacity as a comic book writer and editor. But, considering I was not the author of "The Planet of the Jews," and the real authors were hiding out somewhere in the bowels of Jewish Brooklyn, I was, to say the least, considerably distressed by all the interest. I didn't know what the hell to tell them. The truth – that some Jewish couple I don't know wanted to use my name – seemed both ridiculous and utterly fantastic. Not even my closest colleagues really believed in Moishe and Esther, no matter how many times I vouched for their existence. So I ignored every call, not even referring them to a lawyer or an answering service. I told myself since it really wasn't me – I really wasn't the Judah Loeb who wrote "The Planet of the Jews" – I had no moral obligation, or even right, for that matter, to handle any of the calls. They weren't for me. They'd gotten the wrong number.

But, as I discovered, ignoring the beast is not the best strategy for making it go away. All I did was heighten their curiosity. I created a "mystique." The papers called me a "reclusive genius," a "brilliant but adolescent loner," a "Garboesque, Salinger type," (Salinger! Garbo!). Papparazzi camped out in the lobby of my building at all hours of the night; the tenants association already made it clear to me that I would have to move. I wore a costume – a full beard, sunglasses, and a black bowler – whenever I entered or left the building.

In short, despite my best wishes, despite the fact I hadn't done anything at all worth celebrating, I was a celebrity – with all of the disadvantages, and, so far, none of the perks. Except, of course, for the $100,000 check.

But no matter. Next week I would find a new apartment. I would use the money from Alan, and maybe even some of the royalties money I was saving for Moishe and Esther (why the hell not? The checks were made out to me!) and find a new place to live on the Upper East Side. The celebrity storm would pass. The "Planet of the Jews" sensation wouldn't last another year; even Alan knew that. I'd survive. Meanwhile, I wanted to get back to my own writing. I decided to begin with the *Star Trek* novel I'd started the week before my father died.

I sat down at my desk, flicked on the variously colored lamps, turned on my computer, and waited. I sat for twenty minutes. No ideas. I stared at the outline I'd scrawled on five 5x8 index cards. The plot I'd so carefully laid out made no sense to me at all. I could barely make out the handwriting. I cracked my knuckles three times, took a deep breath, and started to type, the ideas flowing at last. After ten minutes, my hands flew off the keyboard as if they were propelled by an electrical charge. I realized with a growing sense of nausea and desperation that I was writing an almost word for word copy of "The Time Traveling Jews," merely substituting the characters of *Star Trek: Deep Space Nine*, for the Jewish creations of Moishe and Esther. I scrolled back to where I'd started, deleted the whole thing, and tried again. After five minutes, I realized I was re-writing the first chapter of "The Planet of the Jews." This time I hadn't even bothered to change the characters. In my novel, somehow Evan Isaacs and Rabbi Judah Loeb and all the rest showed up on a Federation space station. Captain Benjamin Sisko of the United Federation of Planets was organizing a pogrom against Bajoran Jews.

I drank an oversized mug of coffee, then decided to switch to the script for a *World Justice* comic which was due in three days. Another illustrator had already drawn the pictures; all I had to do was fill in the dialogue. Normally, these scripts took me about an hour to finish. That night, I sat for two hours without composing a word. I couldn't think of anything to write. Actually, I thought of plenty to write, but they were all words that had already been written by Moishe and Esther, and published by Alan.

I started to worry. In fifteen years of writing comic books

and cheap science fiction, I'd never experienced writer's block. I could always stretch my creative muscles enough to come up with coherent ideas which function within completely fanciful worlds. I'd concocted creatures with three eyes who see into the past, future and present, elongated men who travel the galaxy selling substances which induce pleasant dreams, multi–colored androids who solve crimes by analyzing the entire caseload of Sherlock Holmes. I'd always managed to create bizarre – really juvenile – ideas, and fit them, somehow, into a realistic scheme. And I always had fun. I was good at it. Alan often called me his best writer.

But that night I couldn't come up with a single original idea. "The Planet of the Jews" crowded out all other inspiration. I was stymied, approaching panic, because the very notion of a writer's block for a comic book writer – a field so crowded with potential ideas – meant the end of a career. I began to wonder if I would ever write again.

I stayed at it for another hour, downing at least four more cups of coffee, before giving up. I thought about going to bed, but I knew I'd never be able to fall asleep.

Instead, I decided to visit my Uncle Max and interview him some more about his Holocaust experiences. Maybe, I thought, doing some research into my own graphic novel might snap my creativity back into place. It was past midnight, but I knew Max's habits. He fell asleep every night at one o'clock, after Jay Leno, and woke up every morning at nine. If I hurried, I could catch him.

He seemed quite pleased to see me, as pleased, in fact, as he'd ever been. He smiled warmly, hugged me, and then startled me by kissing me on the cheek.

I noticed something strange as soon as I walked in the door: no dust. Normally Max's apartment was as dusty as an ancient library; normally, I had to get about a minute of sneezing out of the way before I could even say hello. But that night, well somebody had clearly been doing some serious dusting. I looked around and saw that someone had indeed tidied up the whole apartment. Every book was in its place on the black wooden shelves; every piece of clothing hung up or put away. Had Max finally hired a cleaning lady?

The next thing I noticed was the smell of food. Terrific smells, like chicken soup and kishke, and tsimmes, kashka, boiled beef, latkes, and gefilte fish – the smell of Jewish foods – wafted in from Max's tiny kitchen. Max cooking?, I thought. Something more complicated than scrambled eggs? Before I could ask, he ushered me into his living room.

"Judah, Judah," he said. "I'm sorry you missed them! They left just a few seconds ago. Did you see them?"

"I don't know who you're talking about, Uncle Max."

"Your friends, Judah. They were just here. You see what they did," he said, sweeping his hand in an arc across the room as if he were exhibiting a great piece of art. "They cleaned, they brought me dinner, they. . ."

"Who, Uncle Max, who?"

"Those two *Yidden*, Judah, your young friends. I'm so pleased, Judah, to meet your friends. You know, with the beard," he said, pantomiming, with his hands, a long beard. "And the black coat. And the girl, that tough looking *maidele*, with the long skirt, and the thing on her head, you know, the wig, the *sheitel*. You must have seen them on the stairs. They left just a minute ago, Judah. What are their names? Mordechai and Esther? Moses and Miriam? Mendel? No, then. . ."

I went pale, as a chill passed through me. It couldn't possibly be. "Moishe and Esther," I whispered.

"That's it, Judah!" he exclaimed. "You know I don't remember things so well these days. Anyway, I was surprised you had friends like these, but I figured your father. . ."

"They're not my friends."

"No? But they're lovely people. They brought me *Shabbes* dinner, and. . ."

"Excuse me?" I said.

"*Shabbes* dinner," he repeated.

I shook my head, perplexed. I didn't understand. He looked at me, himself confused.

"Which don't you understand, Judah?" he asked. "You don't know what dinner is, a meal you eat when. . .? Ah, *Shabbes*," he said. "This you don't know. *Shabbes*. Judah you know what is *Shabbes*. Sabat, you call it I think," he said. "I mean Sabbath. The Sabbath."

Of course. It was Friday night. Still, that didn't explain anything. "Uncle Max, what were they doing here?! Why did they come to you? How did they even find you?! What. . ."

"Shhh, Judah," he said. "Shah. You're turning red. You're raising your voice. This is not like you!"

He was right. I'd been yelling, and I hadn't even realized it. And my heart was beating madly. I shook my head. "Uncle Max, they're just two strange writers. But I barely know them, and I can't understand why. . ."

"Of course they're writers!" he said. "Just like you, Judah. This is the first thing they told me. They're writers, just like my nephew, my brother's grandson. And so they want to know my story, just like my nephew the writer wants to know my story."

"They asked you to tell stories?" I asked. "About Poland? About the Holocaust?"

"What else?" he answered. "What other stories do I know?"

"And did you tell them?"

"Of course," he answered. "I told them everything. Every story. In its proper order. From beginning to end. Like with you, Judah. Don't I always tell you? I always cooperate with writers," he said, as if writers were a regular part of his social circle.

I was suddenly furious. "Do you?" I said. "You haven't told me a damn thing in its proper order! I can't get you to tell a single story straight. I just hope you confused the hell out of them, the way you confused me!"

I sat back on the couch, breathing rapidly, my hands

shaking. My outburst, of course, was totally unprecedented; before that moment, I'd never been anything but respectful to Max. I expected him to yell back, or start crying, or kick me out of his apartment. But I could tell from his face he was merely puzzled. As was I. Where did that burst of anger come from?

We stared at each other for a few minutes, while my pulse slowed down, and my tremors lifted. I waited for a response from Max.

"Judah," he finally said, shaking his head with disappointment. "It's *Shabbes*!"

We made up. I apologized; he asked about my health. Did I miss my father?, he asked. Had I felt lonesome since the divorce? Yes, I answered, to both questions. But I didn't elaborate. Eventually, Max brought me some tea and some left–over kishka. Then he regaled me with some Holocaust stories – some of his best, he claimed, though they were all gobbledegook to me. Either I was too tired and too tense and distracted to really absorb what he was saying, or he was his usual incoherent self. But I wasn't about to press him; I just let him talk. At 2:30 A.M. I finally got up to leave. Max walked me to the door. I noticed, with some relief, that the dust was beginning to reappear in the apartment; it would be back to normal, I thought, in a day or two. I was out the door and almost at the dark staircase when I heard him calling me back.

"Judah," he called out, his voice echoing. "Judah."

I turned around.

"I forgot to tell you. I mean, I forgot to *give* you. To give you this."

Please, not more *tefilin*, I thought. "What is it?" I called out.

"This," he said, and, as if out of thin air, he produced a thick manilla envelope. "Your friends," he said, walking down the hallway toward me. "Mordechai and the girl. Havele. Rivkale. Whatever. Those two writers. They told me to give you this. It was yours, they said."

I took the envelope. I opened it, shook out the twenty or so sheets of paper, though, of course, I knew what it was before even glancing at the first page. It was another story.

6: Teachers

The bulky, rectangular space ship landed on a Friday morning. Four small, roly-poly, human-looking creatures with blue skin waddled out, presenting themselves to the large group of Jews who had been expecting their arrival for the past six weeks.

"*Shalom Aleichem, Yidden!*," the tallest, fattest, and bluest one exclaimed.

The Jews looked at each other, uncomprehending. "An alien language," Alan Shapiro, community president, whispered to Evan Isaacs, his best friend, and former leader of the Jews. Evan ignored him and stared at the blue men, a look of intense, almost religious interest on his face, as if he were staring at angels.

"*Yidden, Farbreingen! Alles shoni some memedino rchoyka, alle spenden Shabbes mit you!*"

The crowd began to murmur. Something about the gibberish seemed oddly familiar, but no one could place it. "It sounds something like German," Alan said to Evan. "But there's a strange kind of. . ."

"They don't speak Yiddish!" Evan yelled out, stepping forward and speaking directly to the blue men.

The aliens exchanged puzzled looks. They moved their broad, round shoulders slightly upward in a move which, to Alan, seemed reminiscent of a shrug.

"*Nein sprken de Yiddish*," Evan said, his voice cutting through the chatter and the murmured whisperings. "*Sprken Englis*," he yelled out.

The blue men huddled together, their four heads touching, their bottoms arching out like the sides of a dreidel. Alan noticed for the first time that the aliens weren't wearing any kind of clothing; yet their nakedness was neither gross nor forbidding. They looked like large, sexless, dwarf dolls.

"How's this?" the tallest one shouted out, in English, without a trace of an accent, as if he'd just arrived from Chicago. "How about this?" he yelled, a hopeful look on his face. "This is your language?" he asked. "This is better?"

Evan smiled. "Much better," he said. "Much better." He looked at Alan. "Mr. President?" he said.

"Oh, uh, yes," Alan said, taking a step forward — trying to look dignified. "This is better. And, uh, welcome. Welcome to our home." Having never greeted aliens before, Alan was unsure of what to do. He bowed his head, and then, embarrassed, merely shrugged.

In perfect imitation, the blue men bowed their heads, and then also shrugged. "Peace to you," the taller one said, his voice booming out as if amplified. "Peace to you, brothers and sisters. Hello, fellow Jews. We received a call — a call from God — and we've arrived. We've come from a long way. To join you for *Shabbes*."

Fellow Jews? *Shabbes*? Word spread like wildfire throughout the settlement. There were Jews on other planets! Odd looking, bluish, and they didn't seem to wear clothing, but still, Jews! And they'd come for a visit — called by God, yet! They weren't alone in the Universe! Astounding news!

Alan had his suspicions. He asked Evan to check with the Planet — was it playing God again? Calling living beings across the light years with a fake spiritual message?

"I did not send for them," said (really thought) the Planet, indignantly.

"Do you know who did?" Evan asked.

"I did not send for them."

"Do you know anything about them?"

"I did not send for them."

Evan shrugged and looked at Alan. "Broken record mode," he said, referring to a rather common trait of the Planet. When it didn't really want to talk about something, it would repeat itself over and over again, until you finally changed the subject.

"Are they for real?" Alan, asked. "What do you think, Evan?"

"They're definitely for real," Evan answered. "But are they Jewish?" He shrugged. "I'm not even sure if we're Jewish anymore. But, look, they're guests. And they certainly seem harmless."

"Hmmm." Alan responded.

It turned out there were 180 of them. They looked exactly alike, except for the variation in sizes. Alan guessed that some were children, some adults, but, when he asked, the aliens didn't seem to have any grasp of the concept of age.

"Older? Younger? Oldest? Youngest?" asked the tallest one, who called himself Dovid Hamelech. "I don't understand you. We're all Jews!"

"Yes, certainly," Alan agreed. "But surely some of you were born before others. I see, for instance, you are in charge. And you are clearly the tallest. Is that because you were born first?"

"Born?" said Dovid Hamelech.

"Born, hatched, come into being, created . . ."

"I was created, you were created, all were created. God creates. Me, you, us, them. All."

"I see," Alan replied.

As it happened, they had a very simple request. They weren't planning on settling down — after all, this was not their home. They simply wanted to observe this Jewish community, compare beliefs and customs, and maybe ask a few questions. They wouldn't stay long, they assured their hosts. No longer than four hundred years.

When Alan explained that no one on the planet would live past 120, Dovid Hamelech quickly apologized. "Ahh, then," he said. "In that case we'll stay no longer than six weeks."

No one, not even the leery president, could think of any reason to object. They were quite a pleasant, polite group of believers. And if what they claimed was true — if they really were Jews — then this was an extraordinary opportunity. Together, they could prove that the essential precepts of Judaism were not tied to any one planet in the Universe. Judaism, they could show, was a truly intergalactic religion.

It became clear fairly quickly, however, that if indeed these were Jews, they were of a different type altogether. Their first night on the planet, Dovid Hamelech and three of the shorter blue men joined Alan and his family for Sabbath dinner. Alan, like the great majority of the community on the planet, was barely perfunctory in his observance of Jewish rituals. But that night, in honor of his guests, he made sure a full Sabbath table was set. He even consulted with one of the students at Evan's yeshiva to make sure he got all of the details right.

The little blue men watched without comment while Alan's wife lit the Sabbath candles, Alan's oldest son recited the blessings over the wine and bread, and while all the human beings washed their hands from the ritual bowls. It was only after the ceremony was done, and Alan was finally beginning to relax, that the questions began. Alan was stuffing a piece of challah in his mouth when Dovid Hamelech spoke for the first time.

"Uh, excuse me Alan. Sorry, so sorry to interrupt, but, what exactly are you doing?"

Alan quickly chewed the challah, swallowed and began to explain. He went through all of the Sabbath table rituals, going into detail about each one. He was grateful he'd thought to ask for explanations at the Yeshiva, otherwise he'd have been as ignorant as these funny blue men.

"Yes, yes, thank you," said Dovid Hamelech. "Thank you so much. Very complete, very intelligent. Much gratitude. But I wasn't referring to those rituals, which we all understood completely." The other three blue men nodded in agreement. "But we're puzzled about what you just did with that substance." He pointed to the bread. "You ground it up with your teeth and sent it down your throat. Why would you do this?"

Alan looked at his wife, who suppressed a giggle, and then at his daughter, who ignored him. Dovid Hamelech, however, stared at Alan intently, waiting for an answer. "Well, Dovid, it's called *eating*," Alan said. "I guess we just assumed . . . seeing how your physiology is so similar . . . that is . . ." He stopped for a moment to study his food. "You don't eat?" he asked.

The three blue "men" opened their eyes wide, their faces reflecting complete bewilderment.

Alan explained the process of eating, digesting and eliminating food. Dovid Hamelech listened, fascinated. Occasionally he interrupted

Alan's narrative with a squeal of delight or a clap of the hands. Clearly, the subject fascinated him.

"And you can eat anything?" he asked, incredulous. "This table cloth, this chair, these utensils, your daughter. . . ."

"No, no," Alan interrupted. He paused for a moment to think, and then to formulate his words in an accurate way. "We eat. . . food," he said, at last.

"Ah," said Dovid Hamelech. "Ah," the others responded. "Of course," they said. They then knocked their blue heads together. This, Alan discovered, was how they communicated with each other, reserving oral language for discussions with their hosts from Earth.

Alan and his family resumed eating. After about ten minutes of complete silence, Dovid Hamelech again spoke. "Excuse me, Alan," he said. "I don't mean to make a pest of myself. I understand how important this eating is to you. But I'm curious — I would very much like to know — what is. . . food?"

Alan sighed. He explained, once again, those elements of human biology associated with the digestive system, putting special emphasis on the concepts of nutrition. Dovid Hamelech and his compatriots nodded vigorously as Alan talked.

"And you can eat any kind of food?" Dovid Hamelech asked. "Any food you desire?" The three aliens leaned forward, as if Alan's answer to this question were of the utmost importance.

Alan remembered that these strange beings were supposedly Jews, and were therefore, presumably, looking for Jewish answers. He stumbled through a brief, and probably inaccurate, explanation of Kashrut — the Jewish dietary laws — for some reason emphasizing, more than anything else, the imperative to separate milk and meat products. The aliens took in his explanations with great enthusiasm — once again, squealing and oohing and ahhing as Alan spoke, simply enchanted with the ideas.

Suddenly, though, a look of concern crossed Dovid Hamelech's face. "But, Alan," he said. "How can you be certain there are no traces of milk product in the meat you eat? Or vice versa? After all, we couldn't help but notice how sloppy your wife was in preparing the food. It seems to me quite possible a bug or a lizard or even a fleck of steak could fall into your butter, or your cheese, and then. . . . why that would be a disaster! A mixture of milk and meat! Unintentional, to be sure, but still, a forbidden mixture!" Alan noticed that while Dovid Hamelech was clearly disturbed, his blue companions were suddenly in a state of near panic. They muttered to themselves in a strange language, and waved their short, thick arms up and down, as if trying to fly away. Alan wanted to reassure them, quickly, but he didn't know quite what to say. The fact is he'd never in his life kept kosher, and he certainly paid no attention to dietary restrictions on this new planet, where — despite the seeming abundance of earth-like grazing animals and earth-like fruits and vegetables — he could never be sure what exactly he was eating.

He thought for a few moments, and then shrugged. "We do the best we can," he said finally. "We're only. . . human."

The three blue men bumped their heads together for several seconds, and then broke out in wide grins.

"Alan," Dovid Hamelech said, "we would like to do this favor for you. It would be our pleasure to serve you in this way. Our vision is much more developed than yours," he explained. "For instance, I can see all of the molecules and atoms of the bread you are eating. I can also see it traveling down your esophagus. I see the various enzymes breaking it down in your stomach, and can watch as the waste products make their way to your bowels."

Alan stopped to examine his slice of challah, and then put it down.

"We would be most willing, while we're here. . . It would be an honor. . . If you would permit us to supervise and then certify for you that your meat products and your dairy products are completely kosher. With our eyes, Alan," Dovid Hamelech said, and Alan could have sworn the blue man winked at him as he spoke, "there would be no doubts. We could ensure that everyone on the planet ate only kosher food." They beamed at Alan, clearly overwhelmed by their own generosity.

Alan thanked them and told them he would relay their kind offer to the religious authorities at the Yeshiva. He was certain, he said, that it would be warmly received.

Meanwhile, Evan hosted three other blue men for the Sabbath. The largest one (his head barely reached Evan's chest) seemed to be the spokesman. He called himself Moishe Rabbeinu.

Evan, unlike his friend Alan, lived a religious life, and observed the Sabbath meticulously. Before dinner, he took his guests to the synagogue at the Yeshiva — the largest of the four synagogues on the planet, and the only Orthodox one. He ushered his new friends into the men's section (deciding, somewhat arbitrarily, that they were male), gave them prayerbooks, and sat with them near the back. Evan closed his eyes, his usual practice, and quickly lost himself in the rhythms and melodies of the service.

Ten minutes later, when Evan looked up for the first time, he was surprised to see the little blue men were no longer sitting next to him. Annoyed, he put down his prayerbook, and walked toward the exit, thinking what a mess it would be to have the three aliens wandering around the settlement alone at night. He was almost out the door when he was startled by the sounds of beautiful singing, the most enchanting, most sublime Jewish praying he'd ever heard. It came from the synagogue's front row. As the remarkable chanting gained in volume, the entire congregation stopped, just to listen. Walking quietly to the front, Evan saw that the noble noises flowed from none other than his blue friends. He was also shocked to see that each of them now wore both a yarmulke — a ritual headcovering — and a tallis — a ritual shawl. Looking more closely, Evan realized it would be more accurate to say they had grown yarmulkes and tallises; the ritual garb appeared to be organically attached to his friends' blue bodies.

Evan nodded to the chazzan, the prayer leader, who had stopped chanting along with the rest of the crowd, in order to gawk at the aliens — and the service continued. The voices of the blue men continued to soar above the rest, but no one felt inhibited or embarrassed, and everybody sang along as best they could. The combination of voices, human and alien, created a harmony which elevated the praying to almost magic, mystical heights. It was as if all the angels of creation — the good, the evil, the demonic, and the saintly — gathered together from the four corners of heaven, just to praise God. The worshippers could practically see all of their most intimate outpourings float through the ceiling and wind their way to the stars. Evan, who had never before cried at a religious service, wept unashamedly by the end.

Afterwards, everyone ran up to Moishe Rabbeinu and his cohorts and thanked them effusively for "the most spiritual Friday night service ever."

At dinner, Evan complimented them. They responded, without a shred of false modesty, that, yes, it was probably the most extraordinary prayer event the Jews on this planet had ever experienced.

"It was also quite fascinating to see how you spontaneously generated a yarmulke and a tallis. Does this happen every time you pray?"

The men looked at each other, puzzled. "Spontaneously generated?" Moishe Rabbeinu asked. "Yarmulke? Tallis?"

"And why a tallis?" Evan continued. "In our tradition, we don't wear tallises at night. Except for Yom Kippur."

The men stared at Evan. Clearly, they had no idea what he was talking about.

"The little caps on your heads," Evan said. "The shawls. These things appeared suddenly on your bodies in the middle of services. Out of nowhere. They weren't there when we first met you. I'm just wondering where they came from, and why it happened."

The blue men appeared embarrassed. They touched their heads briefly and nodded. Moishe Rabbeinu turned to Evan, and then spoke for the group. "Evan," he said, "believe me when I tell you this is how our bodies have always been shaped. Everything you see of us is exactly how God intended us to be. There have been no changes."

"But I saw. . ." Evan protested.

"Perhaps, Evan," said Moishe Rabbeinu, sadly, "this is a cultural misunderstanding which cannot be bridged. But let us not fret about such a silly issue. We're all Jews. We're completely alike in so many ways. We have so much in common."

Evan nodded. "Of course, of course," he said. "I was just trying to learn. But we shouldn't lose sight of what really is amazing. God in His wisdom has blessed us with a visit from fellow Jews! This is a wonderful miracle! And you speak like us, and worship God like us. You obviously revere Moishe and Dovid, as we do. And you understand Yiddish, and you *daven*. We are so very much alike. Please, my friends," he said. "Please. Let's eat."

"Eat?" the blue men all asked together.

Well, they weren't so much alike. In fact, Alan could never really figure them out. Whenever he, or anyone else, asked the aliens about their own history, they would respond with the most confused double talk Alan had ever heard. Moishe Rabbeinu, for instance, insisted he had lived forever, yet at the same time he spoke movingly of his parents. When Alan asked him how it was possible for someone who had lived forever to have parents, Moishe Rabbeinu said, "Well, Alan, I meant to say, had I been blessed to have been given parents, I would have loved them dearly. And, in fact, I do so love and respect my mother." When Alan asked him if, in fact, there were any mothers, or any females at all, on his planet, he responded, "well, of course there is God."

The blue men were equally vague and confusing when discussing details of their own society. Dovid Hamelech assured Evan that there were several religions on his home planet, "though, of course, everyone is Jewish." At first Moishe Rabbeinu claimed that no one on his world had ever heard of the Torah, but the next day described how it was recited, in its entirety, to children every night before putting them to bed. Dovid Hamelech insisted his group was the first of his people ever to travel the stars, while Moishe Rabbeinu, on the second day of his visit, told a long convoluted tale of how tyrannical monarchs on his home world had been exiling political dissidents into space for hundreds of years.

The blue men were no more coherent, nor forthcoming, when discussing their religious customs and beliefs. Whenever Evan asked how the blue men celebrated a particular event, or performed a particular ritual, Dovid Hamelech responded by asking Evan how those ritual were done in his community.

"Ahh," he would then answer. "This is exactly how we do it on our planet."

"But," Evan once responded, "you told me five minutes ago you'd never even heard of that ceremony."

"Of course," Dovid Hamelech answered, with great force, as if he were explaining the most obvious teaching in the Universe. "And yet we do it exactly the same way."

One morning after prayers, Evan asked Moishe Rabbeinu if his people had any stories.

"Stories?"

"Yes," he said. "Well, our central story is the Exodus from Egypt. How God freed us from the bondage of Egyptian slavery and gave us the Torah. This story explains both who we are as a people and what our obligations are to God and to other. . . ah. . . creatures. Our tradition is full of stories: the binding of Isaac, the story of Joseph. Many of us now consider the recent escape from Earth to be the greatest and most dramatic story in our history — a story which fundamentally changes how we think of each other. Stories," he explained. "Are important to us."

"We don't have stories," Dovid Hamelech said flatly.

"None?" Evan asked, surprised.

"We have. . . conversations."

"Ah," Evan responded.

"But, of course, I do have a story. Evan, my good friend, let me tell you my story."

"Please," Evan said, settling back in his chair.

"I was born," Dovid Hamelech began, his voice suddenly acquiring the excitement and timber of a great storyteller. "I live," he continued, in more moderate tones. "One day," he concluded sadly, "I will die."

Evan waited. His blue friend smiled eagerly.

"That's it?" Evan asked.

"You don't like it?"

Evan sighed. "It's a wonderful story, Dovid Hamelech," he said. "A wonderful story."

The third Friday night after the arrival of the blue men, Evan lay in his warm bed, about to make love with his young wife, when he heard strange noises. It sounded like a combination of muffled giggling, and deep breathing. He flicked on the light and peered under the bed.

"Moishe Rabbeinu!" he said. "What the hell. . ? And Dovid Hamelech! How on Earth?"

"Good Shabbes, Evan," Moishe Rabbeinu said, squeezing out from under the bed and pulling himself up next to Evan with surprising grace. Dovid Hamelech, to Evan's great annoyance, chose to stay under the bed, his red eyes glowing in the dark like the headlights of a large truck.

Evan's wife, Esther, a tall brunette in her late twenties, smiled, grabbed a robe and went to the bathroom. They'd been married for just under six months, fixed up by Evan's friend, the planet's Lubavitcher rabbi. It was this marriage — particularly its physical side — which went a long way toward restoring Evan's vigor and leadership abilities. Twenty years earlier, Evan might even have said he was happy. But since the Exodus, Evan refused to look at happiness as a possible human achievement. Still, there was a new glow in his eye which had been absent since the loss of his first family. He was beginning to enjoy certain aspects of life.

Which made it all the more annoying that Moishe Rabbeinu was interrupting the ritual he enjoyed most — sex with Esther on Friday night.

"Why are you here, Moishe Rabbeinu?" he demanded.

Moishe looked puzzled, at least that's how Evan, in his admittedly limited experience with blue Jews, interpreted the scrunched expression on the alien's face. "Everything you do, Evan," he said. "Is a teaching for us. Everything. It is Torah. You are our Rabbi. We must watch."

"Please get out, Moishe Rabbeinu," Evan said, sharply.

"Of course," the blue man responded, and scurried out the door.

Evan waited a few seconds. "Dovid Hamelech!" he called out.

The alien appeared immediately. With Evan still lying on the bed, Dovid Hamelech's eyes stood at the same level as Evan's nose. The two creatures stared at each other. Evan suddenly felt tremendously amused by the situation.

"I would like you to leave also, my friend."

"Of course," he said, and turned to leave. When he reached the door he turned around. "One question, please, Evan."

"Hmm."

"Why do you have sex?" he asked. "I mean, of course, not just you, but all of you, uh, creatures. The whole thing seems so. . . so. . . ridiculous, if you don't mind me saying so. And messy. Why do you do it?"

"To have children, Dovid Hamelech."

"Ah, of course. To have children. This makes perfect sense. It is a wonderful teaching, Evan. It is a pure and good teaching, like the Torah itself. My only question is, well, Evan you have had sex eight thousand seven hundred and twenty two times in your life. But you have only two children."

"You're right," Evan admitted immediately, nodding in agreement. "It's not just for children. We enjoy it, Dovid Hamelech."

"They enjoy it," the alien whispered to himself with a profound sense of awe, as if his teacher had imparted to him a great truth. "Enjoy," he repeated, and scurried out to join his friend Moishe Rabbeinu.

The next day Moishe Rabbeinu and Dovid Hamelech forced Evan to go into more detail. Evan, in a more patient frame of mind, explained the human reproductive system, helpfully dwelling on the concepts of pleasure and orgasm. After intense questioning he admitted that no, the Torah did not allow everyone to take advantage of this pleasurable act whenever (and with whomever) they felt like. No, he responded rather quickly, sexual intercourse was neither allowed nor was it particularly common with animals or with plant life. He carefully explained, in great detail, all of the Torah's sexual restrictions. Dovid Hamelech appeared greatly disturbed to learn that only one mikveh — a ritual bath which cleansed Jewish wives from menstrual impurity, and allowed them to have sex with their husbands — existed on the entire planet.

Evan was not at all surprised that the blue men seemed much more interested in the laws rather than in the biological act itself, which, no matter how he tried to explain it, seemed to confuse them greatly. He was discovering that the while the aliens were either bored or genuinely baffled by human biology, they were fascinated by Jewish law. And they were especially concerned it be carried out correctly.

The next morning, Moishe Rabbeinu reported to Evan that he and his friends had spent the night building mikvehs.

"Two thousand, six hundred and ninety–seven of them!" Moishe Rabbeinu proclaimed. "Of course, we're not absolutely certain of the legal validity of sixty three of them, but still, I must say. . ."

"Moishe Rabbeinu!" Evan interrupted. "Why on earth would we need. . ?"

"And we will do more for you, Evan," Dovid Hamelech interjected. "More to enable you to enjoy this holy mitzvah. With our eyes we will be able to discern blood spots in your women which humans would never be able to see! We will make it our responsibility to ensure that every woman who has intercourse with her husband is completely and absolutely pure! With us, their will be no doubts!"

Evan stared at them, dumbfounded, his mouth hanging open, as if he had only just now realized he was speaking to blue creatures from outerspace, as if the utter strangeness of the exchange – of the whole alien visit – had only just occurred to him.

"Evan?" Moishe Rabbeinu asked. "Are you all right?"

Evan shook his head. He wanted to explain that the planet didn't need more mikvehs; the existing one was hardly ever used. He also felt a need to admit a sad fact: all of the elaborate rituals and laws surrounding sexual relations – the laws Evan had spent hours and hours teaching the interested aliens – were only observed by a handful of the Jews on the planet. Further, he felt he should report that, in fact, only a small percentage of the community regularly observed any of the Jewish laws.

But these blue men were so fervent, so innocent in their faith, so free from doubt and cynicism. How could he disappoint them? A tremendous sadness suddenly came over Evan, a biting sting of grief which for once had nothing to do with the Holocaust. Judaism, Evan thought to himself with a sigh. Even on this far away sanctuary, this Planet of the Jews, even with no Nazis, no threats, no persecution, it still only truly inspires twenty or thirty thousand souls. How can this be true? What could God be thinking?

What he finally said, though, to his good blue friends, was, "We probably won't be needing quite so many *mikvehs.*"

But, in fact, within a month several dozen of the perfectly formed ritual baths were seeing great use. And it seemed like many more would soon be up and running, catering to a whole new clientele. Suddenly, a religious revival swept the planet and spread like wild fire. Jews – young, old, men, women – began flocking to the handful of synagogues in droves, and when those became too crowded, more were built, then more, and then more. At least one blue man chanted the services at each of the synagogues, so their inspired worship could be shared by the entire community.

Also, the demand for kosher meat so outpaced the capacity of the one harassed ritual slaughterer that nearly half the population became vegetarian, practically over night.

And there was more. A third of the planet's population now spent Shabbat resting and praying.

Passover shed its secular political/nationalistic trappings and became a holy day, celebrated by a quarter of the population, not because of ethnic custom, but because it was a way of showing loyalty to God.

Alan remained somewhat suspicious of the new spirituality, maintaining his usual conscientious objector status regarding any form of organized religion. He was, however, not at all puzzled about what prompted the new spirituality. It was the blue men.

They were in every *schull* davening with a fervor and an emotional sincerity, and an esthetic beauty, that even Alan had to admit was simply breathtaking. They knitted *talleisim* with the purest blue dyes anyone had ever seen. Using sand and heat from their breath, they fashioned lovely glass *mezuzahs* and affixed them to every doorpost on the planet.

They examined the kosher meat, and guarded the *mikvehs.*

They told new Jewish stories, tales about Jews roaming the galaxy in fantastic ships, all for the greater glory of God and Israel. They wrote achingly beautiful Jewish songs – in Hebrew, which more and more Jews began to learn – with words and melodies that so captured the imagination of the men and women on the planet, they became a part of the classic liturgy, as if they'd been composed thousands of years before.

The blue men served the humans with great humility, never acting as leaders, never usurping the rabbis' roles as Jewish authorities or Evan's role as spiritual leader of the planet. They served as the catalyst for the new Jewish renewal, but not as directors. We're not prophets or angels, they reminded the people, just simple Jews, like you, trying to live according to God's will. And everyone, even the rapidly shrinking secular population, loved them.

Until one cloudy morning, when everyone woke up and they were gone, along with several tons of food replicators, fuel manufacturers, hydrogen/oxygen converters, hydro—electric synthesizers, and virtually all of the mined Uranium on the planet.

"They stole from you," The Planet told Evan and Alan. After weeks of listless confusion, when no one knew quite what to think about the simultaneous disappearance of their blue friends and some of their most valuable equipment, Alan prevailed on Evan to ask the Planet if it knew anything.

"It was all a hoax," the Planet continued. "They're thieves. This is what they do. They go from planet to planet, insinuate themselves into the local population, win everyone's trust, and then they steal; they take whatever they can load into their space ships in one night. They never gave a damn about Judaism, about your primitive rituals or your obsolete languages. They certainly never gave a damn about any of you."

"Con artists," Evan said.

"Grifters," Alan agreed, nodding. "Blue grifters," he added.

"But wait a minute," Evan said to the Planet. "You know who they are. You know their story. You must have known all along! You knew they were just scamming us!"

"I did," the Planet admitted.

"Why didn't you tell us?" Alan asked softly.

There was a barely perceptible pause before the Planet replied, a beat of such short duration Alan wasn't at all sure he hadn't just imagined it.

"This was to be part of your story," the Planet replied.

"What the hell do you mean by that?" Evan demanded.

"This was to be part of your story," the Planet repeated.

"What story?" Alan asked.

"This was to be part of your story."

"Are there others like them?" Evan asked.

"This was to be part of your story."

It was the only answer they would get. The Planet was back in broken record mode. For forty–five minutes Evan and Alan probed, demanded, beseeched, flattered and begged, asking any question they could think of which might offer even the tiniest bit of information on the blue visitors. "This was to be part of your story," was all the Planet revealed. Finally, the two friends gave up.

Word got out in almost no time; the blue men were crooks.

Alan was surprised at the people's reaction. Naturally the religious revival flagged a bit; there was bound to be some disillusionment. But many, many thousands of Jews stuck with their new found faith. Not a few dug even deeper into their new spiritual selves, finding existential, hidden meanings in both the visit from the blue men and in the enigmatic reply of the Planet. A new form of Jewish mysticism arose, based on the spirited davening of the blue visitors, and the search for the perfect telling of the Planet's "story."

Alan noticed surprisingly little resentment directed at the thieves. Almost no one had a bad word to say about the swindlers; only Evan seemed to bear any grudge at all. Forgiveness, even, astoundingly, some lingering admiration seemed to carry the day.

As far as Alan could discover, the thinking went something like this: Yes, it's true they stole from us, and stealing is certainly not a good thing. On the other hand, we can easily replace everything they took. And, yes, they lied about their religious convictions, and were utterly insincere in all of their multi–faceted spiritual activities. But their counterfeit Judaism was so completely convincing, and so overwhelmingly filled with beauty, that, well, there must be something valuable in the original, something worth exploring. So, in this sense these blue thieves, these cheats, these swindlers, were — in reality, if involuntarily — master teachers.

And in later generations, when families and friends gathered to tell the story of the Great Visit around the Passover table, or under a tree, or on the floor of the wide wooden community center, or in a story circle in the broad meadow, that's what the Jews on the planet called those mysterious blue people. They called them teachers.

7: Saying Kaddish

"Huh?" Alan said. "I don't get it. How were they teachers? They were crooks. Cute little fellows, though." He thought for a moment, wrinkling his forehead. "Make an interesting comic book series, don't you think? Maybe a spinoff?"

"Hmm," I responded. We were sitting in my new office, directly across from Alan's. Since my promotion – I was now Executive Publisher for special projects, a newly invented position which really meant it was now my job to make sure Moishe and Esther submitted a story once a month – I'd been given, in addition to bonuses and a huge increase in salary, a new office with a shiny black oak desk and a view of the East River. We were discussing – what else? – the new Planet of the Jews story.

Actually, I was doing my best to ignore Alan, studying my beige carpeting, wondering if I could change the color. What was there to discuss, after all? Alan would publish the story; I'd make another million dollars.

But this time, as it happened, Alan wasn't so sure. "I think this may be it, Judah." he said, chewing on the leftover ice from his scotch on the rocks. My new office came equipped with a well stocked wet bar. "You've shot your wad. This story," he said, tapping firmly on the manuscript with two fingers, "is filled with *ideas*."

I looked up, puzzled. I thought all science fiction was about ideas. But Alan's tone sounded like he was practically accusing me of heresy.

"Oh, don't get me wrong, Judah. I mean *I* like this stuff. Mysterious blue men discuss the fine points of Jewish behavior, and they end up being phonies. It's great; it's brilliant! It's even a little funny. *I'm* into those ideas. But our readers want action – you know that. Fighting with the Zyclon bomb! Blowing up Hitler! They don't care about Jewish law."

"Alan, I. . ."

"Judah," he said quickly. "I'm not meaning to insult you. God forbid. I love your stuff. *Love* it! You're my best writer. Did I ever tell you that?"

"Yes, Alan."

"Well, all right. But here, in this series, I think you should get back to the stories. There's too much at stake here to blow it on ideas."

I told him, as politely as I could – he was still my boss – that I had absolutely no control over what Moishe and Esther produced. "And," I reminded him, "I personally don't have any ideas at all about Jewish law, or about anything religious. I hated Hebrew School, too, you know!" I grumbled, and looked down again. The only idea I had right then, besides wishing Alan were out of my office, was ripping out the horrid carpet.

"Sure, sure," Alan replied. "They're not your stories. But listen Judah. Tell you *fr–ie–nds*. . ." he said, singing the word out as if it were several syllables, "that our readers don't care about this shit." He winked at me. "Tell them, Judah."

But he was wrong; they did care about this shit. The story of the blue men sold even more copies than the others, and it caused an even greater sensation. I now needed a full–time answering service just to turn away all the calls that came to my three unlisted numbers. I hired six employees just to sort and answer the mail which came in big bags to both my office and my apartment penthouse. *Astounding Stories* quadrupled its printing run. It was now the most widely distributed magazine in the country.

"I apologize," Alan offered the next week. This time we were in his office, lounging on the white velour sofa, negotiating a new bonus for all *Astounding Stories* employees. Alan had received a directive from the chairman of the board to 'spread the wealth around a little.' To my mind, Alan was focussing on the phrase 'a little,' and resisting the 'spread the wealth' part. "You've got the touch," he continued. "I shouldn't question what you. . ."

"Alan," I whispered tightly. "For the last goddam time, I don't write those. . ."

He held out his beefy palm. "Whatever," he said quickly. "But, listen Judah, I got a favor to ask."

I eyed him suspiciously.

He laughed. "No, no" he said. "It's nothing about business, nothing about sci–fi, or comic books. And nothing about money. Listen, it so happens my mom died exactly eight years ago. I've never done it before, but I thought I should say *kaddish*."

"*Kaddish?*" I asked. For some reason, I felt myself going pale.

"Yeah," Alan went on. "You know, the mourner's prayer? You say it when. . ."

"Of course I know!" I snapped.

"All right, all right," he said quickly. "But, look, I don't really want to go to *schull* alone. I hope this is not too much to ask. Could I come with you tomorrow morning?"

"Come with me where?" I asked. I didn't have the slightest idea what he was talking about.

"To say *kaddish*!" he said. "Haven't you been listening?" He looked at me carefully. "Judah are you alright? You look a little sickly. . ."

"I'm fine!"

"Hmm," he said. "Anyway, is it okay?"

"But Alan," I said quickly. "Why on earth would I say. . . "My voice trailed off. Before I even finished the question, I remembered why. My father. I blushed. Still. . . "Alan," I sighed. "I thought you knew. I'm just not that kind of Jew. I mourn my father in my own way. I have my own. . . spiritual. . ."

"Of course, Judah," he put in quickly. "None of my business. I apologize again. But I just assumed, you know, with the ratty old *tefilin* bag you've been carrying to work every day for the past three weeks. . . well. . ."

"I didn't think anyone noticed." I said softly. "They were a gift from my Uncle Max," I explained.

He held up his beefy hand again, our conversational traffic cop. "None of my business!" he said crisply, which clearly meant something more like 'I don't want it to be any of my business.'

In fact, I'd been bringing in the worn out *tefilin* in the hopes of running into Moishe or Esther, who would then show me how to put them on. I could have asked Uncle Max, and now when I thought about it, I suppose I could even have asked Alan, but for some reason, the only people I could trust to offer me Jewish ritual instruction were Moishe and Esther.

"But listen Judah," Alan went on. "Why don't we go together anyway? I need to say *kaddish*, and I don't want to go alone. And you. . ." he stared at me, stroking his fat chin thoughtfully, as if I had a familiar face he couldn't quite place. Then he shrugged his shoulders. "You could call it a research project," he said.

I agreed to go, but only because it finally gave me an excuse to track down Moishe and Esther. After all, this time I did need them. I needed them to show me how to put on those damn *tefilin*.

A few weeks earlier, I'd finally prevailed on Moishe to give me a phone number where I could reach him. I knew not to bother asking Esther, but I thought I saw an opening in her more relaxed husband. I swore up and down I wouldn't give the number to anyone else. I told him I couldn't stand the idea that a deadline could arrive, and I wouldn't be able to reach them.

And even though they'd been meticulous in getting their copy in on time – always in person, always together – you never knew what might come up.

In fact, my argument made no sense at all; even if 'something' (an earthquake? the coming of the messiah?) were to come up, what good would it do for me to call? But I think the beseeching quality of my voice finally got through to Moishe. One day, while Esther stood ramrod straight, staring at the elevator as she awaited its arrival, Moishe shoved a wad of paper into my pocket. "My number," he mouthed to me, as the elevator doors swished open. He smiled and waived goodbye from the elevator, while Esther offered her usual impatient glare.

The first time I called – the night before my *schull* date with Alan – I let the phone ring twenty–seven times before giving up. Five minutes later, I tried again, letting it go thirty two times before replacing the receiver. Five minutes later, another thirty times. Then I found enough inner discipline to wait fifteen minutes, and then, for three hours, I dialed Moishe and Esther every fifteen minutes, always hanging up on the eighteenth ring. A strange but insistent feeling of panic slowly began seeping into my soul after the first hour, and it seemed to grow with every unanswered ring. By 9:30, I was a nervous wreck. I started doodling on my notebook, sketching pictures, first of old comic book characters I'd created in the past: Tiger Man, a superhuman accountant with great leaping ability; Susan Seer, a police woman who could see ten minutes into the future. Then I pencilled pictures of the characters from Planet of the Jews: Evan, Alan, the blue men, the Planet. And then, finally, Moishe and Esther. I drew them both as ten feet tall, each with muscles bulging out of their Hasidic garb. In my sketches they towered over me like monsters; I drew myself as a cockroach. The sketching relieved my anxiety, but just a little.

At eleven o'clock, I finally got an answer.

"*Sholom Aleichem?*" I heard from the other end. It was a

polite, timid voice – Moishe's.

"This is really intolerable!" I said.

"Judah?"

"I never see you!" I continued. I was screaming into the phone. "You don't call! You don't check in. It's almost impossible to get you by phone. What if I need to see you?! What if I need to talk to you?!"

"Excuse me?" He spoke softly. I got the brief impression I had woken him up.

"I need your address!" I said. "I need to see you! Now!"

"Judah, there is something wrong? You are . . . ill?"

"Your address, Moishe!"

He gave it to me without hesitation.

It took me over an hour to get there. My cab driver, who told me he lived in Brooklyn, not far from Moishe and Esther, got lost twice. He ended up circling around Williamsburg for twenty minutes, and then finally let me off for free. It was after midnight when Moishe opened the door.

I was surprised at the looks of the apartment. I expected something rather dark and rundown, something reflecting the rumpled shabbiness of Moishe and Esther. I expected, in other words, a perhaps less dusty version of my Uncle Max's brownstone. But the place was bright, tidy, well–lit, tasteful and even, in some ways, elegant. Somehow, it reminded me of my own new condominium on the Upper East Side. Of course, every decoration, from the carpets to the walls to the ceilings, reflected Jewish themes. There were Jewish stars, and photographs of smiling, bearded Jewish men, and *menorahs* and paintings of dancing *Hasids*, and many, many pictures of Jerusalem. But the overall impression, beyond extreme neatness, was one of light and joy.

I was also surprised at how quiet it was. For some reason, I'd always assumed Moishe and Esther would have at least six children. I thought I'd find a house full of babies. But the only sound I heard was my own heavy breathing.

"Children asleep?" I asked.

"No children," he replied cheerfully. "Just the two of us."

"Esther?"

"Esther is. . . Judah, Esther is out."

"Hmmm."

"But *I'm* very happy to see you." He smiled the warmest smile I'd seen from him, and led me to a comfortable tan couch in the living room.

In fact, he did look happy to see me. He immediately treated me as if I were an old friend. He gave me several glasses of weak, sugary tea, and asked about my life. I answered him. I unburdened myself. I told him about my dissatisfactions, the sources of my vague unhappiness: my job, my relationship with my parents, my artistic troubles with Uncle Max, my divorce. He listened sympathetically, nodding occasionally. It was an hour before I noticed I was doing all the talking. But by then I didn't care. I realized it had been almost two years since I'd last seen Elena – my ex–wife. Two years since I'd truly revealed myself to another human being.

Moishe seemed perfectly willing to listen all night, but I suddenly became terribly fatigued. Moishe offered to let me sleep there – and the soft couch felt awfully inviting – but it didn't seem quite right. Instead, I took out the *tefilin* and asked him if he could show me how to use them.

We tried for an hour and a half, stopping just once for another glass of sweet tea. I almost got it. The head strap was easy; I just fit it on like a headband. It was too small, but it would do; I could wear it. But no matter how patiently Moishe demonstrated for me, I couldn't figure out the arm strap. I'd start off right, tightening a slip knot directly above my right elbow. But then I'd forget how many times to loop the strap around my arm, or how to bring it in between my fingers and on to my palm. I'd end up hopelessly tangled. Finally, I sort of succeeded, though it felt like all I'd done was fasten my forearm to my biceps. Nevertheless, I decided to claim success, and get out of there before morning.

"We'll try again," Moishe reassured me. "Soon." Then he called me a cab. I fell fast asleep on the way home, but the driver managed to rouse me, and my concierge helped me to the elevator. Both men winked at me after saying goodnight, as if they were certain I'd partied the night away. I was too tired to correct the impression.

Early the next morning, Alan met me in the lobby of my building. I was shocked to see him wearing an expensive three-piece suit, and black, newly shined shoes. I hadn't even thought to replace my sneakers, much less wear a tie.

I nodded, mumbled a greeting, then yawned and rubbed my eyes. He grinned. "Late night, huh?"

I ignored the lurid tone in his voice, and resisted the temptation to tease him about his attire, though, in fact, he looked pretty silly. Some people, particularly fat sci-fi publishers, just shouldn't wear fancy clothes.

I suddenly remembered that even though there were probably five hundred synagogues in Manhattan, I didn't know of a single one.

"Where to?" I asked.

He looked at me oddly. "Well, the synagogue at the bottom of our office building seems like the most logical choice," he said. "Unless you've got a preference. . ."

"Oh, no," I said, and quickly shook my head. I was completely unaware there was a synagogue anywhere near the office, even though I'd been working there for ten years. I didn't know how I could have missed something so obvious, and was tempted to ask Alan how long the *schull* had been there, but I didn't want to admit to him I'd never noticed it. Instead I just motioned for him to lead the way, and followed right behind. For a big man with expensive shoes, he walked quickly. I had to strain to keep up.

Alan and I were amazed at how many people crowded into the one-room, dimly-lit *schull*. Nearly every one of the hundred odd seats were taken.

"Is it a holiday or something?" Alan whispered. "*Simches Torah? Shavuos? Succos? Yom Kipper?*" I shrugged. All those words – with the exception of *Yom Kipper*, which I knew was an extremely important Jewish holiday – could have been Greek, for all I knew. "I don't know," I whispered, but a handsome young man – I recognized him as an illustrator who worked three floors below us – assured us this was now the regular turnout for weekday mornings.

"Since those sci–fi stories," he confided to us. "The Planet of the Jews."

We both nodded, and claimed two seats in the back. I picked up a prayerbook and flipped it open, but the illustrator reached over, grabbed it, and turned it right–side up. He smiled at me. I didn't smile back.

For the first ten minutes of the service, I struggled to put on my *tefilin*. I'd forgotten virtually everything Moishe had showed me. At first I tied two of my fingers together, and had to ask Alan's help in unravelling the knot. Later, I even mistook the arm band for the head band, and started wrapping the long, black, slip–knotted section around my neck.

"Judah," Alan whispered loudly. "You're going to choke yourself! Put the damn things away!"

I never did fasten them correctly; I ending up setting them down in a heap on my lap.

But other than that, I quite enjoyed the service. The melodies seemed vaguely familiar and lovely – mournful at points – though not at all memorable or catchy. I wasn't plan-ning to bother reciting the *kaddish*, since I couldn't read Hebrew, but Alan pointed out to me where the prayer was printed out phonetically in English letters, so I had no excuse. I was surprised at how the experience moved me. The words, of course were gibberish; I didn't even bother to look at a trans-lation. But it didn't matter; mouthing the strange words, while thinking of my father (and of my mother, and everyone else I'd ever known who died), was an immensely powerful experience. I felt, for the first time since the funeral, like a mourner, if sadness and yearning were a normal and proper part of my being, as if loss could be enjoyed, even savored.

After the *kaddish*, people started filing out; I didn't realize it at first, but it was all over. I was amazed at how short the service was – it couldn't have lasted more than forty five minutes. My few memories of synagogue as a kid involved dreadfully long services (did they last five hours? six? twelve?) with interminable operatic soloists dreying on in an atmosphere of oppressive decorum. This service was nothing like those. The difference was remarkable and obvious, like night and day. It was as if sometime, in the past twenty five years, every observant Jew in the world had agreed secretly to change religions – to call everything by the same name – *kaddish, yahrzeit, davening*, whatever – but completely alter the content. Or maybe I was just remembering wrongly.

In any case, I appreciated the service, and so did Alan. He couldn't stop talking about it.

"So many people," he gushed, as we rode up the elevator to the top floor. "Judah, did you ever imagine there were so many observant Jews on this one block? And those melodies, they were so beautiful! Did you recognize any of them, Judah?"

"Uh, sort of," I answered. "I mean, they sounded familiar."

"Hum one now!" he asked me, and it sounded oddly like an order from a superior. In fact, I would have liked to comply, even with four other people in the elevator listening in; I also enjoyed the melodies. But I couldn't remember them.

"Too bad," Alan said sadly, as the doors swished open at our floor.

"Judah!" he called out as I turned to walk into my office. I spun around to face him. "Let's go again tomorrow!"

I laughed, though I wasn't sure he was joking. "Maybe," was all I could answer.

"I'll call you," he said. "And Judah. . ?"

"Alan?"

"Thanks for coming with me."

"No problem," I said. "I liked it too."

"Yes," he said. "Good, good! Great. Good! Well, uh, back to work, huh?"

"Back to work," I answered, and retreated into my office. Back to work.

The truth was, however, I didn't have much work to do. My sole assignment now for the company was to insure the production of "The Planet of the Jews" series. That task took me precisely one hour a month – the time it took to read a story, and then walk down the hall and give it to Alan. For this strenuous hour, I was paid $50,000, excluding royalties and bonuses. I never copy edited a single word, never made a single correction. In the third story, I actually noticed several mistakes in grammar, as well as spelling. I also discovered awkward phrasing and run on sentences. In fact, inelegant, cumbersome language infected all of the stories. It didn't matter – not to me, not to Alan. We ran the stories as Moishe and Esther gave them to us. We figured any mistakes were either intentional or just meant to be. Why mess with success?

That particular day was three weeks before printing, so I had exactly nothing to do. The usual batch of phone messages from reporters, publishers, investment bankers etc. . . awaited me on my desk. There was also one from my ex–wife's attorney, thanking me for the final alimony check. But the only ones I intending on returning were from my auto broker who'd finally dug up a new Mazerati, and the house contractor who was replacing the cabinets in my 1200–square–foot kitchen. But even they could wait.

No deadlines loomed. I'd broken all of my writing contracts; I hadn't recovered from my "Planet of the Jews"–induced writing slump. The only project I could work on with any real enthusiasm was *Roach*, the comic book novel about Uncle Max and the Holocaust. But any progress there depended on finally getting a coherent narrative from my Uncle, something he kept on promising but could never quite deliver. I'd decided a few weeks earlier that if Max didn't come through by November, I would just take what I had, do a little research, and make up the rest. One way or another, I was determined to get *Roach* into print, if only to get the world off my back about "The Planet of the Jews."

That morning, I spent a couple of hours making sketches of what I assumed would be the main characters. I had to admit my roaches didn't really look like roaches, because I had to give them faces with real expressions. But I was pleased at the fear and vulnerability I was able to put into the little insects. And I was pretty sure, though they didn't look 'cute' like Disney characters, that they were not disgusting. The Max roach, for instance, bore a saintly, wounded look on his bespectacled face. I illustrated his scatterbrained charm by giving him six different non-matching shoes.

I toyed with the idea of putting myself into the story – maybe give the novel a kind of flashback frame. I spent some time drawing myself as a cockroach – a tall, balding, skinny insect with wire-framed granny glasses, a five o'clock shadow, and sneakers on each of his six feet. I'd be a pushy little roach, constantly hounding Max for the story. While I was at it, I took a stab at drawing the roach version of my namesake – Judah Loeb: The Killer Partisan. I gave him a French Foreign Legion Beret and five different weapons, for five of his appendages: a machete, a knife, a machine gun, a crossbow, and the pistol he used to kill the German. In the sixth hand (or foot, or whatever) I placed his pair of *tefilin*. I knew I would find a way to include them in the story.

I became so engrossed in my illustrations, that, once again, my secretary had to remind me of my appointment with Uncle Max. She asked me if I wanted her to call up the limo service I'd been using recently, but I said no, I'd grab a cab.

I found Max sitting at his kitchen table staring at a thick white candle. Unwashed dishes crowded the sink and counter; the linoleum floor was streaked with long strips of grime. I was pleased; the room had recaptured it's untidy state. Max's apartment had apparently recovered from Moishe and Esther's visit. Max didn't look up, or acknowledge my presence in any way. I pulled up a chair and sat down next to him.

"What's with the candle?" I asked.

"Oh, Judah," he said, startled. "I didn't hear. . . or see, or. . . . Please," he said. "Some tea, some milk, coffee, soda. . ?"

"No thanks, Uncle Max." I jerked my head toward the candle. "What's that?"

"What? Oh, the. . . on the table. This, Judah," he said, waving his hand over the flame, "is a *yahrzeit* candle. You light it when they. . . you see, you understand I lit it when someone dies."

I nodded. "Someone die?" I asked.

"No, no, God forbid, no. No, I didn't mean when someone dies. I meant you light it when you remember someone who died. You remember the dead with this candle."

I was puzzled. "You light the candle whenever you *remember* someone who died?"

"Oh, no, no, no, Judah. You remember the *day*. I meant to say you remember *because* this date. . . this day. . . this is the day they died."

"You mean the anniversary of the death?"

"Ah, Judah," he said nodding. "You *are* a writer!"

We stared at the candle together. Max took a sip of his coffee, which for all I knew was ice cold. It looked like no one had put anything away in a long time. "So," I said, pointing again to the candle. "Who died? Whose anniversary?"

"Today, Judah," Max said, "is September 12th. The Hebrew equivalent is the sixteenth of Elul. On the sixteenth of Elul your great aunt Sylvia, my sister, passed away from typhus. So," he said, pointing to the candle. "Remembering. Mourning."

I was impressed. "You remember the exact day," I said.

Max nodded. "Of course," he said. "Because, you understand. . . it's precisely because. . . well, on the twenty–third of Elul. . . you see it's a week later?"

I nodded.

"On the twenty-third of Elul my first cousin Mendel – Judah, he's your second cousin, I believe. Mendel died on the twenty–third of Elul. The gas chamber," he said.

"You mean he was selected on the twenty–third?" I asked. I doubted Max had actually seen Mendel die in the gas chamber on that very day.

"And on the thirtieth of Elul," Max went on, ignoring me. "Another week, you see?"

"Yeah, I see."

"On the thirtieth my youngest brother Avrum was shot."

"Why was he shot?" I asked quickly. "Were you with him? Did you see. . ?"

"On the twelfth of Tishei," Max went on. "Now this is trickier because it's two weeks later. It's not a week, it's two. Well, actually it's two weeks minus a day. Still, I. . . Well, anyway, on the twelfth of Tishrei, Ziony finally died. Starved to death."

"But how. . ."

"And on the seventeenth. . ." he continued. And he went on to tell me the exact date on which sixteen of my relatives perished in the Holocaust. He also told me how each one died – most in the gas chambers, but some were shot, starved to death, or succumbed to disease. What he didn't give me was a single detail about their deaths other than the raw facts of how they died. No context, no story. Was Avrum shot while running away stealing bread to feed Ziony? Did Mendel puff up his chest and rub blood on his cheeks in a fruitless effort to convince Dr. Joseph Mengele he was strong and healthy, and not a good candidate for extermination? Why did Ziony starve to death, but not Uncle Max? Did he hoard food, keeping it even from his own younger brother? No answers, not from Max. I asked him to elaborate the first half dozen times he gave me a date and a death, then I stopped bothering. Max now was playing the archivist; he was giving me just the bare facts – the name, the date, the manner of death. In a way, I considered myself lucky. This was the first sustained, coherent chronology I'd ever gotten from him. If Max never came through with more details, I could still turn all of his dry statistics into stories. I could, in other words, make roaches out of all those murdered Jews.

"Uncle Max," I asked, when it seemed like he was finally done with his gory list, "why do you light the candle, anyway. What does it do for you?"

"Well, Judah," he said, reaching out again to the candle, as if he were warming his chilled hands in its heat. "I've explained to you, I think. It is a memorial candle. I light it so as to remember."

"Yeah, but you already remember. You know the dates by heart. So why do you bother to light the candle. What do you get out of it?"

He squinted at me, straining to understand. Then, exasperated, he shook his head. "What I get out? I. . . I. . .I don't. . . I don't understand what you're asking, Judah"

"Why do you light the candle, Uncle Max?"

"Because it's the anniversary," he said.

"But you know it's the anniversary, so why. . ."

"To remind myself of the anniversary."

"Yes, but why. . ."

"To remember!" he snapped

"Ahh," I said.

I was upsetting him. I was being a pushy little roach. But I really wanted to know. What was the psychological motivation for this ritual, which he clearly performed several times a year at regular intervals? What was the payback? What did he get out of it?

I was curious (well, more than curious) because I had reacted so strongly that morning to rising in my seat, and then reciting – in a strange foreign language – the mourner's *kaddish*. I had experienced something beyond mere memory. It had been a weird mix: longing, heartbrokeness, impotence, awe, joy, relief. Also, strangely, curiosity – about the lives of my parents. I couldn't fix any one word on what I'd felt. I wasn't even sure if I wanted to feel it again. But I wanted to know more about it. Did Max feel it, every time he lit one of those thick candles? Did all Jewish mourning rituals conjure up these powerful emotions?

But I didn't want to push Max. We'd been snapping at each other too much lately; I'd yell at him, or he'd whine to me. It wasn't right. The day after my father died, Max kept telling me we were all each other had. "It's just you and I," he cried, tears streaming down his cheeks. "Just you and I." I'd never really taken the idea seriously; didn't we have friends, jobs, lives? But suddenly, thinking about loss, and about my parents and – I couldn't deny it – about Moishe and Esther, I felt it was true. He was the only family I had; I was all he had. And he was already seventy–six years old.

For the rest of the afternoon, we played chess, and then took a walk. I let him guide the conversation, and barely asked any questions. Before I left, I washed all the dishes in his sink, scrubbed down his counters, and mopped the floors. During this fit of cleaning – completely uncharacteristic, I doubt I'd ever even rinsed a glass for him before this – he gawked at me like I was a crazy man. To be honest, I felt a little crazy, but I also felt right doing it. When he wasn't looking, I left a check for $10,000 on his kitchen table, next to the *yahrzeit* candle. Maybe he'd hire a cleaning lady.

From Max's apartment, I decided to head over to Moishe's and Esther's. It occured to me their place was within walking distance of Max's. Well, it would be over an hour walk, but it was a nice, crisp, sunny day, and I had nothing else to do.

I did feel strange barging in on them. I wasn't even planning on calling first, and this was a couple who clearly valued their privacy. But after my late night *tefilin* session with Moishe, I felt a bond. I just hoped Esther wouldn't be home.

In fact, neither were home. I leaned on the buzzer, knocked until my knuckles ached, but nobody came to the door. I decided to wait. I was exhausted from the walk, which I'd done at a rather rapid pace, practically running, so I sat down on the floor mat and stretched out my legs, leaning my head against the bottom of the door. In a few minutes, I was asleep.

I dreamt that Moishe had invented a machine which could communicate with the dead. It looked suspiciously like a pair of tefilin, with two solid black cubes, connected by black ribbon–like strips which Moishe explained were antennas. On the smaller cube was a keyboard you could use to punch in the name of the person you wanted to talk to. In my dream, Moishe was demonstrating the machine to me, hoping I would buy it for Astounding Stories Inc. He offered to place one free call to anyone I chose. I was debating in my mind over whether to call my father or my mother, or maybe some famous historical figure like Moses, when Esther shook me awake.

I was alarmed, and a little frightened, when I saw her concerned face; I even recoiled and put out my palms as if I needed to defend myself. But she astonished me by smiling, fully and warmly. It was a dramatic, almost revolutionary change in expression. She looked serene and content. And she appeared – could it really be? – happy to see me.

"Look who's here," she practically gushed to Moishe who was following her up the stairs.

"Judah," Moishe said simply and grabbed my hand to pull me up. He led me into the apartment.

They fed me. I hadn't eaten since breakfast and it was already early evening. Esther made hard boiled eggs, kasha, and lentil soup; Moishe produced a rounded loaf of pumpernickel bread and a huge jar of pickled herring with sour cream.

I ate like a horse. I was starving.

After three cups of strong, sweet coffee, Esther, the absolute picture of friendliness, of cheerful hospitality, asked me what I was doing there.

I thought about saying that some issues had come up concerning their stories – some minor editorial points to discuss, some plot suggestions, or maybe some accounting difficulties. Instead, I told them I was curious about Jewish mourning rituals. Did they happen to know, I asked, looking at their book shelves crowded with Hebrew titles, of any books I could read on the subject? Or, I suggested hesitantly, could they, possibly, talk to me a little about these rituals?

Esther's whole face lit up. She turned to Moishe who also grinned, though not, perhaps, with quite as much enthusiasm.

"Judah," she said graciously, her eyes glowing, "it's one of our *favorite* topics."

"Rituals?" I asked.

"Mourning," Esther answered. Moishe nodded.

They spoke with me for almost four hours, teaching me with great patience and even affection. I learned what I supposed was everything one can know about death and dying in the Jewish tradition. They explained the technical details as well as the emotional resonances. By the end, I was sprawled out on their white sofa, tears filling my eyes, though I was not at all upset. On the contrary, I was elated. I'd finally discovered a context for all the jumbled feelings I'd accumulated about my parents' deaths (and their lives, for that matter). The rituals (along with Moishe and Esther's kind explanations) were like a box, or, better yet, a vase, where I could store those feelings, remove them from the turmoil of my soul, yet still keep them close at hand.

It was almost midnight by the time we finished talking. Once again, Moishe offered to let me sleep on the couch. I was tempted, but again, it didn't seem proper. It would be, I thought, like intruding in a sacred precinct. Esther led me to the door and shoved a stuffed manilla envelope in my pocket. "For later," she whispered in my ear, and for a moment I thought she was going to kiss me on the cheek. Instead she wished me goodnight, good health, and a safe trip home. I thanked both of them profusely – I couldn't thank them enough – and climbed down the stairs.

It was cool outside, and rain threatened. While I waited with my arm up, occupied taxis whizzing by, a sharp, damp wind pushing at my face and hair, I realized I'd forgotten what seemed to me were key points about mourning. I'd forgotten where exactly one is supposed to tear one's garment after hearing of a death. The sleeve? The front pocket? The buttons? Where? More importantly, I'd forgotten the kabbalistic explanation for the tearing. I'd also forgotten what exactly one is supposed to do on the thirtieth day after the death of a parent. Walk around the block? Eat lentil soup? Go the movies? What? For some reason, these seemed like especially pressing questions. I didn't want to go back to my penthouse without knowing the answers. I was about to run back up the stairs to Esther's place, when all of a sudden, as if out of nowhere, a cab appeared. I still thought about heading back for a flash refresher course, but I was worried I wouldn't get another taxi. Reluctantly, I climbed into the back seat and settled in for the long ride uptown.

As the driver turned on to Park Blvd, crossing the Williamsburg bridge, I took out the envelope Esther had snuck into my pocket. It was a new manuscript. I read it on the way home.

8: Talking to the Dead

"You'll find a lake 2.32 Kilometers past this clump of Lujures trees. Head east 34.21 degrees. It's quite a lovely lake, really. Potable, well stocked with edible fish." The Planet spoke to Evan and Alan who were leading a mission to chart and explore the planet's southeast continent.

The Jewish refugees had really begun exploring the planet the day of the Landing, but no one ventured too far at first. The landing site was so beautiful and so hospitable that there didn't seem to be any point in wandering around. Everyone was too busy building the first settlement, which they eventually called Loebville, after Rabbi Judah Loeb. But now, fifteen years later, a kind of curious wanderlust had set in. What, people wondered, is this planet, our new home, really like? They decided to find out.

Three weeks earlier the first official expedition headed north, across the ocean, and discovered a benevolent ecosystem of exceptional diversity, far more diverse than anywhere on Earth. For instance, the explorers were able to catalogue one hundred and fifty bee–like creatures which produced one hundred and fifty types of edible, delicious honey. They also noticed seventy–five different cow like creatures, each producing its own potable, tasty milk. There were also forests consisting of hundreds of trees, where no two trees were of the same kind. Overall, the adventurers discovered an extremely lovely and hospitable continent. The mission was such a great success, that dozens of families began making plans to start a new settlement.

At first no one even thought to ask the Planet for help in the explorations. No one, not even Evan or Alan, had been able to get the Planet to talk at all about itself — not of its origins or history or feelings or, most importantly, why exactly it chose to rescue this group of Jews and bring them to the planet. It wasn't until Evan and Alan put together their own expedition that the Planet, without being asked, began to contribute.

Then it was hard to shut it up; it became positively promiscuous in giving out information. Nothing, of course, about who it was, or the ultimate nature of its existence. Nothing about why it was "alive" in the first place. In other words, it continued to offer no information about its spiritual state. But it was happy — it certainly seemed happy — to blabber on and on about its physical self — its geography, geology and topography.

Evan and Alan's group consisted of nine men and nine women. They were charged with no particular mission other than to see what was out there, and report on the physical characteristics of the southeastern corner of their new homeworld. The planet was extremely useful to them in this goal.

The first day they set out — their rovers packed with provisions, tools and fuel — the Planet, who hadn't spoken to anyone in several weeks, suddenly told Evan to head 26.6 degrees southeast and drive for 212.0436747 kilometers.

"Why?" Evan asked, a bit suspicious of the Planet.

"There's a wonderful field of what you would call wild mushrooms. They are edible, and I think even you, Evan, would consider them to be delicious. They also constitute a fine form of vegetable protein."

Evan turned to Alan. "It's the damn Planet," he grumbled. "It wants to tell us where to go. It says there's some nice mushrooms not far from here."

Alan noticed that Evan seemed annoyed. He could tell that Evan didn't much like the Planet lately, though he couldn't understand why.

"It sounds like a good enough place to start," Alan offered.

Evan scowled, but pointed the rover in the right direction — 26.6 degrees southeast for 212.0436747 kilometers. "We'll go pick mushrooms," he muttered.

They looked like mushrooms, but to Alan they tasted more like biscuits with butter and honey, one of his favorite dishes.

"They stay fresh for twenty-three days without refrigeration,

Alan," the Planet said. "And reproduce themselves quite easily." Alan ordered the crop to be harvested immediately.

The Planet gave detailed descriptions of all the wildlife and the reptiles and the fish and the insects of the region, leaving nothing out. It also described all of the lakes, rivers, streams, mountains and valleys. During each hike, the Planet gave step by step descriptions of everything which came within visual range — every rock, tree, bug, reptile, and weed.

Evan, Alan noticed, became extremely irritated with the constant chatter.

"Look," Evan said, after three straight hours of reptile reproductive systems and the molecular composition of different types of soils. "Do you have to tell us *everything* at once? Can't we just explore on our own for awhile? Can't you just answer questions when we ask?"

There was a small pause. "I can do that, Evan."

But it couldn't, not really. It was, Alan thought, like a proud parent, jabbering on about a gifted child, or like a body builder obsessed with its own physique. It would shut up for awhile, but then a particularly lovely glade would come into a view, or an interesting rock formation, or a rare mammal, and the Planet would be off, bragging about every detail.

Alan's group found the lake to be every bit as lovely as the Planet's promise. At the Planet's suggestion, they camped there for the night, in a level clearing just fifteen or twenty meters from the water's edge. Alan ordered most of the group to go fishing for dinner, while he and Evan set out to explore the caves towering above the western shore.

The Planet's chatter accompanied them as they wandered from cavern to cavern. "To your immediate right, Evan, .38 centimeters from the ground, you'll see an important kind of fungus forming, something you'll be able to make use. . ."

"What's that?" Evan suddenly yelled out, shining his flashlight directly in front of him.

Alan squinted and tried to see. It looked like. . . he rushed over for a closer look.

"Bones," he said, kneeling down to examine them. He looked up at Evan. "Human," he said.

Evan shone his flashlight through the cave; it was littered with human bones. Some of them were connected to each other and formed skeletons, but most were just scattered. It's a graveyard, Alan thought, or a massacre site. He noticed many relatively small skeletons mixed among the larger ones; the cave, he concluded, held the remains of children as well as adults. He figured they were looking at as many as 50 dead people, of all ages.

"Those," the Planet answered, responding in it's most matter-of-fact voice to Evan's shouted question, "are the remains of the last settlers who attempted to colonize the planet. But they're all dead. Now," it continued, "if you'll look to your left, 22.8 degrees, you'll find an interesting form of. . ."

"Settlers!?" Evan and Alan yelled out, both at the same time.

"Yes, Evan and Alan," the Planet answered. "But if you'll just look. . ."

"When did they die?" Alan demanded.

"35 years, 4 months, and 14 days ago. This is according to your calculations of time."

"They all died at once?!" Evan asked.

"Yes, Evan."

Evan and Alan looked at each other. Alan fought an impulse to bolt from the cave. Evan, as if reading his mind, grabbed him by the arm and whispered, "wait."

"Planet," he said. "How did they die?"

"Why don't you ask them?" it responded.

Alan raised an eyebrow. The Planet could be quite exasperating, but he never remembered it being a smart ass.

"What do you mean by that, Planet," he asked slowly.

"I can communicate with the dead, Alan," it answered. "I'm sorry to surprise you. I thought you knew."

After Evan and Alan finally fled the cave/graveyard, the Planet explained. Every one hundred and twenty years the Planet was able to arrange communication between any live human life form and any dead one; the live one, of course had to take the initiative. There were limitations. It could only set up conversations with ten dead people in the course of two weeks. The dialogues could last no longer than thirty-six minutes. And there could be no group interviews, only one-on-one conversations.

It so happened, by coincidence, that exactly one hundred and twenty years had passed since the last two week period. That very day, the Planet explained, a new two week window of necromancy opened up.

"Let me speak to the leader of the last group of settlers!" Evan blurted out, as soon as the Planet finished its explanation.

"Evan," Alan said softly. "Do you really think this is the best. . ."

He shut up when he saw the apparition. It was a tall, strikingly handsome, commanding-looking male, sculpted jaw, penetrating blue eyes – human in every way except for two features: he had bright orange skin, and you could see right through him. He was completely transparent. Alan thought at first it was a holographic image. He even looked around for a projector. Evan just stared straight at the ghostly alien, who wore what looked a lot like black jeans and a white t-shirt.

"Why doesn't he say anything?" Evan asked.

"He can't initiate conversation, Evan," The Planet answered. "He can only respond to your questions. Oh, and Alan," the Planet added, "he's not a holographic projection at all. But you're right to understand he's really not here, at least not in body. This, though, is the form he's given in order to talk with you."

"What can I ask him?" Evan asked.

"Whatever you'd like, Evan."

"Evan," Alan said. "I don't think. . ."

Evan cleared his throat, keeping his eye on the tall orange man. "Why were you on this planet?" he asked.

"Hejad lloco dimn siholwi ikko." the man responded, looking confused.

"I'm sorry, Evan," the Planet said quickly. "He doesn't speak your language. But I can adjust that. Wait. Okay, Evan, ask again."

"Why were you on this planet?"

"Our world is overcrowded, is it," the man answered, in a surprisingly high, melodic voice. Probably was an excellent singer, Alan thought. In fact, many of his answers sounded more like songs than stories. "Many expeditions go," the man continued, "go on searches every year. We look for habitable worlds, to look. Here is one we find." He looked as if he wanted to say more, but instead shut his mouth and started looking around the area.

"Evan," Alan said, touching his friend's shoulder. "Ask him. . ."

"How did you all die?" Evan asked.

A dark, pained expression came to the man's face, as if he were experiencing both physical pain and an unpleasant memory at the same time. "Were attacked, we were," the man sang out sadly. "We camped, camped by the lake. Catching fish, to catch. They came out of nowhere, from behind the clouds, shooting. They had light beams, some kind of weapons we couldn't even understand, we could. Ran, all of us, we ran into the cave." He pointed at the cave and looked at it for a long time, his expression changing from sorrow to wonder. Alan assumed he'd answered the question and wouldn't be able to talk until the next one. But the orange leader went on.

"It seemed like our only chance. We couldn't fight, we fight," he said. "But we died anyway."

"Who attacked you?" Evan asked.

"It was too quick," the man answered, shrugging his shoulders "I know, don't know."

"You have no idea?"

"No idea to have, we have. We know, don't know."

Does he know, or doesn't he? Alan thought. But Evan continued the interrogation. "You all died in the cave?"

"We all died in the cave," the man said, shaking his head slowly. "We died," he sang.

Evan took a deep breath, and glanced quickly at Alan. "Do you think," he said, turning back to the alien, "the Planet anything to do with the attack?"

Alan practically gasped. What an idea! And didn't Evan realize, anyway, that the Planet could hear the entire conversation? Alan expected the Planet to say something, to protest, but the transparent man was already answering.

"Impossible!" he said, shaking his head. "The Planet helped us, it helped. The Planet told us where we could catch fish, where were the best places to camp, it told. We catch, we camp. We trust the planet, trust, trust, trust, trust, we trust."

"I don't want to talk to this man anymore," Evan said, still looking right at the alien. "Thank you," he added. The man gave a courtly bow, then winked out of existence.

Evan said nothing as he and Alan hiked back to camp. He did nod in agreement when Alan told him it would be up to the ruling council, not any one person, to decide what additional nine dead people to contact. It was too great a decision, Alan continued, for just one man, even Evan, to make. Evan nodded again, without apologizing for unilaterally using up one of the ten conversations. Or saying anything, for that matter.

The council debated a long time about whom to contact. It was similar to the debate about time travel. A few scholarly types suggested they use the opportunity to interview some of the great geniuses in history — Einstein, Freud, Moses. We could finally learn something, they said, an opportunity we lost when we destroyed the time machine. But after the fiasco of Pesek Z'man, there was little enthusiasm for exploring ancient history.

On the other hand, nearly everyone on the planet had left a loved one behind on earth. Most assumed these loved ones were all dead — killed in the Nazi conquest of Earth, and the subsequent destruction of the Jews. But they couldn't be absolutely sure. A rough consensus developed around the idea of contacting at least one relative from earth who died at the hands of the Nazis and asking him or her what had happened, if only to satisfy the morbid curiosity of the surviving Jews. But they couldn't agree on who the dead person should be, and they finally admitted that, come to think of it, they didn't really much care about what had happened on Earth. Their old planet was light-years away and far in the past.

In the end, the council decided not to decide. They voted unanimously to select eight people at random and have them communicate with whomever they chose. But beforehand, they would contact Rabbi Judah Loeb.

Evan insisted on it. He reminded them that the rabbi's unsolved murder remained a significant security issue for the Jews on the planet. Someone from inside the community, Evan maintained, had killed him. Until we apprehend the killer, Evan insisted, none of us is safe.

Evan spoke forcefully, but it's unlikely the council would have gone along with his idea. For the most part, they all just wanted to forget the traumas of the past. But the Planet intervened.

"Evan thinks I killed Rabbi Judah Loeb," it said. "He also suspects I killed those poor settlers who came before you. He can't explain exactly why, but he *is* suspicious of me. And if he's suspicious, sooner or later, many others of you will be — maybe even all of you. And this is certainly not a good basis for any future relationship. So, contact Rabbi Loeb and ask him. We're going to be together a long time," the Planet continued. "Your community and I. It won't do for you to suspect me as a killer. Let me call up your Rabbi Loeb. Ask him yourselves."

And so they did.

Evan was surprised at the rabbi's appearance. There were very few streaks of gray in his brown beard, and almost no lines of age on his face. His black coat and black pants looked new and freshly pressed. He was relatively trim; what bulk he did support gave the impression of authority and spiritual weight, not gluttony or neglect. He looked, in other words, like the Rabbi Judah Loeb Evan had first met more than twenty years ago, before the ravages of the Exodus years. He was also transparent. Through the rabbi's thick torso, Evan could see three Lujures trees, as well as the purple and white Judah Loeb Memorial Chapel — the first synagogue the settlers had built, shortly after landing.

The two old friends stared at each other. Evan got the impression that Judah was annoyed about something. He waited for his old friend to talk, and then remembered the rules: the dead could only respond to queries; they couldn't initiate conversation.

A few questions popped into Evan's mind: 'How are you?' 'What's it like being dead?', but it seemed somehow sacrilegious, also impolite, to engage in small talk. So he got right to the point.

"Judah," he said. "Who murdered you?"

The ghostly image shrugged. "I didn't recognize the man," Judah said, matter-of-factly, as if he were discussing what he'd had for breakfast that day. "I only saw him for a split second. I assume it was a Nazi."

"But why would the Ukrainians want to kill you?" Evan protested. "It didn't accomplish anything! The plan was set. We didn't need you in order to leave!"

"They hated Jews, Evan. Some of us they would blow up, some of us they would gas, some of us they would stab." The transparent man looked around, as if he were searching for a chair. He gave up and looked straight at Evan.

Evan rubbed his smooth chin, then took a deep breath. "Okay," he said. "Let's assume it was the Nazis. Doesn't that mean we had a traitor, or that a spy had infiltrated the project? Who planted the bombs? Who tried to kill you those other times? Whoever did it must have had inside contacts, or they must have been part of the project. How else could he have gotten to the ships? Or to you? We spent fifty million dollars on security. Don't you remember? We were absolutely paranoid! No one could have just walked into the office and knifed you!"

Judah shook his head and chuckled. Evan was taken aback. It was quite odd to hear a dead transparent being laugh about his own murder.

"Evan," Judah said. "You were in prison! You'd been gone for months. You have absolutely no idea how insane everything got when we realized we were actually going to leave. Everyone, Evan, *everyone* was completely panicked. We ran around the compound like chickens with our heads cut off. Rumors reached us that the Ukranians had vaporized Israel. Every Jew on earth was knocking at our door. The United States government stopped functioning. Nuclear sirens were blaring on every radio, every holo-set. Our whole organization nearly collapsed! It was a miracle — and yes I mean this, a *true* miracle, from God — that you were able to lift off in the first place. Evan, there was *no* security in my office that day. A Ukrainian soldier in an SS uniform could have walked right through my door waving a bloody knife. No one would have stopped him."

Evan persisted. There *must* have been a spy, he insisted. He pointed out that attempts on the Rabbi's life had begun years before the pandemonium of the last weeks, when security was at its tightest. "You remember," Evan said. "Those attacks you never told me about. Back then, no one could have gotten through. We had the best security on the planet."

Judah shrugged, smiled at Evan, then seemed suddenly to relax. Evan wondered if the Rabbi was able to smoke a pipe in Heaven, or wherever he was.

"Those attempts were not so serious after all, Evan." Judah said. "They didn't succeed. I'm not so sure they were even related to my murder. Remember, my friend, for many of those years, I was a criminal; I was the head of a vast illegal enterprise. I was not so surprised, frankly, that I ran into violence. It seemed an inevitable part of the criminal world. And this is why, Evan, I never told you about those attempts. What could you have done? We couldn't tighten security any more; we simply didn't have the resources. And I needed to continue my role as an outlaw — this was clearly my destiny. So?" he said. "I took the risks. As did you."

Evan took a few moments to absorb everything his friend had said. Could it have been just some two-bit Ukrainian terrorist, just a vicious hate crime? Was he merely being paranoid, looking for Nazi conspiracies millions of miles away from Earth? Was the Planet really some benevolent but lonely celestial being, with their best interests at heart? He looked at his watch. There wasn't much time left.

"Rabbi," Evan said. "Let me ask you one final question — flat out. Were you killed because you found out about a spy in the Exodus project? Were you murdered because you uncovered information which someone, or some . . . thing. . . didn't want known?"

"You've asked two questions, Evan," the ghost said. "But I will answer them as best I can. I cannot recall discovering any kind of dangerous information. And I certainly did not detect a spy. So? I do not believe I was murdered for those reasons."

Evan gave up. Either he really was speaking to the late Rabbi Loeb, or this whole necromantic spectacle was some kind of charade put on by the Planet. There was no way to know for sure. In any case, there was no sense in badgering this poor transparent creature. He glanced at his watch. There were only twelve minutes left in the communication. He took another deep breath.

"Judah," he said. "Rabbi Loeb. What. . . what should I be doing now?"

"Evan," the ghost answered, smiling with tobacco stained teeth, his voice suddenly saturated with warmth, "you should be doing exactly what you are doing. Exactly. Nothing more or less. You are fulfilling your part perfectly, Evan. You are perfect, my friend. Perfect."

Evan felt tears well up in his eyes despite his suspicions that the whole thing was a hoax. "It wasn't. . ." he continued. "It wasn't God, at all, Judah. It was the Planet, this strange. . ." He shook his head. "You know," he continued. "Of course you know; you know it wasn't God. But my question is, did we do the right thing, anyway? Maybe we could have stayed? Or tried to rescue more Jews? Or fought back?"

"Evan," the apparition responded, "You saved hundreds of thousands of lives. Millions of lives in generations to come. You preserved an entire people, Evan, a great culture. You have no reason to be afflicted with doubts. We succeeded tremendously. Because of you and your efforts. You are a great, great hero, Evan, a kind of biblical hero."

Evan wiped away his tears, and looked again at his watch. So little time. "I want to keep helping, Rabbi. What do the people need? What should I give?"

"The people need healing, Evan, just as you do. Concentrate on healing and letting go of the past as much as you can. Love the people, Evan, love yourself. I do not say these things as slogans, or as trivial generalities. I cannot be more specific because I am not there with you. But, Evan, these are what you need to give, and what you must provide for yourself: Love. Healing. Love. Love."

He smiled again, and put up his finger, as if to make a final point. "And," Judah said, "say Kaddish for me. Please, Evan. Say Kaddish"

With that, he faded away.

Staring for several minutes at the empty spot where moments ago an image of his friend and mentor had stood, Judah felt a tremendous sense of relief. Somehow all the ghost (what else could Evan call it?) had to do was mention healing, and letting go, and a huge burden was lifted from Evan's soul. Suddenly all the mental torment — the unspeakable anguish of each of the six million, his own sorrow at the loss of family, of community, of home, the horrible pain in his head — suddenly these stinging sensations fled to a remote corner of Evan's brain where he could manage them, keep them in a separate compartment. Evan felt a great healing power invade his psyche, like benevolent bacteria. In the back of his mind, Evan thought maybe he should resist the intruder. But then he said to himself, enough, enough. Why shouldn't I have peace? Why shouldn't I have life?

Finally tearing himself away from the spot, Evan went home and collapsed in his bed. He slept for twelve straight hours.

Melinda Carrey's mother had died of cancer three weeks before the Exodus from Earth. On the day of her death, Melinda had been hard at work at the Exodus headquarters, dealing with the rush of Jews suddenly eager, because of Ukrainian pronouncements, to become space refugees. At the time, she served as an important executive at Exodus.

She'd signed on the very first month — when the project had virtually no chance at success, and when everyone was calling them crazy — because she saw something powerful and sincere in Judah Loeb's eyes. Over the years, she steadily moved up the ranks. Exactly one year before liftoff, Melinda discovered from her younger brother, that her mother had developed an inoperable form of lung cancer. The day after receiving the grim news, Rabbi Loeb offered her a promotion; he wanted her to manage his own senior staff. She would have to move into the compound in Arizona, far away from her parent's home in San Diego. The job would require virtually twenty-four hour dedication.

Rabbi Loeb had listened sympathetically to Melinda's sad story. Terrible to lose a mother, he acknowledged. But his advice shocked her.

"You mother will die soon," the rabbi noted sadly, his big gray eyes clouding up. "But the Jewish people can survive. This is our task here, Melinda."

She nodded, sat silently for a few minutes, and then agreed to take the job.

She visited home as often as she could – which wasn't very often. She'd tried to relieve some of the burden of care from her father and two brothers. But she wasn't at all familiar with her mother's needs – the calls to doctors, the CT scan appointments, getting the right drugs, arguing with the insurance companies, arranging for home health care – the –day–to–day routine of caring for a dying patient. She was out of the loop, the morbid circle of information. So, on her rare trips home, she sat around befuddled, watching helplessly as her family engaged in frenetic, and, to her, barely comprehensible activity, and her mother coughed, gasped for breath, and gradually wasted away.

She felt guilty. She felt guilty when she was visiting, and felt guilty when she was away. She felt guilty as her mother lay dying, she felt guilty when she died, and she felt guilty after her death. She had never stopped feeling guilty, even as the spaceships blasted themselves into the wide universe, even as she helped build this new and safe community for her people.

When Melinda won the lottery which gave her the right to talk to one dead person, she knew, without even thinking, that it had to be her mother. Evan had explained the rules to her very carefully, especially how the departed could not respond to statements, only to questions. Nevertheless, Melinda began the encounter by saying "I'm sorry," five times in five different ways. Finally, she remembered the instructions and asked a question.

"Do you forgive me?" she asked.

Her mother answered yes, of course she forgave her. She assured her she always understood the importance of the Exodus project. She had never, ever, resented the time Melinda devoted to it, and she was tremendously proud of Melinda's great role.

Great, burning tears swelled up in Melinda's brown eyes. She asked her mother, who appeared statuesque and youthful, not the emaciated cancer victim of her final weeks, how could she possibly still love her? How could she excuse the neglect? How could her mother absolve her from the sin of letting the family down? Of leaving all the work to her father and her brothers?

Because, her mother explained, love contains it's own healing. There was always love between mother and daughter – while the mother lay dying, while the daughter toiled far away in the Arizona desert, and after the mother passed on. In this love was the potential to heal any breach, to conjure up forgiveness from the worst estrangements. Feel no guilt, she instructed her daughter, because all sins – real or imagined – had long been washed away. Now there was only healing, she told her. Now there was only love.

Melinda gasped and fell to her knees. She wept in great convulsive heaves, as years of poisonous self-hatred fled from her soul like salty fluids escaping through her pores. The massive cathartic joy she felt was almost painful, almost too pleasurable to bear. Melinda felt something inside of her struggle to staunch the flow, to prevent the guilt from escaping. But the outpouring was too strong, too forceful, and so she stopped resisting, without really putting up much of a fight.

After ten minutes of being washed in cleansing tears, she dried her face with a handkerchief and pushed herself up – recovered and rejuvenated. Healed. She asked her mother how she could sustain this feeling. How could she *maintain* the love, the healing?

"*Kaddish*," her mother told her. "Say *kaddish* for me at my *yahrzeit*, and at every *yizkor* service. And light a candle, Melinda, a *yahrzeit* candle. Do this faithfully, Melinda," she said. "And the love will always be there."

Melinda was puzzled. Her family had never been religious. It had never occurred to her that these mourning rituals would mean anything at all to her mother. But she didn't argue. She thought about asking why, but it was too late. Melinda's mother popped out of existence.

Melinda went home in a state of exhausted euphoria. She collapsed on her bed and slept for twelve hours. She woke up a new person.

Seven other members of the community took advantage of the Planet's gift and contacted lost loved ones. They spoke, each in their turn, to a brother, a cousin, a sister, a father, and three mothers. Evan told them how the dialogue worked, then left them alone. They didn't report much of the conversations to Evan, and he didn't ask about them. He did, however, notice that all of the dialogues shared two elements in common: each live participant experienced a profound and immense sense of resolution by the end of the encounter — old wounds were healed, old sins forgiven — and each of the dead participants, in one way or another, requested that their loved ones among the living perform all of the Jewish mourning rituals. Each living relative was surprised by the request, since none of these dead people had ever been observant Jews. But no one begrudged the request, and they all intended to honor it. It didn't seem, after all, like much to ask.

Evan, naturally, had many questions to ask the Planet about the strange phenomena. He didn't expect to get many good answers, but he decided to give it a try.

"Why," he asked, "only ten dead people? And why only every one hundred and twenty years? Why can't you just do this. . .thing, provide this service whenever you want, whenever anyone asks you?"

"Evan," the Planet responded, "it's no good you asking me these sort of questions. It's like me asking you why you breathe oxygen and not helium. Or why you have to breathe at all. Or why you aren't able to fly. I was created with these limitations, Evan. This is how God made me."

Evan raised an eyebrow. This was the first time he'd heard the Planet mention God. He was surprised the Planet would admit to being created by anyone.

"Can you provide this gift to people on Earth?" Evan asked.

"No, no," the Planet answered quickly. "They're much too far away."

"Too far away from you?"

"Well," the Planet answered, "actually, too far away from the dead."

Another shocker for Evan. He felt a sudden chill. "You mean this planet. . . I mean you. . . you're close to where dead people go? We're close to Heaven, the World to Come, the Other Side, Valhalla – whatever? Here? On the Planet of the Jews?

The Planet hesitated just a moment. "This is all a bit difficult to explain, Evan," It said. "I'm not sure we should talk about this anymore."

"Are we dead?" Evan asked.

"Not. . . not exactly," the Planet answered.

And that's all the Planet had to say on the matter. Whenever Evan – or anyone – asked, the Planet would, so to speak, clam up. It wouldn't say anything at all.

In any case, a great calm descended on the community in the wake of the episode with the dead. As stories of healing and forgiveness spread, the community itself felt the beginnings of a great healing. The building, the working, the settling, the living, it all went on, but without the panicked energy of before, without the dreadful anxiety, and without the great, great sadness. Alan felt the healing inside his own soul. Even Evan felt it, at least partially.

"You have to admit," Alan told him one day – about a month after Evan's chat with the dead Judah Loeb. They were walking home together from Shabbat morning services. Alan normally didn't attend, but that day was his mother's *yahrzeit*, and he'd wanted to say *kaddish*. "Even if the whole thing was a hoax," he said, "even if the Planet is malicious and has some evil plan in store for us, you still have to admit, these. . . interviews, these. . . conversations with the dead. . . you have to admit they did a lot of good."

Evan nodded. "Hmm," he said. He was noncommittal, though, in fact, he did agree; the conversations had done a great deal of good. For himself and for everyone.

"So," Alan continued, "we may as well trust the Planet. Even if it's wicked. Even if it's out to get us. Since we landed, it's been entirely benevolent. So we may as well act as if it really *is* benevolent. Give it the benefit of the doubt. Even if there's a chance it's evil, let's act as if it's good."

Evan nodded. "That's a good idea," he admitted.

But even as he said goodbye, and wished his friend a peaceful

Sabbath, he knew this was a formulation he could never accept. Alan wanted to act as if the planet were benevolent and good, even though there was a chance it was wicked and harmful. But for Evan, everything in the universe was wicked and harmful until proven otherwise. That went for planets as well as for people. It went for the dead as well as for the living.

9: Max's Story

"There's no sci-fi in this story, Judah!" It was Alan speaking. We were meeting in my penthouse apartment on the Upper East side of Manhattan. He was sitting on my pure white George S'zard sofa, sipping from his snifter of port and rummaging through the pages of Moishe and Esther's latest story. I'd called him as soon as I returned home with it, and he grabbed a cab and came right by.

"There's just this one alien," he continued. "But he doesn't do much, and I can't make heads or tails out of what he says. And this girl, this Melinda? Her mother, Judah, her mother dies of cancer? *Cancer* Judah? Wouldn't you think by the year 2100 – that's the year we're talking about, isn't it? – they'd have found a cure for cancer? There's no cancer in the future, Judah. It should be some futuristic kind of disease. The woman should die of zyrteularisis, a strange alien parasite. Or some kind of genetically engineered super microbe. You know what I'm talking about!"

I nodded.

"And right here," he said, flashing a page of manuscript at me like a switch blade knife. "Here you have Evan looking at his watch. A *watch*, Judah? This is a civilization which can transport tens of thousands of Jews to a distant solar system. Wouldn't you think they'd have come up with something to replace the wristwatch? At least, Judah, at least call it a chronopiece. Now, wouldn't that be better? Judah?"

"I suppose," I said.

"Anyhow," he went on. "It's not about *anything* having to do with sci-fi. There's no fancy gadgets, no battles. . . no social predictions. . . no science. It's just about. . . well, I guess it's about death. Isn't it, Judah?"

"Yes," I answered. "I guess it is."

"No sci–fi elements," Alan repeated. "Nothing exciting, no violence," he said, counting out with his thick fingers. "No melodrama, no real mysteries, unless you count the double talk at the end. And it's a story about death." He sighed, leaned back, and polished off his drink. I poured him another, as he stared at the manuscript, his glasses slipping down his nose. "But this is gonna be the biggest one of all, isn't it Judah?"

I nodded. "I think it will, Alan," I said softly.

Alan placed his drink on my custom–made black cherry–wood coffee table, stood up, yawned loudly, and stretched. It was odd to watch this fat person extend all of his limbs, looking rather like a pregnant acrobat. I stood up also; I assumed he was leaving. But instead he disappeared into my kitchen. A minute later he reappeared with two bottles of Samuel Adams lager. I looked at my watch; it was two A.M. I sighed, took the beer from Alan, and sat down. He wanted to talk.

"Judah," he said. "I. . . I need to meet Moishe and. . . what's her name?"

"Esther," I said.

"Yes, of course," he said. "Esther. I need to meet Moishe and Esther. There's a few things I need to. . . ask them.

I shook my head. We'd been through this. "Alan," I said. "They don't want to meet anyone. *Anyone*. They want to be completely anonymous. They don't want anyone but me, and I guess you, to know they're writing the stories. They don't want to be bothered. You know, I can't blame them. With all the publicity, the newspapers, all the bullshit since the stories came out, I'm not surprised they don't want any part of it. They don't want anyone to know. This way they can avoid all. . ." I looked around the big room, with the expensive furniture and pricey wall–hangings. ". . . all this," I said.

Alan scrunched up his eyebrows, giving me a puzzled look, but then nodded. "I understand, Judah," he said. "But, look, I'm not gonna blow their cover. I just want to meet them. I just. . . I just want to *talk* to them, Judah. There's just so many things I need to ask, to clarify. . . "

"Alan, I promised them." I said. "I told them. . ."

"Goddamit!" He yelled, throwing the manuscript across the room. Papers flew all over, landing on my couch, my coffee table, on two of my three Persian rugs, and in my bonsai trees. Alan was breathing heavily. I stared at him, and he stared right back, his glasses fogging up the way they did when he perspired or became emotional. He took them off and wiped them on his shirt.

"You know, Judah," he said, a sly smile suddenly appearing on his face. "Your refusal to let me meet them. The fact you won't even let me *talk* to them. It just adds credence to my original theory. There really is no Moishe and Esther, no strange Jewish couple. It's just you, Judah. Just you. You write the stories. You. . ."

"I dreamt the last one," I said.

"Huh!?"

"I did, Alan," I said. "I dozed off on their doorstep, and I dreamt about a way to talk to the dead. I dreamt about a debate raging in my mind. Who do I talk to? My dead father? My dead mother? Moses? How do I use this gift?" I looked at Alan. His mouth was open, his eyes peering at me through his glasses. "Pretty weird, huh?"

We looked at each other for a long time. Finally, he pushed himself off the couch, and wandered around the room collecting the pages of the manuscript. I got up and walked him to the door.

"Fuck it," he said, reaching out and touching my shoulder. "Let's just publish this thing."

I nodded.

"Let's make another million dollars," he said.

And, in fact, the story did make its usual million or so dollars. Like the others, it was an enormous hit. It broke all the previous sales records, records which had only recently been set by the earlier "Planet of the Jews" stories.

But the impact of this issue went beyond just sales. Suddenly, everyone in America developed a fascination for Judaism. The other stories had sparked a fairly serious Jewish revival among Jews. Alan and I had seen the evidence with our own eyes, at the *schull* on the bottom floor of our building. But with the publication of this story, even non–Jews wanted to learn about Judaism.

A week after we published the "Speaking to the Dead" story, *USA Today* ran an article interviewing over a dozen rabbis in the New York metropolitan area from all of the different American Jewish denominations. Each rabbi reported a marked increase in *gentiles* calling and asking about Judaism. Each rabbi attributed the new interest to the publication of our magazine. The next day the *New York Post* reported that this odd phenomena wasn't limited to New York City. Rabbis all over the country had similar stories to tell.

But the strangest effect was how the press suddenly started to treat me. Before this last story, reporters had hounded me about my personal life. They dug up stories about my divorce, my other few romances, my parents. They asked my few friends about what kind of guy I was. Since no one would talk to them, they invented all sorts of sordid tales – wild sex parties, illegitimate children, four movie star wives.

Or, they'd ask about money: how much was I making? What was the company's share? They wondered about the rumors that all profits from the stories went to the State of Israel, or to the Holocaust Museum. They were curious if I had any other deals going; they'd pester me about movie rights, television specials, book deals. In other words, they didn't have the slightest interest in the content of the stories. I suspected most of the reporters who tormented me in those few months hadn't read a single line of what Moishe and Esther had written. They just wanted to know about me and my money.

But now they hungered after my opinions on Judaism and religion in general. It occurred to them, suddenly, that I might be a profound thinker. After all, thousands of people were exploring Jewish spirituality because of my words. This was religion; this was serious business. Reporters left messages with my answering machine begging for my views on the afterlife, or on the coming of the Messiah, or on sin and punishment. One intrepid writer for the *Daily News* told me it was my *responsibility* to give interviews. After all, she said, I was a teacher.

"You?!" Esther snapped. "A teacher?" She had reverted to her old form, which is to say she was short, nasty, and impatient with me. Our night of warm communion was suddenly forgotten. She and Moishe had burst into my office the day after the article in the *Daily News* appeared. They were furious – or, it would be more accurate to say that Esther was furious – that their little fantasies were being taken so seriously. Esther, all five foot two of her, stood imposingly over my desk, Moishe a half step behind.

"How can they call you a teacher?!" she yelled. "This," she said waving a manuscript at me. "This is science fiction, it's stories, it's fairy tales, it's. . . .it's drivel! It's not *serious*! And you," she said staring at me with angry green eyes. "You write. . . you write comic books!" she said, spitting out the last two words like they were epithets.

"People see these stories as much more than sci–fi," I explained, patiently. "There's. . . something, I can't begin to understand, but there's something people are finding. They think these stories are true. . . ."

"True!?" Esther cried, and took a step toward me. Moishe took her by the arm, and gently led her away from my desk. Otherwise, I think she might actually have slugged me.

"Yes," I said. "You have no idea how many questions I've

gotten about death since the last story. People want to know. They want to know about death, about what happens after we die." I took a deep breath, and picked up our latest issue, weighing it in my hands and holding it gently, like a newborn baby. "People *believe* in this, Esther."

"But don't you understand how completely ridiculous this is?! Mr. Loeb," she said, "it is a completely insane development. It's. . ."

"Yes, I know," I said. "But. . ." I shrugged. I couldn't possibly explain what was going on. I didn't understand it myself. "Listen," I said. "Even *I'm* affected. I'm. . . I'm *moved* by these stories. In fact, I've wanted to ask you something since I read this last one."

She waited, her arms at her side, fists balled up, as if she hadn't completely given up on the idea of hitting me.

"All this stuff about talking to the dead, and the stuff about love and forgiveness. About the dead forgiving the living. Is this," I said, holding out the magazine like an offering, "is this true?"

"How on Earth should I know if it's true?!" she screamed. "Have you lost your mind completely?! This," she spat out, grabbing the magazine from my outstretched hand, "is just a stupid *magazine*! It's not the Torah!"

"I know," I said. "Of course. It's a magazine. But a lot of people see it as much more. They see it as. . ."

"What do I care what a bunch of *meshagoyim* think!" she exploded. Here, Moishe finally tried to quiet her, whispering in her ear and taking her elbow. But she twisted away and started shaking her finger at me.

"Has everyone in the world gone completely crazy?" she burst out. "Finding God in these ridiculous illusions, in this flat, this superficial literary form? In science fiction, with its idiotic machines, it's superhero dialogue? What is the matter with everyone?" She was breathing deeply, and I saw sweat trickling down her forehead. We stared at each other, her infuriated features imploring me for a response, but I couldn't begin to answer. I didn't have anything to say.

Finally Moishe managed to take her hand and lead her toward the exit. He told me he would see me in a few weeks, when they dropped off the next installment. I told him I just had one question, and he nodded, waiting.

I eyed Esther warily, then directed myself to Moishe. "Moishe," I said softly. "Do you believe this stuff? I'm not asking if it's true, I just want to know if you believe it."

Esther looked as if she were about to spring on me like a wild animal, but Moishe touched her shoulder and she drew back. Then he answered me, polite as a priest. "Of course we believe it," he said. "Every word." He led Esther out of my office.

About an hour later, he reappeared. He looked around the office nervously, as if he had snuck in, as if he were afraid of being followed. Then, looking like a spy, or a drug courier, he reached into his breast pocket, and pulled out a folded manilla envelope.

"I wanted to give this to you," he whispered, and set the thing on my desk.

I looked at him.

"It's a comic book," he explained. "I've always wanted to write comic books, it's what I really love. But Esther, she doesn't. . . she thinks. . . well. . .uh. . . anyhow," he said. He looked around again, peering over my shoulder and out the window as if someone might be watching him from the ledge. "Just read it, Judah," he said. "I'd like you to read it."

I nodded, and he shuffled off – out the door, and down the elevator.

It was a pretty damn good comic book. Of course, I could never publish it; there wasn't a comic book publisher in the world who would print anything like it. But I quite enjoyed it.

It was about a young attorney named (of course!) Judah Loeb. One day two angels, real angels with wings and halos, pop in and visit with Judah at a local Chinese restaurant. While he is deciding what to order (there are so many choices at this restaurant!), they take seats at his table. The angels quickly explain that no one but Judah can see them; they're his personal angels. They tell him they would like to sit and observe for awhile, if it's all right with him. He has no objection. They peer at him closely as he studies the menu, then pop out of existence after he finally orders.

For the next few weeks, the angels suddenly materialize whenever Judah is about to decide something. He contemplates who to ask out on a date, and they show up. He struggles to decide what shirt to buy, or which cereal to eat for breakfast and they appear. Finally he figures out what's going on; they're interested in choices, or in the process of choosing. The angels, after some hemming and hawing admit that, yes it's true – but, they say, it's more than just mere interest. They *worship* choices. Choices are like God to them, because they, being angels, and therefore automatons, cannot ever choose.

At first, Judah is flattered that these celestial being are so enamored with his choices; he figures there must be something especially profound and attractive, or at least wise, about his own decision making process. But the angels say, no, they're interested in Judah's choices only because Judah is their responsibility, since they are Judah's angels. It wouldn't matter what choices Judah ultimately made in life, they explain. He could decide to join the circus, or elect to become a mass murderer. It didn't matter. They worship all of his choices – good and bad.

For the next couple of weeks they continue to appear during moments of choice, like when Judah decides to quit his job and become a writer, or to break up with his girlfriend. After awhile, they show up less and less, and eventually they vanish altogether. Judah guesses they've gotten all they need.

One day, though, Judah's father is badly hurt in a traffic accident. Judah, the only surviving relative, has to decide whether to keep his coma–ridden parent hooked on to life support machines, or let him die. As he finally decides to grant his father a natural death, and doctors enter the room to pull the plug, the angels pop into existence. They stare at Judah with reverence and awe, and the comic book ends with them chanting songs of praise and devotion for Judah's holy choices. Moishe called the story "Pro Choice."

I liked the comic for many reasons, though I have to say I didn't exactly understand the plot. I liked the character Judah. Insecure and alone, he reminded me much more of myself than the confident, heroic Rabbi Judah Loeb. I was also particularly impressed with the artwork; in fact, I was jealous. Moishe was clearly a better artist than I. His depiction of angels in particular seemed to me to be especially inspired; in fact for several minutes, I could hardly take my eyes off of them. With flaming, bright orange wings, jet black halos, white webbed toes, and dark blue robes, they looked like no angels I'd ever seen, yet they were immediately recognizable as angels. Also, the scenes at the hospital bed – the pale dying father, the stained white sheets, the grieving son, all the tubes, IVs, and blinking machines – were drawn with great sensitivity; they looked more like a series of intimate photographs than comic book drawings. I wondered for a moment if Moishe had really done the illustrations. For some reason, I suspected that while he might have written the script, Esther must have drawn the pictures.

I also loved the idea that every human being is granted two angels, though it wasn't at all clear from the comic what, exactly, your angels do for you. I called Moishe that night and asked him. After twenty–two rings, he picked up the phone.

"Well, Judah," he answered cautiously, "you understand this is just a comic book."

"Yes, yes," I said, impatiently. "Of course."

"Okay, then," he answered, sighing with relief, as if we'd gotten a major point of contention out of the way and could now really get down to business. "Well," he continued, "the primary function of our angels is to argue on our behalf before God. That is," he said, "after we die."

"Why," I asked, "would they do that?"

"You see, Judah," he answered, "all our lives we sin, and we do *mitzvehs* – good deeds. When we die we're punished for our sins and rewarded for our *mitzvehs*. But before either the reward or the punishment, we're brought before the Heavenly Court. In other words, we're brought before God. Our angels try to convince the Holy One that our sins really weren't so bad, and that our *mitzvehs* were really very good."

"Convince God?"

"We–e–e–e–ll," he said, switching to the sing song voice he always used whenever we had a conversation which lasted more than ten minutes. "Maybe not exactly convince. They *push* God. They encourage God to be merciful."

"Push God," I mumbled, mostly to myself. "Our sins really weren't so bad. Hmmm," I said. I pondered this for a few moments. It occurred to me that, in fact, most of my sins really hadn't been particularly bad. On the other hand, I couldn't remember doing too many *mitzvehs*. This would be something to work on.

"Moishe. . ?" I asked.

"Yes, Judah?"

"You believe this stuff?"

"Of course, Judah. You see, this is one of the points I was making with the story. Our angels have no choice but to intercede for us. They are created for this function. They can make no independent choices of their own. So I asked myself, how would they feel about the human ability to choose? So I. . ."

Here, I must admit, I tuned Moishe out. He spoke for several minutes without interruption. He was explaining to me how angels could never make choices, yet, at the same time, were able to choose to examine other choices. The whole discourse hinged on Talmudic dialectics and mystical paradoxes and, to be honest, I've always been extremely impatient with these kinds of metaphysical puzzles. He lost me right away. In any case, I was busy trying to form a mental picture of my own two angels. In my mind's eye, they looked a lot like Moishe and Esther, but with bright orange wings and black halos.

Moishe concluded his little religious lesson, and then informed me that Esther wanted to speak with me. I was surprised; I assumed she was still furious.

"I apologize," she began. "Of course, none of this is your fault."

"This?" I asked.

"Very upsetting," she said, her voice picking up an ominous edge. "Distressing!"

"Hmmm." I said, not wanting to trigger another outburst. But, as usual, she surprised me. We had a nice, pleasant conversation. She told me she was worried about me; lately I'd seemed sickly and haggard. She said I should go out more, enjoy myself, try to meet a nice Jewish girl. Settle down, she said.

I told her I would like nothing better.

With all of my money, she said, I could certainly afford to court many pretty young Jewish ladies.

I agreed.

She also told me I should be nicer to Alan. In his own way, she remarked, he's really trying to be your friend. And wouldn't you agree, she said that there's really nothing more important than a good friend, except for maybe your health? I concurred and assured her I would take a second look at Alan.

She also told me she was happy I was now being so kind to my Uncle Max.

"It's a *mitzveh*," she said, her voice now as calm and comforting as a summer's day. "He's your only living relative, Judah, your only family. You don't need to badger him to get his story. Be a nephew to him," she urged. "Be a *son*, like you were the other night, when you washed his dishes and gave him money. Then, after awhile, he'll gladly tell you anything you'd like to know."

I was about to ask her how she knew of the other night,

how, in fact, she knew anything at all about my relationship with Uncle Max, when she told me Moishe was summoning her and she had to hang up. She assured me she'd talk to me soon, "in a week or two. Or maybe even in a couple of days. You'll come over," she said. "We'll eat, we'll drink, we'll chat."

In fact, I never spoke to her again.

I had dinner that night with Uncle Max, at my place. I'd invited him several times before, but this was the first time he accepted. Since I couldn't cook, I made it a point to order in all of his favorite Jewish foods: roasted chicken, heavily spiced with garlic; kishke; stuffed cabbage, latkes and potato knishes. Max gorged himself, sighing and smacking his lips with appreciation after each bite. He ate with enormous appetite; he ate more than I'd seen anyone eat in my life.

"Judah," he said. "This food is. . . . well it's. . ." He shook his head; words escaped him. He grabbed his fork and continued shoveling it in. I enjoyed watching him, though I have to say his massive (and noisy) enthusiasm dampened my own hunger. I mostly watched.

After the meal, I offered him tea. I told him I would make it the way he liked it – weak and sugary. I was about to put the water on to boil when I saw him eyeing a bottle of peppermint schnapps on my bar counter. Coyly, he asked if I could, perhaps, put some schnapps in the tea, maybe use the schnapps instead of the sugar, maybe make it half schnapps, half tea, maybe, on second thought, forget the tea altogether and just bring him a glass of schnapps. Or maybe two glasses.

In the end, he finished off the bottle, and then drank another couple of glasses of raspberry brandy. He got drunk. Not falling–down, stinking, plastered. He didn't slur his speech or throw up, or pass out on the rug. He was not even disoriented. His only symptom of serious intoxication was that he finally told me – cogently, clearly – his story. If I'd known that booze was all it took, I'd have used it months ago.

"You understand," he began, as always. "You understand I couldn't follow my parents, my family. The border closed the day after they left."

I nodded.

"So," he said, "it was the beginning. I was stuck in Poland when the Germans came." He sighed deeply, and settled back into his chair. By this time, he was drinking straight from the bottle. "Voytek, my gymnastics teacher, my friend, he understood the Germans, he understood what they would do to the Jews. He hid me, Judah. You understand?"

I nodded. What was there to misunderstand?

"But his house, well, this was too small. And, you must understand, there were many, many Jews in the village. Most had left, but many were left behind, including my brother, your Uncle Judah. So, you understand, Voytek helped. He helped a great deal, Judah. But we couldn't stay. We went to the forest. And. . . " he took another swig from the bottle, then replaced it gently on my coffee table. "We started a. . . a little group."

"A partisan band?" I asked. A few minutes before, I'd snuck out my pocket recorder and turned it on.

He chuckled. "You understand, Judah, we didn't know from such things. Partisan! I'd never heard the word! We were whatever you want to call us – a group, a band, refugees, schlemiels – we were hiding! And hoping to survive until this crazy time would pass."

"But you fought, didn't you? My father told me. . ."

"Yes, yes, yes, okay Judah. We fought. A little. We had to do something, no? But you have to understand, this was not our main purpose. We had a purpose, but fighting – this was not it."

I waited. I assumed he would tell me without asking.

Max got up and helped himself to his first glass of brandy. "We helped Jews escape, Judah," he said, plopping down on the sofa and sighing, as if he were finally getting something off of his chest. "We became part of a network that moved Jews – through Poland, south to Bulgaria, which was not at war with Germany, and then, in airplanes provided by the Swedes, to Switzerland. We were a kind of – what is the term Judah, the same thing that happened in the American south when they rescued black slaves – we were an underground subway?"

"An underground railroad," I said, my face clearly showing my growing fascination. This was a part of the story no one had ever told me.

"But don't exaggerate this, Judah." he said. "Please. Through this very inefficient method we only saved a few dozen Jews, at the most. And many of them were caught and killed along the way."

I promised not to exaggerate. But still! Here was, finally, a story. And a story with heroism, even some hope. A brave bunch of partisans, who saved others, and with the help of a non–Jew!

Max went on to say it was his brother Judah who was the true leader, the brains of the operation, though when I pressed Max about his own role, he admitted he was also an important figure.

"Perhaps you might say," he acknowledged, his face flushing a bit, "there were times when I was co–leader *with* Judah. But everyone helped, Judah. You understand we had to work together."

"But what about Rabbi Boronsky. You said. . ."

Max laughed. "Of course, he was helpful – a good man, a good worker. But you see already how these things get exaggerated. It makes for a good story to say we were a group of fighting partisans, and we had a rabbi for a leader. This story gives you a strong, heroic rabbi, not just a *yeshive bocher* – a scholar, but a *shtarker* – a fighter. But the truth. . ?" he shrugged. "He was a good man," he said.

Max also told me to be sure and mention that there were many, many good Poles.

"The *Polisher* people," he said. "They've been treated very unfairly. In some of the books I read, you would think it was the Poles who murdered the Jews, and not the Germans. Even my own friends, my own crowd, I hear them say 'damn Polacks,' or 'Polish pigs.' This is very wrong, Judah."

I blushed. I'd been planning on using pigs to represent the Poles in my comic book.

"But the Poles in Stashov, Judah," he continued, "most of them helped us. They were good people, this was a good town When the forests were unsafe, we slept in many of their homes. We stayed with. . . what's his name. . . Krysinzke the lawyer. Or with Voytek – you know him. Or. . . well, we stayed in many houses. We even used the church as a kind of meeting house. And not the basement, Judah, the sanctuary! By the statue of Jesus Christ! It's where we picked up new refugees and tried to send them on their way. The priest in this church, Judah," Max went on, shaking his head, still astonished after all these years. "You must understand the risks. This stooped over, gray–haired *goy*, with his dirty collar. He was a very brave old man, this Pole." Max stared at the ceiling for awhile, as if trying to see straight into heaven to catch a glimpse of this courageous cleric. "Between you and me, Judah," he said finally. "He was braver than our Rabbi Boronsky."

I asked him if he had any close calls. He told me yes, of course there were close calls. All the time. I needed to understand. He described one occasion when someone in town – as it turned out, one of the few informers – overheard plans for an evening meeting at the church. When the first SS soldier marched into town Father Jszionsky, the brave town priest, ran all the way to the forest hideout, through three miles of damp woods, to warn the group. "And Judah," Max said, "this priest was not much younger than I am now. Think about it."

But there was one time, he said, when it really seemed like the end. He and Judah had left the forest hideout to forage for supplies. To make a long story short, it was bad luck *and* stupidity, Max assured me, they were caught.

"At this time, Judah," he said, "you understand they weren't shipping Jewish captives to prisoner of war camps. They took us to a ravine, to be shot. And all those movies, those pictures about poor Jews taking off their clothes so the Nazis could shoot them down naked? This did not happen to us, Judah. They did not even want to wait until we took off our clothes. We thought – I thought – for certain we were done for."

"And?" I asked.

"It was luck, Judah. No heroics. We didn't fight these men with our hidden knives and pistols. It was very simple. One of the soldiers who was about to shoot us down, he had been a school friend of mine – we had grown up together in Stashov. He took one look at me and told me to get lost. I didn't ask for permission, you understand, but I grabbed Judah's hand and took him along with me. We ran, as fast as we could, for as long as we could." He shrugged. "In a couple of days we made it back to our group. But it was. . ." He exhaled deeply and shook his head. ". . . it was close, Judah."

There was so much more I wanted to ask him. For instance, I wanted to know how Judah was finally caught. I'd learned that he died at Auschwitz, but how did he end up there? And I'd heard Max had met his wife, my late Aunt Aliza, in the forests among the partisans. A forest romance? What was their story?

But it was late, and Max's speech was starting to slur. I was delighted finally to receive a true, comprehensible narrative. And Max, too, seemed happy, almost elated, to have unburdened himself. All evening long he'd spoken with great animation and emotion – with wild hand gestures, deep belly laughs, sudden outbursts of tears. He was as alive as I'd ever seen him. But it was enough for now; it was time to go. How many bottle of schnapps could he drink in one evening? I called a cab, and sent him on his way.

It was past midnight when Max left, but I was too charged up to sleep. I spent two hours listening to parts of Max's story on my cassette player – enjoying the musical cadences in his voice, his still charming Yiddish accent – and working on my graphic novel. Normally, when writing a comic book, I'd do the script first and then the pictures. But that night words escaped me entirely. Even though I had a pretty good idea of the story I wanted to tell and what I wanted my characters to say, I wrote no dialogue. But I drew hundreds of pictures: of me, Max, Uncle Judah, Father Jszionsky, Voytek – who would be an important figure in the novel – and Aunt Aliza, Max's partisan wife. They were the best, most life–like pictures I'd ever drawn. My pig version of the brave Father Jszionsky, in particular, seemed to leap off the page; I gave him a flaming red robe, and a huge silver cross which slung loosely down from his pink neck. Even without dialogue, it was a good night's work. I went to bed happy and satisfied. There was plenty of time, I thought. I would start filling in the words the very next morning.

It was not to be. Alan called me at 6:00 A.M., waking me up as usual, and told me to be sure and read the story about "The Planet of the Jews" in the *New York Times*.

I felt a little sick to my stomach picking up the paper from the front hallway. I always felt apprehensive before reading anything in the paper about "The Planet of the Jews," and something in Alan's voice made me especially wary of seeing this article. But I mustered up my courage, opened the paper (thank God it wasn't on the front page), poured myself some orange juice and coffee, and read the thing. My pulse raced dangerously, quickening with each paragraph.

At first, there was the usual hype – the amazing sales statistics, the odd cultural effect, the enthusiastic endorsements of many academics and intellectuals. But the article went on to report a clearly documented phenomena: since the last issue of "The Planet of the Jews" hit the newsstands, conversions to Judaism increased by over 300 percent. Random surveys of American rabbis showed this was no coincidence. Nearly all of the new converts mentioned "my" stories as the major factor in their decisions to abandon Christianity, Islam, Buddhism,

Paganism – whatever – and embrace Judaism. "The Planet of the Jews" series, according to the *New York Times*, was creating converts. I was now editing a sci–fi magazine with a new specialty: we proselytized. We converted the Gentiles.

Moishe and Esther. The thought came to me suddenly like a bullet to the brain. They're not going to like this. Did they read the *New York Times*, I wondered? Maybe not, but probably. Thinking of another explosion from Esther, I wondered briefly if I could sneak into their neighborhood and buy up all the newspapers within a five block radius. But this didn't seem practical. Instead, I grabbed all of my drawings, took a taxi to the office, and waited.

Sometime in the late afternoon, I received a tightly wrapped package from Moishe and Esther, sent by special messenger. It contained three items. One was a clipping of the *Times'* article. Another was a manuscript entitled "Our Last Story."

The final item, on cream colored bonded stationary with light blue Jewish stars in the place of a letterhead, was a two word note. It said "We Quit."

10: The Last Story

Every man, woman, and child on The Planet of the Jews attended President Alan Shapiro's funeral. Six rabbis officiated, each representing six different denominations. Rabbis from the other two denominations refused to take leadership roles in the ceremony; their full participation, they feared, would only confer legitimacy on the other six. But they did insist on their respective flocks showing respect to the great leader by attending the service.

The wind blew hard from the north; the sky was overcast. It was one of those rare unpleasant days on the planet — cool temperatures, humidity, and a fog so thick that Evan couldn't see the internment, even though he sat with the other dignitaries and their families in the front row. They buried Alan on the southern edge of Loeb Park, a vast, grassy twenty-acre treeless expanse which spread south from the base of Mt. Sinai. It was the first public park on the planet, and now the rabbis sanctified it as a cemetery for one; only the president would be buried there.

Evan held his wife's hand and struggled to hold back tears. Alan had been a young man, barely fifty–five, a full fifteen years younger than Evan. Dead of cancer. Cancer, Evan thought. That old killer. You'd think, he reflected, with all our great technological advances, we'd have finally found a cure.

Alan had been a dear friend, possibly Evan's closest friend. It's true their relationship had become strained ever since Evan began pushing his plan to leave the planet. That suggestion, along with his increasing suspicions (some said paranoia) about the nature of The Planet, had eventually gotten Evan booted off the ruling council. But he'd remained cordial, if not close to his old friend.

They'd had one serious argument. Two weeks before Alan dropped dead, Evan gathered a group of eccentric, but brilliant scientists, and announced he was forming a political party of his own.

"This is not personal, Alan," he'd explained.

"No," Alan responded. "but it's idiotic. Evan, I can't imagine why, but there's still people on this planet who respect you, who listen to what you have to say! And that's okay, I guess. Everyone has the right to pay attention to raving lunatics. But now, to take these brilliant minds – some of our most talented scientists, our best computer specialists – and corrupt them with your, your. . ."

"Lunatic ideas?" Evan finished for him. "About leaving, about not trusting the Planet. . ."

"You *brought* us to this planet!" Alan exploded. "Evan, it's been almost thirty years! The Planet's only been good to us! You haven't been able to prove a single instance of malevolent thought or action! Now it's even helping us grow food, it's providing energy resources. . ."

"That's exactly my point, Alan," he said. "We're become dependent on a . . . a *thing*! A bizarre creature we can't even begin to understand! Where's the wisdom in trusting a thought creature, Alan, where's the. . ."

"But, Evan, to uproot the entire society? Again? When we're just now settling down? And to demand that we rely entirely on our own technology, on machines, for life support, for energy. To refuse all help from the Planet, all of its resources, it's. . . "

"Lunatic," Evan said flatly.

Then he'd offered a deep, warm smile. Despite everything, he liked Alan, and didn't enjoy arguing with him. He hoped they could just agree to disagree.

But Alan was angry. He'd shaken his head, disgusted, and walked away.

This was an especially difficult memory for Evan, since it had been their last real conversation. He couldn't get it out of his mind as he watched Alan's wife and two sons grab shovels and finish the burial. After the last bit of dirt was heaped on to the coffin, Evan finally took his face in hands and broke down in tears. He wept for forty–five minutes straight. Not even the cool ministrations of his wife, whom he loved more than life itself, could assuage his grief. After the funeral, he retreated to his house next to the Yeshiva, and didn't emerge for six days — until the space ship from Earth arrived.

This wasn't like the invasion of the blue men; they'd been expecting this particular visitor. Four months earlier, several lines of Hebrew lettering suddenly popped up on the screens at the planet's main communication facility, on top of Mt. Horeb. The young technician on duty, part of the first generation to be born on the planet, didn't understand Hebrew and had to rush a print out to the local rabbi, who quickly translated the message. It said:

"We've beaten our swords into ploughshares and our spears into pruning hooks. Shall the sword forever devour? We seek the peace of Jerusalem, a great peace for the people of God. He who makes peace in the heavens has made peace for us and for all of Israel. The war's over. The Nazis are no more. We're coming to visit. See you in four months."

The message was signed: "The People of Earth: Pursuers of Peace."

Over the next few weeks, several more messages arrived, all in Hebrew. These communications assured the Jews that the visiting spaceship would arrive entirely unarmed. It would transport only one passenger, who would come bearing a single, simple message. The Jews could take it or leave it. In fact, if they so desired, the messenger would turn right around and head back to Earth, without even spending the night. There would be no threats, no coercion, said the messages from Earth. No reason at all for suspicion.

Evan, naturally, was extremely suspicious, and suggested building a laser weapon to blow the ship out of the sky. But no one, except his small group of fanatics, listened to Evan. He was appalled to discover that his former colleagues on the ruling council were not even planning on meeting the Earth ship with an armed party. Instead, they planned on announcing the date, time, and place of the landing, and allow anyone who wished to come and watch the ship touch down. With one proviso: there would be no weapons; no one could be armed.

Evan considered bringing his own pistol and encouraging his loyalists to follow suit, but he had no interest in a potentially dangerous conflict with the planet's government. Instead he planned on boycotting the landing. He would stay at the Yeshiva and teach a special Talmud class on the sacred obligation to kill your enemies before they kill you.

But the day after Alan died, another communication came from Earth, specifically requesting Evan's presence at the landing. "If," the message read, "the old man is still alive."

"I'll show them who's still alive," Evan grumbled to Mark Green — the tall blond interim president who'd come to deliver the invitation. "I'll show them what a survivor is!"

"Of course we'd be honored if you would accept this invitation," the interim president said, in a tone of voice suggesting he would be horrified if Evan accepted the invitation.

"I'll accept it, all right!"

"Of course. But, Evan. . ." the young president said, nervously "You remember the rules. No guns. Right?"

Evan grunted, and the young administrator fled.

On the day the ship arrived, Evan sported a shiny leather holster on the outside of his pants housing two oversized laser pistols. He kept his right hand poised on one of the guns, looking like a cowboy, waiting to draw. He'd also deposited two laser knives in his boots. He stood next to Mark, who frowned, but said not a word about the ostentatious weapons display. Together with three hundred thousand Jews, they watched the ship from Earth touch down.

The hatch slowly eased open and a tall, thin, elderly, gray–haired man with kind eyes and a slight stoop climbed out. He wore a silver *yarmulke* on his head, and a gold star of David on a chain around his neck.

"Greetings to you all," he said, in what Evan immediately recognized as an Eastern European, Yiddish accent. "*Sholom Aleichem.* My name," he said slowly, pointing at his own chest with great animation, as if the crowd didn't understand English, as if they needed gestures in order to comprehend, "is Max. Max Loeb."

Evan slid his hand away from the gun.

But, as everyone quickly discovered, he was neither Jewish, nor related to Judah Loeb.

"Loeb is a common name, now," he said. "In tribute to your former leader, the late Rabbi Loeb. And these. . . these, uh, decorations," he continued, pointing to the gold star of David and the skullcap, "are fashionable all over Earth now. Everyone wears them, from Mongolia to California. Ever since the end of the Nazi regime."

"And the accent?" Evan asked. The Earthling, along with Evan and the other Jews, was sitting in a small reception room in the central administrative building, drinking coffee and eating the chocolate bars Max had brought with him as gifts from Earth. President Green had arranged a small party for the visitor, inviting only Evan, and, at Evan's insistence, the old scientist Ziony Zevitt.

"An affectation, I'm afraid," he said, reverting suddenly to the slight Central European accent which Evan assumed was his true manner of speaking. "I'm a professional diplomat. I studied many, many old holos in preparing for this trip. I tried to get a grasp of several of the old Jewish dialects. But," he said, "the truth is, Jewish accents are also now quite fashionable. As are Jewish languages. Hundreds of thousand of university undergraduates all over Europe and the United States are now majoring in Yiddish, or Hebrew, or even Ladino."

Evan blurted out a line in Yiddish. "You are a lying bastard," he said.

Max smiled politely.

Evan smiled back. "You are a murderous gentile," Evan said, in Hebrew this time.

"Ah," Max said, laughing. "I see what you're doing. You were speaking to me in a Jewish dialect. But I don't understand any of those languages. And I'm afraid I'm too old to start learning them."

President Green frowned. He, also, could not understand what Evan had said, but he suspected it had not been exactly polite. He wondered again why the Earth people had been so insistent on including Evan in their discussions. "Ambassador Loeb," he said, putting aside, with genuine regret, the candy bar he'd been eating. "I'll speak to you in English; it's the only language I know. Why don't you just tell us why you're here."

It was simple, Max said. He'd come on behalf of the New World

Government to invite the Jews back to Earth.

"Now," he quickly added. "I don't expect all of you, or any of you really, to jump at the opportunity. In fact, President Green, my space ship can only accommodate five other travelers. So my suggestion is this: Send a delegation back with me to Earth. They will be treated like royalty, I assure you. Let them explore for a week, a month, a year — whatever they'd like. They will discover a peaceful, prosperous planet where Jews participate in the general welfare as completely equal citizens. After some time, let this visiting delegation then return and report back to you other, uh, Jews. Then, should any or all of you people want to return to Earth, my government will provide transportation free of charge. Anyone returning will receive their own large house wherever they choose to live, their own university computer so they can study and receive an Earth-style degree, and enough funds to live comfortably for at least ten years. These items will come to you as gifts from my government. They'll carry no obligation whatsoever."

When President Green asked why the Earth government was being so generous, Max responded gravely, "The expulsion of the Jews into outerspace was one of the great crimes of the last century. Since the Nazi rule ended, there has been a great desire to somehow repay the living Jewish community on Earth. . ."

"Living community?" Evan asked. "You mean some Jews actually survived the Nazis?"

"Oh," Max responded, "most of them survived. There were some excesses the first year or two, but even those were greatly exaggerated. Unlike their German predecessors, these Nazis never had a program to exterminate the Jews."

The three Jews stared at their guest, utterly dumbfounded. From the very beginning — since the first spaceships landed on The Planet of the Jews — it had always been assumed that their little band of space refugees represented the galaxy's last surviving Jews. The story of the complete destruction of Earth's Jews had grown into the central myth of the community. To the men and women on the planet, the notion that "most" Jews survived the ravages of the Ukrainian

Nazis would be simply beyond belief.

Evan, of course, *didn't* believe it. But he decided not to say anything.

Ambassador Max went on to describe how, after decades of peace, a united Humanity finally acquired the ability to explore the stars. The very first use of this technology, Max told the Jews, was an effort to find some trace of those unfortunates who had fled the planet so long ago. Of course everyone expected the worse. No one dreamed they would find a living, breathing bunch of Jews. The effort took years, but finally physicists were able to retrace the original course of the escaping spaceships. Then a few interstellar messages confirmed the "marvelous news." The Jews were alive and flourishing, on a hospitable planet. And with the new technologies, they could send a spaceship to visit in only six days.

"You can't imagine," Max said, with great emotion, "the jubilation, the ecstasy. We hadn't killed you! We hadn't doomed you to die a horrible death in space! We felt redeemed. Almost. . . well, almost forgiven."

Evan noticed tears forming in the ambassador's eyes. He looked over at President Green, who seemed to be struggling not to cry. Even the normally cynical Zevitt brushed a tear from his cheek. Evan shook his head, exasperated at the naivete. But still, he elected to say nothing.

After a question from the president, Max went on to describe Earth's current political structure. "You know," he began, enthusiastically, like a professor teaching a particularly interesting graduate seminar on political science, "in a strange way the Ukrainian conquest was almost a blessing. It introduced us to the idea of World Government. It forced us finally to work together, to trust one another. A world wide democracy followed the fascist government — a democracy which ushered in an era of world peace and prosperity."

Democracy, Max explained, brought a sense of shared destiny to the people of Earth. At last humanity could strive together to eliminate the world's most stubborn evils. "There is no more hunger, " Max claimed, with great pride. "Or serious environmental pollution. And cancer," he continued, triumphantly. "We've finally found a cure, a fairly simple cure, for all cancers."

The ambassador spoke for nearly three hours, telling tales of Earth. They'd invented a machine, he said, which could travel through time, though they were still afraid to use it. On the first trip outside of the solar system, he related, they'd encountered this marvelous race of blue men and — get this — they were all Christians! Max's office was now negotiating a trade agreement with this enchanting new species. Max went on, reciting stories of new religions, of wondrous new forms of literature. He even hinted that scientists on Earth were about to discover the ultimate secret: what happens when we die. Ziony and Mark listened with rapt attention, and even Evan had a hard time maintaining his cynicism and suspicion.

Finally, Max requested an adjournment. "I'm not as young as I used to be," he said, yawning. "I'll need to sleep. But please," he continued, putting out his hands, "consider my proposal. A small delegation — no more than five of you. Take plenty of time to think about it." He gathered up his different computer discs. "If it's not inconvenient, I'll stay on your charming planet for a few weeks. You can get to know me. And I you. And then you can decide." He smiled warmly as the president offered to escort him to the Green guest cabin, where he would be sleeping. "Oh," said the ambassador, as Evan and Ziony headed out the door. The president had already extinguished the light; the only illumination in the room came from the stars and the unusually bright moon. "One more thing. Anyone you choose can be on the delegation. That's your business. But my government insists on one condition. One of the travelers must be Mr. Evan Isaacs." He turned to look at Evan. "You are a great hero on our world, Mr. Isaacs. Many, many of our citizens are simply dying to meet you."

Evan stared at the old diplomat. Max's eager, affable features were now almost entirely obscured by shadows. Evan was about to say something, but then he looked away, and slipped out of the room.

Evan, of course, had no intention of ever returning to Earth. He no more trusted the smarmy ambassador than he trusted Adolph Hitler — or the Planet, for that matter. But, as usual, Evan was in the minority. In fact, except for himself and about a dozen of his most dedicated disciples, everyone on the planet was completely charmed by Ambassador Max Loeb. And the competition to be selected as a member of the Earth delegation was fierce. Everyone wanted to make the trip. Even Evan's young wife Penina was eager to go.

"I haven't been to Earth since I was a little girl," she said. "I barely remember it. But — it's hard to explain, Evan, but ever since Max came, I've had this longing, this urge, just to swim in the Atlantic Ocean. Or to fly over Jerusalem. Or just to step on the surface. . ."

"You won't even make it to the surface!" Evan snapped. "He'll kill you in outer space. As soon as you leave orbit!"

She smiled at her husband, accustomed to humoring his darker impulses. "How," she asked. "How can you. .?"

"A feeling," he explained. "Just like with. . . " he drew a circle in the air, his symbol for the Planet ". . .You know who. A feeling. A bad feeling. And far too many unanswered questions."

Evan waited for her to say, "such as?" or "for instance?" or even to cock a curious eye at him. He was prepared to regale her with his suspicions. But instead Penina tightened the kerchief around her hair and headed out. She was going, she told her husband, to a lecture about Earth's new religions. Given, she said, by the delightful Ambassador Max Loeb.

Evan walked next door, to the Yeshiva. He burst into Rabbi Chaim Boronksy's office — the old Rosh Yeshiva who'd helped found the institution, and who'd first talked Evan into teaching Talmud. Rabbi Boronsky was one of the few people left on the planet who Evan still trusted, mostly because ever since the Exodus, the old Rabbi refused to talk about anything but the Talmud. Evan found the wrinkled, gray-bearded, black-hatted man staring at a computer screen.

"Why," Evan exploded, "does that goy Loeb keep saying the Jews were expelled from the planet? No one expelled us. We ran away! And why," he continued, almost shouting, "does the mumzer say most Jews survived the Nazis. We saw the explosions going off from space! We heard about the bomb that destroyed Israel! And how," he demanded, "does this shmuck even know Judah Loeb is dead? We took his body with us! We buried him in space! And if all the Jews survived," he went on, "why the hell would anyone be interested in studying Yiddish, or Hebrew! If Jews are not rare or exotic, why would yarmulkes suddenly be a fashion rage? And why. . ."

"Evan," said Rabbi Boronsky softly, almost murmuring. "Did you hear about all the new Yeshivas they've built on Earth in the last twenty years? Dozens, I've heard, Evan, dozens. Evan, my friend," he said, "do you think it would be possible to include me in the Earth delegation? For me, Evan, to speak to other Rabbis, other masters of Talmud, or to walk on the Holy Land, or even go up to Yerushalayim. Oy," he sighed. "It would be. . ."

But Evan left before the poor old man could finish his sentence.

And everywhere Evan went that day — to the massive communal dining hall where many on the planet still ate lunch, to the telescope center where, ever since the landing of the blue men, the community kept watch for alien space ships, to the bright yellow buildings of the Institute for Planetary Security where a group of tough young men and women designed weapons in case the planet were ever attacked, to the old Pesek Z'man campus where scientists still carried out massive historical research, to the ruling council gym where Evan still retained a membership — everywhere Evan went, all anyone wanted to talk about was the visitor from Earth. Almost everyone Evan spoke with beseeched him for help in securing a spot on the precious delegation. When he would respond by ranting and raving and screaming in their faces about Earth's vile intentions, they would either smile condescendingly or ignore him completely. No one argued with him, but no one wanted to hear it. They were lovestruck, Evan thought, warped. Sick with longing for their old planet.

Meanwhile, Ambassador Max Loeb was making friends as fast as Evan was losing them. The genial old Earthling had a way about him, a warmth, a certain kind of smile. He exuded trust and good feeling. He had a fine sense of humor, and was an accomplished storyteller. Besides, he was able to bestow favors on almost anyone he met. At the hospital he offered the cure to nearly one thousand terminally ill cancer patients. He delivered, in microdisc, over five thousand new volumes of literature to the planet's only library. He added reams of memory to the central computer core. He helped repair, with his own hands, all of the damaged solar generators. In less than one hour, he revamped the community's water distributor, making the water purer and more plentiful. He visited schools, and taught young children — all native to the planet — about their Earthly heritage. He gave everyone he saw a bar of Earth chocolate. He seemed to have an endless supply.

By the end of the first week, it was clear that ninety–nine percent of the population was ready to accept Max's proposal. They'd send a delegation to Earth. The only question was who would go.

Evan refused even to discuss it. At first Max stuck strictly to his government's instructions. If Evan refused to go, he said, shrugging affably, as if commiserating with parents of an especially bright but stubborn child, "then there can be no delegation." But finally, he was just "too companionate" to refuse the pleas of these Jews. "All right, all right," he said. "I suppose I could get in trouble for this, but if Evan doesn't want to go, he doesn't want to go. Why should he ruin it for everyone?"

President Green nodded, sagely. Evan looked away, disgusted.

"If our friend and hero won't visit his home planet," Max went on, "if his suspicions are just too enormous, then someone else must lead the delegation." He looked at Mark and grinned "You, Mr. President. . ?"

Mark smiled back.

"They've given us no choice," Evan said to Bart Gordon the next evening. Bart, a slight, swarthy young man, whose parents had been born in Israel, was one of Evan's most fanatical followers. He was also the most brilliant computer programmer on the planet, and a crucial player in the techno–underground Evan had been creating.

They were sitting in Evan's Yeshiva office, whispering in each other's ear, in case the room was bugged. "You'll have to break into his computer," Evan whispered. "Print out anything that looks important. We have to find out what he's up to before it's too late. Now, Bart, this Loeb, he's a shrewd guy, a slippery guy. I'm sure his programs are the most secure in the galaxy. He'll have all sorts of encryptions, traps, codes. This could be very dangerous, and very time consuming. We may have to try for several weeks." He looked into the young man's eyes. "It won't be easy."

Bart nodded, the slightest of smiles on his face.

But in the end it was easy, ridiculously easy. Bart was back in Evan's office in less than an hour, with one computer disc and several sheets of paper. Breaking into the spaceship was child's play; no one, apparently, had thought to create a lock for it. And getting the information was just a matter of turning on the computer and calling up Max's orders for the mission.

Evan first glanced at the pages, and then read with growing intensity.

By the end, his hands were shaking and his heart pounding. "Wait one hour," he whispered, handing the sheets of paper back to Bart. "Then bring copies to President Green and the rest of the council."

It was worse than Evan could ever have imagined. Infinitely more diabolical. He grabbed one of his laser pistols and went to find the ambassador.

Max was at the hospital demonstrating Earth's latest computerized, all-purpose antibiotic. "It's a machine," Max was saying. "It's inorganic. So you can program it to attack any germ, and it will, of course, attack that germ, and that germ only." Several dozen spectators gathered around, awestruck.

Evan waited until Max handed over several boxes of the microdevices to the doctors. Then he unholstered his gun, aiming it at the ambassador's midsection.

"The Museum of an Extinct Race," Evan said, taking several steps toward Max. "Complete with live exhibits. You'll be able to watch real, live Jews, interact in a 'Jewish habitat.'"

Max stared at Evan's pistol, his face turning red. Evan handed him the computer disc. "Here are your orders, 'Ambassador' Loeb," he said. "To deceive as many Jews as possible. Trick them into returning to Earth, where they will be imprisoned in 'The Museum of an Extinct Race: The latest in a series of mega-museums designed by the Reich Historical

Society.'" He stopped an inch away from Max, his gun practically touching the ambassador's chest. "And what would the Nazis have done with the rest of us?" he asked. "After you kidnapped the first five?"

Max answered without hesitation, also without emotion. "They will come soon," he said. "To kill you. We can't allow Jewish bacteria to spread throughout the galaxy. We have to complete the great cleansing we began thirty years ago. The extermination of Jewish filth from every corner of God's universe. The annihilation. . ."

Evan shot him square in the stomach. Max fell, his entire body quivering slightly for several seconds, as the laser's electrical charge made its way to the brain. Then he died, wrapped in a fetal position, his eyes stuck open and facing the heavens.

Should they run away or fight? They had to decide right away; for all they knew an Earth fleet was on its way at that very moment. But, of course, they had no choice. It would take months to repair the old spaceships, and more months to pack up everything they'd require for survival on some strange new world. Besides, Earth obviously had the technology to track and pursue them, wherever they fled. They'd have to fight, to make their stand on their new adopted homeworld.

There were weapons. Alan had always insisted the community devote some of its resources to defense; he had agreed with Evan that an attack from Earth was always within the realm of possibility. But they weren't fooling themselves. Even a cursory glance at 'the ambassador's' ship showed that Earth's technology had advanced far beyond their own capabilities. The Jews had weapons, but everyone knew they'd prove useless. It would be like using sling shots against laser beams.

A great, great panic descended on the planet as the reality of impending slaughter sunk in. There was only one chance for salvation. They begged, they pleaded, they beseeched, they prayed for their ally and benefactor The Planet to intercede for them. "Make the atmosphere poisonous for the attackers!" they demanded. "Change your gravitational pull so the enemy ships crash," they suggested. "Make the sun stand still, so they'll all burn up and die. Give us dark clouds, so they can't see us!"

But the Planet didn't answer, not even to say no. As the days passed, depression and a melancholy fatalism replaced the panic. Everyone went about their business, preparing to defend themselves and their homes. But there was no point in denial. They would die. The last pogrom was coming, the final Holocaust. The end of Jewish history.

Eventually President Green prevailed on Evan to try and communicate with The Planet. "It's our only hope," he said.

And Evan had to agree.

But he didn't even need to try. The Planet initiated the conversation, that very night, while Evan lay in bed waiting for either sleep or death, whichever came first.

"The fear is great," the Planet said, its voice, as usual, sounding like an echo in Evan's head.

Evan nodded. "They're afraid," he said. "They're all afraid of dying."

"And you, Evan?"

He shrugged. "I haven't been afraid of dying in years," he said. "To be honest, I'm sad. I never admitted this to anyone, but I really wanted to go back to Earth. I miss Earth. To me, this is what's depressing. I knew it was a dangerous hoax, but somehow I hoped. . ." He looked over at his wife, sleeping next to him. For some reason his talking had not awakened her. He considered, for a moment, that he was just having a dream, but dismissed the idea. He didn't speak to the Planet in dreams. "I wanted to think there might actually be a place for us on Earth," he continued. "I wanted to believe I could trust my own homeworld. But now I see through my delusions. We don't belong on Earth. We may not belong anywhere."

"And that saddens you, Evan?"

"Yes," he answered. "But just a little. I don't need to belong anywhere."

"But you need to trust, don't you Evan? If not the people of Earth, then your fellow Jews?"

"Not really," Evan answered.

"But belonging to some form of society, Evan? Being part of a great people? This is extremely important to you, isn't it?"

"It used to be," Evan admitted. "But I haven't been a part of things here for years. I don't need it. I've had two friends in my life," Evan said. "They're both dead now."

"Your wife, Evan?"

He shrugged. "Of course I love her. But you know, I lost two wives already. One of them I just pushed away. I pushed away a whole family. Someday, one way or another, I'll have to give up this wife, too. Either I'll die, or she'll die." He looked at her, curled up — listened to her soft snoring. He was surprised to feel almost nothing. "I love her," he admitted. "But I don't need to belong to her, and I don't need her to belong to me. The fact is I *don't* need her at all."

"Who *do* you need, Evan."

He paused for a second. "I don't need anyone," he said flatly.

"That's good, Evan," the Planet said. "Because I have something to tell you."

"I'm listening," Evan said calmly, though his palms were starting to sweat.

"No other human being exists here," said The Planet, "except for you."

Evan bolted up in bed. He looked over at Penina, but she was gone.

"I'm sorry to shock you, Evan, but it was time for you to understand the truth."

"Earth. . ?" Evan said.

"No other person existed on Earth, either, Evan. It was always just you. Just you."

"But you. . ?"

"Yes, I exist, Evan," The Planet said. "But it's just me, Evan. Just me and you. We're the only life in the Universe. Just the two of us."

Evan slowly got out of bed. He removed his pajamas, pulled on a pair of pants and a t-shirt, and walked out barefoot into the warm night air. The buildings and homes, he noticed, were all still there. But there were no lights, no sounds, no sign of human life. He stared up at the stars.

"You understand intuitively that I'm telling you the truth, Evan." The Planet said. "I can tell you see it now, you're beginning to accept it. You see, Evan," The Planet explained, "everyone you've ever met, anyone you've talked to, yelled at, made love to, heard, smelled or seen — Evan they're all just manifestations of your own personality. You constructed them from your own rich subconscious. Don't you see, Evan? You required these fantasies so you wouldn't have to feel alone. But it was time, Evan. Time for you to move on to your next phase."

"The crisis on Earth," Evan whispered. " The Nazis, The Exodus. . ."

"Yes, yes, Evan!" The Planet replied. "I can see you understand! You're beginning to comprehend everything now. That's good Evan. You see, those events were not real in a physical sense. But for you, they were the beginning of a profound spiritual process. I created the scenario of the new Ukrainian Nazis as a way for you to begin the awesome task of detaching yourself from false human connections. I wanted to release you from your illusions. You had to break free from Earth's gravity. Earth was your prison. And Evan, Evan, of course I had to kill Judah Loeb! Because he was truly your alter ego, the false manifestation most like yourself. Don't you see, Evan? He was your spiritual side, your heroic side, your thoughtful side. Evan, he was your *Godly* side. But now you comprehend, Evan — you can see now, can't you? He was you all along. He was you, and you he. You are *one*. And you understand now that you don't *need* these illusions, these phantoms. You can whisk them away, like space dust. Oh, Evan, Evan, I can't *tell* you! I'm so very proud of you, of how you finally accomplished this promethean task! Bit by bit you've chipped away at the mirage you used to think of as the human race. You achieved almost complete alienation. You stepped out of the fog. And you did it yourself, Evan. I just had to push you a little."

"But. But you. . ." Evan said, trying, but failing, to form some thought of protest in his mind.

"It's just you and I in this limitless Universe, Evan. And now — with your spiritual evolution nearly complete, this Galaxy of wonders is open to you. There are no other human beings, Evan, but there are marvels beyond number. There are the cords of Pleiades, Evan. The reins of Orion. The clouds with their abundance of water. The wisdom of the hidden parts."

Evan felt the blood rushing to his head.

"Evan," the Planet continued. "There are the vaults of snow, the vaults of hail. The rains that saturate the desolate wasteland. The lions, Evan, the lions that crouch in their dens. And, Evan, the Behemoth. And the Leviathan. Evan, you will deck yourself now with grandeur and eminence. Robe yourself in majesty. In your light, you will see light. Learn the laws of Heaven, Evan. Impose your authority of Earth."

"What. . ?"

"Do I seem to be speaking nonsense, Evan? It's because language itself is an illusion. And Evan, you're *beginning* to understand. Evan, Evan, listen to me. Why is this night different from all other nights? We were slaves to Pharaoh in Egypt, Evan. Because of our sins, Evan, we were exiled from our land. Because of your sin. Evan, you grasp so much. You see. You're starting to see. . ."

But Evan could only close his eyes and will himself not to see. If only, he thought, he could force himself not to hear, not to think. . .

"Evan," the Planet continued, "go from your land, your native land, to a mountain I will show you. Sacrifice your son to me, Evan. Sacrifice your sanity to me. One more illusion to kill Evan. Then we'll be together. Truly together. For eternity."

Evan screamed, a loud, long scream that pierced his eardrums, shattered his voice box and tore at his intestines. He threw all of his human strength into a desperate, wordless howl, even as he understood it was a scream no one would hear.

Evan Isaacs woke up in his king-size bed. Traffic noises from Park Avenue floated up to his thirtieth floor penthouse. Pain throbbed through his brain. The dreams, he thought. Again, the dreams. Vague, dark nightmares had invaded Evan's sleep for the past two weeks. They'd affected Evan profoundly. His wife Mary had complained of the thrashing, the moaning, the screaming, all of which would wake her just before dawn. Bruises appeared on his elbows, small cuts on his legs. But when Evan awoke, he could never recall a single concrete detail. All that would remain were inchoate feelings of horror, which lasted exactly twenty minutes, and a splitting headache which lasted only slightly longer. Then, as Evan went through his day as the world's most successful real estate mogul and financier, he'd forget all about the dreams. But they'd return the next night.

That particular day, after showering and shaving, Evan facilitated three hundred and twenty-five mergers. He acquired seventy companies, and sold forty-two. He bought eleven thousand shares of stock, and sold eight thousand. He made $5,765,982 for himself that day and another $12,345,987 for his two children. He returned home at eight o'clock, watched his wife put their kids to bed, ate a cheeseburger with onions, and drank a tall glass of red wine.

He was bored with his life. Long ago, he'd lost the passion for making money, the thrill of the deal. His wife bored him. He was convinced she was having an affair; he didn't really care. His sons annoyed him; he tried — as much as he could — to stay out of their way. He longed for meaning in his life, for a higher purpose, for a mission. He went to bed unhappy and restless. That night he had the strangest dream. . .

Mad, ugly screams woke Penina on the Planet of the Jews. She sat up in bed and turned on the light. It was Evan — another nightmare.

"The Holocaust?" she asked. "Again?"

Pale as a ghost and breathing hard, Evan nodded. He shook off his damp sheets, and groped for a glass of water.

"Do you remember any of it?" Penina asked, grabbing a washcloth and dabbing her husband's forehead. She noticed his sad eyes, windows to burdens she could never imagine. "Would you like you to tell me about it?"

"I remember every last detail," Evan replied, still struggling to catch his breath. "Every damn thing." He gulped down the glass of water. "But I can't tell you," he said.

She nodded, secretly grateful. She didn't really want to hear about it.

They sat in bed listening to the crickets. She heard Evan's breath begin to soften. He would recover; he always did, though each night it took a little longer.

"Alan's funeral," she said, finally. "You were thinking about Alan's funeral. It made your dreams even worse, Evan. He'd been such a dear friend." She sighed. "And to die so painfully," she commented. "Ghastly, really. Cancer," she said, and shivered slightly.

He looked at her and blinked twice, but didn't respond.

He looks so old, Penina thought. Where did all those wrinkles come from? Did they just form overnight? And was his hair always *completely* white? Lately, she thought, he even smells old. How much longer can it be, she thought. How much longer for him?

"Funerals," she said, shaking her head strongly, as if she were evicting thoughts from her brain. "They're so hard, aren't they?"

"Yes," Evan agreed, clicking off the light and turning away, waiting for his next set of dreams "They're hard."

11: The True Story

For three days and nights, I tried to contact Moishe and Esther. The first day, I stayed on the phone for eight straight hours, letting it ring for so long, that a representative from the phone company knocked on my door to see if I was still alive. I spent the next day camped out on Moishe and Esther's door step. I read through a stack of thirty–five comic books while I waited for them to return home. They never did. I went back to my apartment and let the phone ring all night. The next day, sleep deprived and unshaven, I wandered around Williamsburg looking for them in every store, synagogue, and Yeshiva. Just before dawn the next day – I hadn't shaved, showered or brushed my teeth in three days – I returned to their apartment. I started knocking lightly, then gradually increased the force until I was banging fiercely at the door. To my utter astonishment, it flew open.

Their home was precisely as I remembered it, only neater and emptier. The bed was made, the kitchen spotless, the bathroom fresh as a spring forest with clean towels folded neatly on polished bars. Moishe and Esther, of course were gone, and so were all of their books. Everything else was exactly as it had been, except the apartment was now mysteriously free of all dirt – as if Moishe and Esther had taken it with them along with their library.

I searched the apartment for awhile, looking under the bed, in the closets, and the kitchen cabinets. No Moishe and Esther. I was about to check behind the bookshelves when a faded blue object caught my eyes. My teflin bag. It was lying on the corner of the coffee table, like a hidden time bomb.

I hadn't realized the bag was missing, and I certainly didn't remember leaving it at Moishe and Esther's home. But there it was. I reached quickly for the bag, fondled it, felt the soft velvet and slowly unzipped it. The *tefilin* were still there, wrapped up tightly, snug as newborn babies. I was about to remove them when I heard breathing behind me.

A tall, thin man dressed in a pressed gray suit stood in the doorway. He looked old, well into his seventies. He had Moishe's eyes. His father? I thought. But no, I blinked and all resemblance vanished. But he still looked familiar.

"*Vas mach di yoren?*" he said. I noticed he had a slight stoop, like Uncle Max.

I stared at him. I'd heard that voice before.

"*Sprein ill geiz un tact,*" he said softly, smiling.

Then I remembered. My father's funeral. Some old Jewish dignitary – I never learned his title or his name. He'd given a eulogy in Yiddish, the one I couldn't understand.

I shook my head. "English!" I said, shouting the word as if he were hard of hearing. "I only speak English!"

He pointed to the *tefilin* still in my hand. "*Ahbeit macht zu freilig villshon,*" he continued, in a friendly manner, completely oblivious to the fact I couldn't understand a word he was saying. "*Zor azai il nodker zeit?*"

"Moishe and Esther?" I asked.

"*Zor nit shon gist shon felich gein,*" he said, and shrugged.

A lunatic, I thought. He was beginning to give me the creeps. I gripped my *tefilin* tightly, and headed toward the door. The bent old man straightened out, and put his hands up as if to stop me. But I scooted around him and ran down the steps.

Outside, on Roosevelt Avenue, I noticed a group of black–clad Orthodox men streaming into a small synagogue. I decided to join them. While everyone ignored me, I sat in the back and tried, again without success, to fasten the *tefilin* to my arm. Finally I gave up and listened to the a–tonal, mumbling melodies of the service. About half–way through, a young boy with an oversized black hat and long, greasy side curls walked up to me. Without saying a word, he plopped a *yarmulke* on my head.

That night, I dreamt about Moishe and Esther. They were dressed as angels – in orange wings, blue robes, and black halos. Moishe appeared worried; he kept looking around, as if he were afraid to be seen with me. But Esther looked as serene as a fairy godmother. She smiled at me, and her countenance seemed to envelope me, as if I were being pulled into her face, her brain, her heart. I put my arm out to touch her, but she was transparent. My hand went straight through her.

"Write some more!" I begged.

"We can't," they both answered, sadly.

"Who are you?" I asked.

"We're you!" they both answered. "We're *you*," Esther repeated, and they both disappeared – Esther and then Moishe.

Then I woke up.

Alan looked unwell. He was perspiring and hadn't shaved. It was hard to tell, but he may even have lost weight. There were bags under his eyes.

"Find them!" he ordered me.

"I can't, Alan."

"Tell them I'll double their percentage. I'll *double* it, Judah! Do you have any idea how much money I'm talking about?"

I reminded Alan of something I'd told him several times before: Moishe and Esther weren't taking the money. They didn't care about money. "Alan," I said, "they're giving the money to *me*."

He stared at me from across his desk. He fished around in his breast pocket, put on his glasses and studied me some more, as if he wasn't really sure who he'd been talking to.

"Judah," he said. "Do you like this job? Do you like your new salary, your new office?"

"Alan, I. . ."

"Judah!" he yelled. "Goddamnit! Motherfucker! This is *millions* of dollars! This isn't some crap comic book novel, some asshole scheme about the Holocaust and bugs! This is like a drug we've been selling, Judah, an addictive drug! This is nicotine we're peddling, my friend, but it don't cause cancer! It's a goddamn hundred–proof narcotic! And more chumps get addicted each month. Judah, Judah, listen to me. These junkies, they need their stuff. That's why they pay us. They need their fix. *I* need my goddam fix, Judah! Now, you get off your Jewish ass and get me those. . ."

I fled. I didn't have to listen to his rantings, or, for that matter, look at his fat, ugly face. I didn't need the job anymore. I had enough money. In fact, I'd been planning on resigning for days, ever since Moishe and Esther quit. In any case, I had an appointment with Uncle Max. Moishe and Esther weren't the only authors in the world. I was a writer, too. It was time to start working on my own stuff.

Max, bless his soul, had made me dinner. Well, not exactly *made* dinner, but he had brought home two thick corned beef sandwiches from the deli and two cans of creme soda. He'd set mine on a paper plate – his only meat dishes, he told me – next to four or five soggy potato chips. His lay on a napkin, without potato chips; he'd run out of paper plates. Nothing glamorous or particularly appetizing about the meal, but it's the thought that counts. We dispensed with small talk – Max was never much for small talk – and I ate hungrily. After dinner, I cleared the dish, while he banged around the kitchen making coffee. He told me to ask, ask, he could talk to me while working.

I didn't really have much more to ask. Max had been so lucid, so detailed in our last discussion, and the story, without him really knowing it, had been so fine, so inspiring, that I could have just gone home and written a script. But there was one small inconsistency, and it bothered me. I wanted to include Rabbi Chaim Boronsky as a character. A rabbi who was also a fighting partisan appealed to me, as I'm sure it would appeal to my readers. But I still wasn't clear about his role.

"Max," I said, looking over my notes, "when you first mentioned Rabbi Boronsky, you called him a 'hero.' You said he was the heart of the group, the toughest of the bunch. And all those guys with you, all your comrades in the kitchen, they all agreed."

Max, his back to me, kept on fooling with the coffee apparatus, banging around spoons, rinsing out cups. He didn't say anything.

"But the other night," I continued, still flipping through my notebook, "at my house, you told me you and Judah were the real leaders, and that Boronsky was really a nothing." I looked at my uncle – at his rear end, actually. "Uncle Max," I said, "I don't mean to badger you. I'd just, well, like to *know*. For my book. What was the real story with Boronsky?"

Max was still puttering with the coffee, measuring out sugar, flipping through his cabinets looking for the Sanka. He didn't miss a beat. But he surprised me by doing something I'd never seen him do. After pouring out two steaming cups of weak, sugary decaf coffee, he reached under the sink and took out a pack of cigarettes and a book of matches. After wordlessly offering one to me – I refused – he lit up and inhaled deeply.

As far as I knew, Max didn't smoke. In fact I remembered that he hated smoking. But there he was. While I sipped my coffee, he stood there puffing, using his fresh cup of coffee as an ashtray. It took him two minutes to finish one cigarette. He quickly lit another. Finally he grabbed the whole pack, the coffee cup with butt floating in the middle, and joined me at the table.

"Judah," he said, not looking at me, staring at his coffee cup, as if in a trance, "did you know I had a wife and child before the war?"

I was stunned. "You were only. . ."

"Nineteen years old," he said. "Not so young, not for those days, not for my village." He lit another cigarette. "I made them go into Russia. My wife, she begged to stay with me. She knew Voytek had room to hide her, and the baby also. And it's true, he did have room, Judah, he had quite a large house, and no one would have suspected *him*, of all people, of hiding Jews.

But I forced her to go. I knew," he said, in calm, measured tones, as if he were giving me the weather report. "I knew they would die. My whole family would die."

I didn't know what to say. But I didn't have to talk at all. Max spoke for two hours straight, chain smoking the whole time. I guess he was speaking to me – I was the only other person in the room – but he never once looked at me. He stared straight ahead, at a space in– between the refrigerator and the stove, and recited his new story in the expressionless tones of a bored court reporter.

Voytek, he told me – Max's gym teacher – was a Polish army officer with fierce Nazi sympathies. He appreciated Hitler's racial policies. Far from aiding Jews, he helped the Germans hunt them down. He saved Max, but only because Max agreed first to steal for him, and then later to procure prostitutes. In addition to being a Nazi, Voytek was a thief and a pimp.

"Rabbi Boronsky," Max said, "disapproved of my actions, of course. How could I abandon my wife, my baby while I sought shelter with this Nazi? And Judah – not you, but my brother, your uncle – he hated me with a great passion. To him, I was a worthless coward. I'd betrayed my whole family. But this, Judah, you understand, this was my way of surviving." He took a long drag on a cigarette, finished it off, and then lit another. "This Chaim Boronsky you are so concerned with, Judah. From the moment my family left Poland, he despised me. Can I blame him?" he shrugged indifferently. "No."

Boronsky was the leader of the group in the forest. And, yes, they went on some raids, harassed some Germans, but mostly they struggled to survive. The 'Underground Railroad' Max had described to me – the mission to rescue Jews and whisk them to safety in Switzerland – this was a complete fiction.

"You understand, Judah," Max said, without irony. "It's very far from Poland to Switzerland."

Max was not an active participant in the underground. He was more like a prisoner. After Voytek grew tired of him,

Max fled to the forest, living on berries and rainwater for three days. Finally he ran into Judah. He begged his brother for help, for food, a way out of Poland. But Judah brought him to the partisan band led by Rabbi Boronsky. They agreed to shelter him as much as they could – he was, after all, a fellow Jew. But they couldn't trust him because of his relationship with Voytek. They never discussed operational plans with him; in fact they mostly kept him under guard.

"Judah wanted to shoot me," he said. "But Boronsky wouldn't let him. Still, I was in constant fear of my life. My brother, he slept next to me, and every morning he would wake up and express sorrow that I was still alive. And every night he would wish me a pleasant death in my sleep. I knew one day he would kill me. It was worse than withVoytek."

But Judah died first, caught by the Germans on a raid. "I knew," Max told me. "I was the only one who knew, you understand, where Judah kept his few valuables. Because, you understand, I slept next to him. He'd buried them next to a decaying oak tree. The night after his capture, I dug them out. Mostly it was gold coins, and I shoved those in my pockets. I would need them later. There was also some cans of food. I hid them. I would not share the food; I, myself, was too hungry. And," he said, "there was the *tefilin*. I kept them, also. Who knows, maybe they were valuable? Maybe I could one day trade them for some food. Of course, I was wrong, no one wanted them. But I kept them; for many, many years I kept them. I'm not sure why. Finally, Judah, I gave them to you. I am glad now, Judah," he said, "to finally be rid of them."

"And Judah," he said. "I told you wondrous lies about the Poles. Glorious lies. A whole village of saints I described to you, good, good people risking their lives to rescue Jews. A brave and wonderful priest, running through the forest." Here Uncle Max actually showed some emotion – he smiled. But it was a mirthless, almost cruel, crooked smile. It caused me, for the first time in my life, to be afraid of my Uncle Max. "Such a comedy, I told you Judah. You understand," he said, "the Poles cared nothing about the Jews. They cared about us the way you care about the termites in your building. It wasn't, Judah, that they hated us so much. The Germans, *they* hated us. To the Poles we were like insects. They could ignore us if we stayed out of their way, or they could step on us, exterminate us. But, you see, this killing would be done without any emotions, because we were nothing to them, we were bugs, we were. . ." he said, smiling again, chilling me to the bone. ". . .Judah we were like cockroaches."

There was more to the story, but I stopped listening. I got the point. Max's story of survival was sordid, ugly, cowardly, and utterly without redemptive value. Max was a liar; a man who would deceive his last living relative without a speck of remorse. He made me sick – literally. A blinding headache attacked me, and I felt an overwhelming urge to vomit. I rushed to the bathroom and retched up the night's meal. Gasping for breath, holding tight to the toilet, I threw up lunch too. The pain in my stomach stabbed so sharply, that I was unable to take a breath. Finally, I fell to the floor, curling up in agony until the spell passed. Slowly, I regained the ability to breathe. I rose from the cold tile of the bathroom floor.

Then I returned to the kitchen. Max was smoking, still staring straight ahead. I gathered my papers, and left. Max watched me leave through the smoky fog, an impassive, vacant look on his face.

A few days later, I was in my office, sorting through old manuscripts, trying, unsuccessfully, to get some work done, when I noticed Alan standing in front of my desk. I pointed to the couch, and he plopped himself down.

"It was never you, was it Judah?" he said.

"No, Alan."

"You didn't write 'The Planet of the Jews.'"

"I didn't."

"You just took the money?"

"I just took the money."

He lay down on the couch, his hands raised as his head hit the cushion, looking like a Jewish Sumo wrestler signaling surrender.

"Judah," he said. "You have no idea. You don't know what those stories meant to me. I mean to *me* personally. Listen, you and I both know the stories weren't any good. They were amateur stuff, Judah. But the quality of the writing never mattered to me. There was just something there. It was like I'd discovered Truth with a capital 'T,' like I'd figured it all out. And now," he said, closing his eyes, "it's gone." He sat up and brushed himself off, straightening out the creases in his pants. "I don't understand shit, anymore, Judah." he said. "I tried reading over some back issues, but it's just not the same. My whole sense of identity, Judah, of certainty, everything those goddamn stories gave me, it all just disappeared." He took off his glasses, and starting wiping them with his tie. "You know," he said sadly, "I had a brother once, a younger brother. Died when I was twelve. Leukemia. He went fast, maybe six months from when we discovered he was sick." He leaned back, and again shut his eyes. "Used to cough his brains out every night. We shared a room, in the Bronx. I don't think I slept a wink for two months with all the racket. And every night I prayed to God that the coughing wouldn't stop. 'Cause I knew when it stopped, it meant he'd be dead. You know Judah, I still miss the little kid; I still think about him, nearly everyday, to tell you the truth. And I never understood. Why? For what goddam *purpose*? Why should a young boy like my brother, an eight year old kid. . . why should my parents, myself. . . why. . . why does shit like this *happen*? Judah, I know this sounds insane, but I think I was finally starting to *get* it! I was beginning to understand why my brother had to die! And, dammit, I was starting to accept it. I even had some idea of where my brother is now, Judah, and I was damn happy for him! Now, Judah, you *know* me. I never gave a shit about religion, about Judaism. But those goddam stories, Judah, they started explaining stuff to me! Stuff I wanted badly to know! Judah, I started to *comprehend*! And now. . ." He opened his eyes and looked at me, his face as forlorn and lost as any sick child's.

I understood exactly what he meant, though I didn't want to tell him, because I felt the same way. After pouring through the first couple of issues, I understood who I really was, what my essential identity conveyed. And later, like Alan, I started to grasp something about death: why my father had to die, or my mother; where they went when they died; what they meant to me; what their lives stood for. But apparently the whole feeling was as fragile and disposable as the paper in the sci–fi magazines. Moishe and Esther stopped writing, and that was it. All of our spirituality, all of our answers, all of the sooth-ing enlightenment went up in smoke.

I saw that Alan was in mourning, but I was mourning also. We'd both lost something precious, something irreplace-able, and now neither of us could even describe what it was that had died.

"Judah, look," Alan said suddenly. "Maybe you could just try to write something. You knew them, you had *contact* with them. Maybe some of. . . whatever they had, maybe it rubbed off on you. You're a fine writer, Judah, my best. You could do it."

His voice was imploring, beseeching. His head was now slightly bowed, so it was as if he were praying to me. For just a moment, the ungenerous thought popped into my brain that he was just scheming for ways to milk more money from the fran-chise. But when I looked again at Alan's round, hopeful face, I knew I'd misjudged him. He didn't want to *publish* these stories, he wanted to *read* them. And he thought I could write them. I suddenly remembered my dream. "We're you," Moishe and Esther had told me. Were they really? And now Alan wanted me to be them.

I didn't want to. I still hadn't recovered from the writer's block that had wiped out every scrap of my creativity. I was still reeling from Max's fresh revelations; it was as if he'd torn my *Roach* project to shreds. I had absolutely no ideas.

But I told Alan I would try. I'm not sure why; probably just to get rid of him, so I wouldn't have to talk to him anymore. But I did promise, and I decided there was no time like the present to get started.

I kicked Alan out of the office, fished through my desk drawer, and took out my Uncle Judah's stolen *tefilin* bag. I set them next to my writing pad, figuring I could use them for inspiration. But my storehouse of stories remained utterly empty. So, instead of writing, I took the *tefilin* out of the bag, unwrapped the black leather straps and tried, once again, to put them on. The headband was easy; I looped it around my forehead, letting the black straps hang down my shirt. But the longer strap? I had no idea. I played with the smooth leather ribbons, curling them around my fingers; I bounced the little black box in my hands. Finally, I used the straps to tie my two hands together. I sat at my desk, bound, for almost four hours until inspiration finally hit.

I'm basically a comic book writer, I thought. I was never as comfortable with pure prose. I would write a "Planet of the Jews" comic book! Alan would grumble, but he'd publish it. At this point, he'd publish anything by me. I sat still for another hour until a story finally hit me. I freed my hands and wrote it down.

This was it. Archaeologists, digging for ancient civilizations on the Planet of the Jews, unearth a perfectly preserved set of *tefilin*. They resemble earthly *tefilin* in every aspect but one; this pair measures over eight feet in circumference. Experts, using carbon dating, suggest that the artifact is nearly a million years old. No one knows quite what to do with these massive phylacteries, until one day, a bar mitzvah boy decides he would like to try them on. He unwinds the long, thick straps and attempts to wrap himself properly. But, in the process, he becomes hopelessly tangled, and it takes many strong men and women several hours to release him. Next, different volunteers – men and women – try out the *tefilin*. But each time, the victims just become more and more tangled. The *tefilin*, it seems, have a life of their own. It's not clear whether they are consciously ensnaring their victims, or if it's just an automatic reflex, like a Venus Fly Trap. In any case, the community has no choice but to destroy the things, "before they entangle us all!"

That was the story. It went on for three pages. It took me thirty minutes to complete. I have to admit, I rushed the illustrations a bit; I did them in black and white, and portrayed most of the characters as stick figures.

I stuffed the whole thing in an envelope and mailed it to Alan.

Two days later he popped into my office, waving the manuscript and wrinkling his nose like he was carrying a dead fish. "Is this a joke?" he asked.

"You don't like the drawings?" I responded.

He dropped the pages on the floor, then slowly stepped forward and traced his stubby index finger along the front of my desk, staring at the accumulated dust. He took a deep breath. "Judah," he said, still looking at his finger. "My friend. My good friend. Maybe you should get out of here for awhile. Go to the beach, Judah. We'll pay for it. Go to Florida. Or better yet, Mexico. Or Hawaii. Relax. Get some sun. Eat some good food, Judah, you're too damn skinny. Check into a fancy hotel – with room service and a hot tub. Go dancing with beautiful women. Get yourself drunk, Judah; get drunk every night. Get laid. And write. Write. Write me a story, Judah, a good Jewish story. Write me a story I'll want to *read*. We don't need to talk about. . .about that," he said, pointing down at the manuscript, his face frozen in disgust, as if someone had vomited on the floor. "Something will come to you," he said. "I know it. You have a great, great imagination, Judah. You're my best writer. Did I ever tell you that?"

"Yes, Alan."

"Of course. Well then, write. But go away, Judah. Do go away," he said. "Judah, you. . . you. . . ." He shook his head. "You deserve it, Judah." he said.

I flew to Kauai the next morning. I toured the burnt-out volcano at Hihola. I rode in a helicopter through the rugged, green interior of the island. I went snorkeling and gaped with fascination at the rainbow-colored Ono, and the florescent blue coral. I bought a crate of honey-roasted cashews at Hilo Hattie's. Every morning and every evening a young and beautiful Asian masseuse pounded on my back. I ate expensive, room service meals: steak and lobster, blackened tuna, shrimp scampi. I drank three Manola Rums every night at dinner. I bicycled down Mt. Kona. I climbed Mt. Kinalao. I hiked the Ulaho crater. I sat down at the hotel desk and wrote this story: One morning, every citizen on the Planet of the Jews wakes up with a pair of *tefilin* attached to their heads and arms. No one can remove the things, and doctors quickly discover that these black straps and square boxes are organic growths, a new body part generated by some unknown evolutionary force. Any attempt to surgically remove these strange new appendages would result in almost certain death; they are linked to every system in the body. So no one does anything. The Jews live out their lives with *tefilin* tumors fastened to their bodies.

I wrote the story in script form (let Alan find an illustrator); it was approximately a page and a half in length. I faxed it to my office in New York, and went parasailing.

After two days, when no one responded to my fax, I wrote this story: A mysterious disease on the planet of the Jews leads to a mass outbreak of partial memory loss: everyone forgets how to recite the mourner's *kaddish*. As a result, none of the dead are able to move on to the next world. Confused corpses remain stuck on the Planet of the Jews. Inevitably, all sorts of arguments break out, but the worst problem is this: overcrowding. There is simply not enough room on the Planet for both the dead and the living.

This time I drew the pictures my self – black and white stick figures, once again – but I appended a note explaining I wouldn't be offended if they chose a different illustrator. One hour after faxing the story, I received a two word e–mail message from Alan. "Come home," it said.

On the airplane ride back to New York, I composed eighteen new "Planet of the Jews" stories. They all concerned either the bizarre outbreak of tefilinitis, or the tragic inability of the dead to move on to the next world. Each story lasted no longer than one page.

I took a taxi from the airport directly to Alan's office, and handed him the manuscripts, along with a letter of resignation. He glanced at the letter and nodded. I left without saying a word.

Several weeks later, toward the end of December, he called to ask how I was doing. I looked out the window; snow started to fall. I was rich, I told Alan. I wouldn't have to work another day in my life. No wife, I said, no alimony; I didn't have a care in the world. I was doing just great, I said, as tears flooded my eyes, and streamed down the phone cord, soaking my hand. I was doing great. On the other side of the line, I could hear Alan choke back sobs and then erupt in bitter weeping. We bawled like orphans for nearly five minutes, neither of us, I'm sure, with even the faintest notion of why we were crying.

After we finally pulled ourselves together, Alan suggested I forget about Jews for awhile, maybe even forget about comic books. Write a real novel, he suggested. A normal science fiction novel, or a western, or a romance. I was a good writer, he assured me – his best. Forget about Moishe and Esther, he urged. Forget about your father, about your Uncle Max. And for God's sake, forget about *tefilin*. Write about the moon, he said, write about nuclear physics. Write a book about cats, he proposed, or jazz, or motorcycles. Write about elephants. I promised to try, but I knew it was hopeless. It was too late. I could only write comic books. I could only write about the Jews.

Rabbi Philip Graubart is a writer and a rabbi living in Northampton, Mass. He received his BA from Northwestern University, his MA from Hebrew University in Jerusalem and rabbinic ordination from the Jewish Theological Seminary. He has published articles and short stories in many journals including Shma, Tikkum, Midstream, Emek, Response, Tomorrow, Beggar's Banquet, Potpourri, and Kerem. He's served as co-editor of Emek: A Jewish Literary Review. His monthly column, syndicated by the Jewish Telegraphic Agency, recently won a Jewish Journalists Association award for commentary. His collection of short stories, My Dinner With Michael Jackson and Other Stories was published by Aegina Press in 1966. Rabbi Graubart has led numerous workshops and taught several courses on subjects such as Jewish Healing, The Afterlife, Jewish Mysticism, Narrative in the Talmud, and Jewish Literature. He's taught at several Universities, including University of Colorado, Florida State, Amherst College, and The University of Judaism. He currently serves as spiritual director of Congregation B'nai Isreal in Northampton. He's married to Rabbi Susan Freeman. They have two children, Benjamin and Ilan.